EARLY PRAISE FOR IMAGINARY BOYFRIENDS: SHORT STORIES

Imaginary Boyfriends is bursting with intoxicating characters and unforgettable stories, featuring gay men caught between their dreams and desires and their working-class lives and struggles to survive. With witty, handsome prose Igrejas transports us to bars, baths, beaches, businesses, and bedrooms where these clever fools search for passion and deeper emotional connections. A marvelous debut!

~ Jameson Currier, editor Chelsea Station, author of *Why Didn't Someone Warn Me About Prince Charming?*

What I love is that wild punch. the punch of Igrejas's descriptions—curly hair you have to "finger-fuck to get just right," a Frenchman whose body acts like a map of France itself—but, even more, that punch of sheer *life* delivered to each and every character. This eclectic cast of lost yet spirited souls never fails to dizzy us in turn, with their wit, their sympathetic histories, and most of all, their charisma, somehow never empty, yet always oozing out. Igrejas makes sure they slip on their spillage in all the best ways, leaving us the ones utterly knocked out.

~ Michael Narkunski, Playwright, essayist, author of *Bad Homos Have Macaroni Hearts*

MANUEL IGREJAS

RUNNING WILD

RUNNING WILD PRESS

♥

IMAGINARY
BOYFRIENDS

S H O R T   S T O R I E S

Imaginary Boyfriends: Short Stories
Text copyright © 2025 Manuel Igrejas
Edited by Cody Sisco

ISBN (pbk) 978-1-963869-29-3
ISBN (ebook) 978-1-963869-30-9

"Midtown Manhattan was like a stifling greenhouse filled with exotic human orchids that couldn't survive anywhere else and its streets were littered with their broken blossoms. Adele, bless her heart, was one of them."

In his first collection, *Imaginary Boyfriends,* Manuel Igrejas spins eight tales of love, loss, sex, fantasy, and delusion, where characters who think they're clever often do foolish things.

In *Hassan and Sylvia,* a former boy toy navigates a new world after the loss of his longtime lover. He meets a glamorous, mysterious couple, Hassan, a handsome young Moroccan and Sylvia, an elegant older woman. In *Tiago, My Love,* Joe, a lonely middle-aged restaurant supply salesman wins a trip to Lisbon, Portugal where he stumbles up Lisbon's joyous Gay Pride celebration and falls in love with his handsome, unhappily married tour guide. *Lovey* is the upper half of a beautiful, bald mannequin "Ribs" finds in a garbage can as he drives the recycling truck for his town. She becomes his companion, confidante, and sometimes judge. *Inside Chateau Arbogast* finds Ribs in a new job as a bartender at an ornate catering hall. With Lovey still his companion he connects with a series of younger boyfriends and discovers the wholesome charms of the local gay sauna.

In *Egghead Payne* two boys, one black, one white, have their unlikely friendship tested in the tense, pre-riots Newark of the early sixties where the adults are as dangerous as the streets. In *The Little Trooper* Frank is a gay police officer in suburban New Jersey who meets Ed, a handsome gym teacher, at a bathhouse Christmas night, 1978. The story tracks their passionate, unlikely relationship in the sexually charged time before AIDs, when there were few rules and fewer limits.

Brett, an actor, gets a temp job at a financial magazine in *Madam Cluzet*. His tough, stylish boss confesses her big secret: she is married to a famous French actor while Brett struggles to hold on to his partner who suffers from RDS (Restless Dick Syndrome).

Inside the Show Business is the story Elijah, the lonely only child of Baptist ministers in Oxford, Mississippi. On a class trip to New York, he falls in love with the theater and gets a job as a publicist where he meets an untalented singer and her adorable piano player.

CONTENTS

Hassan and Sylvia   13

Tiago, My Love   53

Lovey   93

Inside Chateau Arbogast   133

The Little Trooper   157

Egghead Payne   195

Inside the Show Business   225

Madam Cluzet   257

ACKNOWLEDGMENTS

For Michael, the steadfast moonbeam who illuminates all the dark spaces.

This book is dedicated to the memory of Andy, Emily, Sindina, and Nana.

For all their help along the way, Jameson Currier, Robert Teague, Edward Field, Christopher Eaves, Liz Alterman, Laura Paz, Donald Weise, George Stambolian and especially Cody Sisco.

Egghead Payne first appeared in 34th Parallel.

Tiago, My Love first appeared in Image Out.

Lovey and *Inside Chateau Arbogast* first appeared in Chelsea Station.

The Little Trooper first appeared in Men On Men 4.

HASSAN AND SYLVIA

I am nobody from nowhere, and I have nothing, I thought as I looked in the mirror at my blurry face on a rainy Monday morning. Three months ago, on June 6, 2000, my lover, Vincent, had a heart attack in the kitchen of his restaurant, Bella Italia, and died on the way to the hospital. He was fifty-five years old. We lived together for twenty years.

Vincent called me that night, a slow one at the restaurant. He left a message, "Hey Punkin'. It's me. I just want to remind you that the recycling goes out tonight."

I was watching *The Women* on TCM, and I wasn't going to pick up. I hated that *It's me* bullshit. Two hours later, the hospital called.

I met Vincent when I was eighteen and snuck into The Male Box, then the hottest gay bar in New Jersey. Vincent was the stocky, raffish bartender with soulful hound dog eyes, dark floppy hair, and permanent facial scruff. It was love at first sight.

Vincent put me through school and subsidized my haphazard acting career, so I never had to have a day job, though I did help him out at the restaurant and on catering jobs from time to time. He ate, drank, talked, and smoked too much. He could be a bully and was not the most tactful man in the world. The last few years, there wasn't a day when I didn't think about leaving him, and, Lord knows, I wasn't faithful to him, but at least once a week, he leveled his droopy brown eyes at me and pinned me to the wall with the depth of his love. I didn't know how to live without him.

Vincent's family, the Azzopardis, snatched back the restaurant and sold it. They sold our little house, too. It was in Vincent's mother's name. Vincent's leased Cadillac was repossessed, and then my little Honda Civic too. There was no will and my name wasn't on any documents. At age thirty-eight, I had to finally grow up. I got a studio apartment in an ugly tower on the other side of Cedar Chips and a temp job doing data entry at International Flange in an ugly tower in Midtown Manhattan. I slouched back and forth across the Hudson River by bus, from one cubicle to the other, and forced myself to attend to the homework of living. An invisible zombie. I drift by, and it seems that no one really sees me. What do you call this state of unseen being? Maybe, like a chameleon, for survival, I blend into the beige and maroon background of the bus, the ashen landscape of Manhattan. Will I ever be visible again? I don't know.

My friend, Ozzie Potter, called me The Widow Azzopardi. I liked the title. It was like a comfy old sweater I could wrap around myself. Ozzie called on that gloomy Monday and asked me to come hear him sing at a new club called The Hideaway on Tuesday night. I said yes. I had nothing else to do. I never had anything else to do.

The Hideaway was a narrow room with hushed lighting and dark green walls in a shady Midtown hotel. It had a noisy kitchen and a tiny stage with a piano tucked in the corner. Ozzie's glamour headshot stood on an easel at the entrance, his mouth wrapped around a long vowel, his dark eyes moist. The sparkling mic in his hand offset his handsome brown face.

Ozzie and I were in a terrible revue, *Two Left Feet*, off-off-off Broadway, years ago. We had a brief romance that turned into friendship. His lover, Dennis, had financed *Two Left Feet* and probably financed tonight's show. Dennis, a furrier, picked Ozzie up in St. Louis, where he was a singing waiter. They have an enormous loft in Williamsburg.

I stood in the doorway and froze. There were two occupied tables. Ozzie had a party of six, and at another table, a striking young man and a striking older woman ordered dinner from a very unhappy-looking waiter. At first glance, this couple looked too glamorous, like movie extras miming gracious dining. Ozzie spotted me and bounded over to give me a hug.

"Jesus, you feel like a bag of bones," Ozzie said.

"Grief has no carbs," I said. I hadn't seen him since Vincent's funeral, and I missed him.

"Come have dinner with us."

I shook my head. "No, thanks. I had a late sandwich at the office. Do you mind if I sit by myself? I want to take it slow. But I will be sitting right over there, loving you."

I settled at a table between Ozzie's party and the glamorous couple. Ozzie went to the men's room to change. Dennis nodded at me. He was a big man with a fine head of wiry gray hair and a cosmetically smooth and startled face. The rest of the table was his repertory company, friends of fur, who attended all of Ozzie's shows.

"Hello!" It was the man at the next table, waving at me with his napkin. Rings sparkled on his long fingers. He was young, bronzed, and exotic in an expensive dark suit. The woman had disappeared.

"Are you alone?" he asked in a small, high-pitched voice.

"Yes."

"You look like you have a lot to think about." His accent was familiar but hard to place. Brazilian? Middle Eastern?

"Oh, not really."

"Would you care to join us?"

The woman made her way to the table. She was slender and wore a satiny green cocktail dress with a deep, wing-tipped neckline. Her dark hair in a short pixie cut framed her handsome face and showcased her big gray eyes. She seemed vaguely contented with everything and twice the age of her companion.

"What did I miss?" she asked.

"I am asking our serious friend to join us," her companion said. "He looks very interesting, don't you think?"

She reached into her bag and put on her glasses, pretending to study me. "Yes. He does look very interesting."

"It is better to sit with friends, don't you think, than to sit unhappy alone," the man said.

"Yes. It is," I said and sat at their table.

"I am Hassan, and this is Sylvia." We all shook hands.

"I'm…" I started to say.

"Have dinner with us!" Hassan said.

"Oh, I'm not hungry." I looked at their big plates. Hassan's contained an artful arrangement of medallions of pink meat with tiny vegetables in a translucent brown sauce with capers. Sylvia had the same arrangement with beige meat.

"Oh, please. It is much more fun if we are all dining. Try the lamb. It looks very good," Hassan said, his cutlery poised over his plate.

"I don't like lamb."

"The chicken then," Sylvia said. "Please. We insist."

Hassan snapped his fingers for the waiter. "The chicken for my friend."

"Do you know Ozzie?" I asked.

"Who is Ozzie?" Hassan put down his fork and gave me his full attention. His eyes were very large and a glowing amber. I imagined him as a magician or mentalist: The Great Hassan on a poster with those shining eyes. The table's rosy candlelight bounced off his perfect cheekbones.

"The singer."

"Oh. I do not know him, but we did come to see him," Hassan said.

"Why?"

"To see if he is good. Then I can use him for my parties."

"Do you give a lot of parties?" I asked.

"I give the most wonderful parties in New York. Would you like to come to my parties?"

"Hassan gives the most wonderful parties," Sylvia said.

"Is that what you do? Are you one of those party promoters?" I asked.

Hassan narrowed his eyes and flexed his cheekbones. "I am not one of *those* anythings. I like to have a beautiful life with beautiful things. I like to know beautiful people."

"Oh, the beautiful people," I said. "How are they?" Fuck him and the beautiful people.

Sylvia raised an eyebrow and Hassan took a breath. His full upper lip puffed up with anger, and his lips parted over small, white teeth.

"It is my art, to make this beautiful life, to make, to bring everything, to make all one…"

"To combine these elements and create exciting, memorable events," Sylvia said. "Hassan is the event, and things… coalesce around him."

"Yes! Yes! I am the event and things collapse around me!"

"Do you get paid for it?" I asked.

"Yes," Hassan said. "I get money, but it is not why I do it. It is for love." He placed his hands over his heart. "You are very American. Very bourgeois. Always money. How much money?"

"I'm sorry," I said. "I know these parties happen all the time. I see pictures of them or online, but I've never been to that kind of party. My life is very, um, Spartan."

"What is Umspartan?" Hassan said.

"Simple, I think," Sylvia said.

"Simple is stupid, no?" Hassan said.

"Sparta is a city in Greece," I said.

"You are Greek? I love Greeks!" Hassan said.

"Spanish. My parents were Spanish, I mean."

"I love Spanish people," Hassan said. "España! Do you know Almodovar? He has been to my parties. He loves me. Would you come to one of my parties?"

"Sure."

"Sure. I love Americans," Hassan said. "Always with this answer that is no answer. Not yes. Not no. Just sure."

"I would love to come to one of your parties."

"Good. On Thursday, I am giving a beautiful party at an art gallery. It is a party of colors, everywhere will be colors. You must come."

"Your supper is getting cold," I said.

"Some like it cold," Sylvia said. I looked at her, admiring her creamy skin. The fine lines around her eyes and mouth were like quotation marks that put a spin on every expression crossing her mobile face. I liked her strong, bare shoulders, and I loved her perfume, like a blossomy spring breeze.

"Do you go to all of Hassan's parties?" I asked.

"Sylvia is always with me. I cannot do without Sylvia," Hassan said.

"You have magnificent shoulders," I said.

"Thank you," Sylvia said, her gray eyes glittering. She absorbed the compliment handily, and a smile spread across her generous mouth. "How do you know Ozzie?" she asked.

"I go to the gym every day. I have ten percent body fat," Hassan said.

"Ozzie's a chum. He's very talented," I said.

"We will see. Do you go to bed with him?" Hassan said, taking a small forkful of lamb.

"Hassan! Really!" Sylvia said.

Hassan continued, "And what do you do when you are not being a chum?"

"I just go to my job," I said. "Let's talk about *you*. How did you two meet?"

Hassan and Sylvia shared a sly look and were transported to the site of their first encounter, throwing the green wall behind them into soft focus.

"I am giving this brilliant party at Balthazar, and I keep seeing this fascinating woman in the edges of my eyes. I see she is standing alone, so I bring her a glass of champagne." Hassan squeezed Sylvia's hand.

"I had come with someone, a terrible man, and he left me to talk business with some people," she said. "I thought everything was so beautiful, so thoughtful. I wondered who was responsible for this delightful bash, and I kept seeing Hassan in the center of everything, looking very official and displeased."

"If I relax one minute, the staff will drink and smoke and put their cigarettes out in the caviar," Hassan said.

"Then Hassan was standing next to me, and I knew my life was going to change." Sylvia ran her hand across Hassan's cheek and gently tugged his ear lobe. They gazed at each other tenderly, then turned their glowing faces toward me. I felt, momentarily, like a pink forkful of meat being raised to their lips. I was being hustled, and after months of what felt like solitary confinement, I liked the attention.

"Hassan has taught me so much," Sylvia said. I wondered if they were lovers.

"You teach me so much," Hassan said, raising her hand to his lips.

"And you've both taught me so much," I said.

"Yes?" Hassan said.

"Oh, you are wicked," Sylvia said.

"What is wicked?" Hassan asked.

"Evil," Sylvia said. "Bad."

"No. Impossible. He is an angel," Hassan said.

The gloomy waiter brought my dinner. The chicken was tough, the sauce like bitter glue. Vincent would have marched into the kitchen with the plate and given whoever was working there an impromptu cooking lesson.

A large young man who had been sitting at the Dennis table wedged past us, sat at the piano, and smiled absent-mindedly as he noodled at the keyboard. The lights dimmed, and the waiter's somber voice announced the song stylings of Mr. Ozzie Potter. Ozzie bounded out of the men's room onto the tiny stage. He launched into "I Love Being Here with You," and I relaxed as his strong, smoky voice washed over me. From this angle, I was able to check out all the expensive dental work, courtesy of Dennis.

Ozzie's set of romantic ballads was soothing and made me feel vaguely romantic. Hassan and Sylvia nibbled quietly at their dinner, their attention drifting further away from Ozzie the longer he sang. Ozzie took his bows to slight, enthusiastic applause.

"He's very sweet, and he sings well," Sylvia said, "but there is no *oomph*."

Hassan dabbed at his mouth with his napkin. "Boring!"

Ozzie came to our table. "This looks like an interesting party," he said.

"Oh, it is!" Sylvia said, clapping her hands.

"What did you think?" Ozzie said.

"Delicious!" Sylvia said.

"I'm trying something new. The old act was more inner-directed, you know? This one is more outer-directed."

Sylvia interrupted him. "You mean instead of singing to yourself, you're singing to other people?"

Hassan started to say something, and I interrupted him.

"The pipes are in great shape, and you look *fabulous*. It was a great set, sweetie," I said.

Ozzie kissed me and went back to Dennis.

Hassan frowned. "I do not like it when you act so... so... what you say... girly." He fluttered his hands.

"But I am so... so... girly," I said, fluttering back.

"Gentleman, put away your parasols," Sylvia said.

"This place is enough for me," Hassan said, snapping for the waiter. He looked at me and smiled. "What now, my new friend?"

"Back to Sparta."

"Come with us," Sylvia said.

"Where?"

"I have to check on a party. To make sure my people do not goof out," Hassan said.

"Up," Sylvia said, "Goof up."

"You see why I love Sylvia," Hassan said. "Please be our guest." He scrupulously examined the check, running a finger down its columns, his lips moving. He frowned, looked at the ceiling, and counted on his fingers. Satisfied, he handed the check to Sylvia. "It is outrageous," he said.

"Oh, stop," she said, laying the check on the table without looking at it. She dug into her small black bag, withdrew a Black American Express card, and placed it on the check.

Hassan leaned forward and grabbed both of my hands in his. It sent shockwaves through my body. Vincent and I liked to hold hands, and I hadn't been touched, anywhere, since I lost him. "I think you are very interesting, very desirable. I do not know why I feel this way. I do not want to feel this way. I feel how sad you are, and it hurts my heart. I do not know what it is about you. Just holding your hand, my cock is so big, it would knock over this table if I stood up."

"Hassan, really!" Sylvia exclaimed. She turned to me and said, "Somebody had their couscous today."

Hassan took a business card from his wallet, wrote on the back of it, and handed it to me. It read "Oasis Travel" with several locations in the Tri-State area. On the back, Hassan had printed his name and phone number in big, wobbly letters.

"Cheer up!" Sylvia said to the waiter as she signed her receipt.

"I want you to call me and don't just say sure," Hassan said. "Give me your phone." Mine was cheap and flimsy, and he looked at it disdainfully as he entered his number.

He handed my phone back to me.

"Are you very poor, my darling?" he asked.

I shrugged.

There was a clump at the narrow door as we all made our exits. The piano player was still on duty and played the "One Note Samba." Sylvia glided between Dennis and Hassan, and I was surprised at how petite she was. Hassan draped a black lace shawl over her shuffling shoulders as she moved to the music. He took her hand, twirled her, and they danced out into the street and got into a big, black car.

The encounter left me a little breathless. They were real people in real time—and they liked me! I wondered if they were trying to recruit me for some obscure religion or a sex ring of aging male losers. Vincent would have flirted with them for a bit, then dismissed them.

❤

I got a naked pic from Hassan late that night. He was very... impressive. He called me while I was at the office the next morning, his voice sleepy and small over the receiver.

"Good morning, my darling. Did you like my picture?"

"Yes."

"You did not send me one."

"I don't have any pictures like that."

"Will you come see me tonight? I would love for you to see my apartment."

"No. No. Not tonight."

"I like you very much. Do you like me?"

"Um, yes. What is Oasis Travel?"

"My family has many businesses. They are very smart. So, *do* you like me?"

"I do like you. I just don't know you very well."

"You will know me, and you will love me. Will you come to my party tomorrow?"

"I love your accent. Where are you from?"

"East Fiftieth Street," Hassan said.

"I mean, what part of the world are you from?"

"Why? Do you think I am from Iraq? Do you think I am a terrorist?"

"Of course not."

"I am from Morocco. Beautiful Morocco. My family is descended from great kings. I am named after one."

"How wonderful," I said. I never met anyone from Morocco. That made him more interesting.

"So, my darling, you will come to my party on Thursday, yes? I will text you an invitation with all the details." He did and included another naked picture.

"Yes. I have to go. I have another call," I said.

It was Sylvia. "You know, Hassan is crazy about you. Promise you'll come to the party." Her voice was like an insinuating woodwind with a merry vibrato weaving through it.

That night, I took the bus home, picked up a sandwich at the nearby Subway, and fell asleep on my futon with the TV on, as usual.

Thursday, I wore a blazer and tie and, after work, took the subway down to Howard Street. Near Mercer, I saw bright lights, a crowd, and double-parked vans in front of the New Lite Gallery. The crowd, which spilled out into the street, was composed of boy and girl model types who pressed against the velvet ropes with decorous urgency, eyeing the gallery's door where two glowering Nubian princes stood guard.

The party was tantalizingly on display through the gallery's tall windows, fueling the forward motion of the crowd. The cavernous room was bathed in golden light that splashed onto the darkening street. Inside, floor-to-ceiling canvases leaked color from the top down in thick drizzles. The paint seemed to crawl down the white canvases as if it were alive. The guests looked like human art, positioned at perfect intervals, draped in beautiful fabrics, holding golden glasses throughout the huge, white room while a DJ in a hot pink body suit blasted EDM that got into our bones even out onto the street. Through the window, it looked like the set of an important film, both alluring and daunting.

I spotted Hassan darting about inside, dressed in a dazzling cream-colored suit and a hot pink shirt, then I saw Sylvia in a long halter dress of brilliant red. She stood next to a giant red, white, and blue drizzle and smiled at it, looking like its elegant coda. While I looked at the Big Drizzle, she disappeared.

I smelled Sylvia's perfume. She stepped up behind me and hooked her arm through mine.

"Hey!" some of the crowd said as we breezed past the Nubian guards and through the door. I was breathless when I entered the room, its scope and colors hitting me in a rush. It was like walking into a painting. Sylvia held onto my arm and snatched a glass of champagne from a passing waiter's tray. We stood before a canvas that bubbled with rust and corrosion. I read the plate next to it. "Toxic Spill #17."

"You look smashing tonight," I said.

"Thank you," Sylvia said.

Hassan floated toward us in his cream-colored suit and hot pink shirt. He extended his hands and held onto mine, kissing my cheek. "Thank you for coming, my friend."

"I love your suit," I said.

"It's Zegna!"

"You look like an ice cream sundae," I said.

"Would you like to lick me?" Hassan squeezed my bicep.

His eyes darted around the room. A posse of adorable young men with longish dark hair and goatees swarmed through the room with a variety of cameras, filming the event.

"Where's Chloe Sevigny?" one of the camera cuties asked Hassan.

"She just left," Hassan said, winking at me. His gaze landed on a makeshift bar draped in white cloth a few feet away from us. A young, ginger-haired bartender poured half a bottle of Champagne into another bottle. Hassan ran to the bartender and shrieked, "No! No! No!" The bartender froze.

"Do not mix them together!" Hassan hissed at the bartender, yanking the bottle out of his hand. "Never mix them together! This is not a Polish wedding!" He turned to Sylvia. "What is the word for mixing bottles together?"

She shrugged. "Mixing?"

"Consolidate," I said. Something I learned from Vincent.

"*Consolidate!* Yes!" Hassan clapped his hands. "Do not *consolidate* the bottles!" he said to the rattled bartender.

"He likes you very much," Sylvia said.

I watched Hassan scold the bartender, then put his arm around him and kiss him on the lips. "He is beautiful and charismatic, but he's a little too much for me," I said.

"He's very dear," Sylvia said, smiling at Hassan as he approached.

Hassan put his arms around us. "My two favorite people. I need you both right now. Chloe did not come; Patti LuPone did not come."

"Yes, but Amanda Lepore is here. Anthony Weiner is here," Sylvia said. Hassan left us immediately to walk around the room again and scold the staff, stopping occasionally to kiss a guest. Sylvia and I wandered through the party, her arm draped through mine.

"He's very nervous because you're here tonight. Be patient with him," Sylvia said.

"Why are you pimping for him?"

She flinched, then appeared amused. "I want him to be happy."

"Are you happy?"

"I just revel in the pure joy of being," she said.

"Oh, brother! Whatever you're on, I want some of it." We stood before another spill, thick blue lines sprinkled with little blue stars.

"I'm serious," Sylvia said. "I was in terrible shape for a few years, as unhappy as anyone can be. I was married to a vile man. I had a gruesome divorce, lost my two girls to him. They're grown up now, and, thanks to him, they won't talk to me. I wandered around in a daze for a long time doing very stupid things. Oh, sweetie, I was a mess."

"You seem like a woman with a secret," I said, wondering if her gauzy good spirits were chemically induced.

"Many secrets."

Hassan scooped us up, saying he was hungry, and, arms entwined, pushed us through the door. "We'll go to my favorite place." He led us to a big, black limo at the curb and held open the rear door.

"Jimmy, take us to Rocky's, please," Hassan called to the driver as we slid into the plush back seat. I sat between Hassan and Sylvia, and each held my hand as the limo whispered uptown. Hassan moaned about the party, the incompetent staff, the flat champagne.

"Consolidate! I will always remember that!"

I looked at the back of the driver's thick neck and the curly blond hair peeking beneath his cap. His right ear was pierced. I tried to imagine his face.

"It was all lovely, as usual," Sylvia said.

"I liked it," I said, breathing in Sylvia's scent. "And I really like your perfume."

"Thank you." She squeezed my hand. "It's my own special concoction."

"What's it called?"

"Sylvia!" she said, and we all laughed.

"I have something special for you, too," Hassan said and guided my hand to his crotch. His pics were not exaggerated. I was surprised at how glad he was to see me. "And that's just from sitting next to you. Imagine when I have you in my bed."

While I was down there, I gave his cock an extra squeeze, but it meant less to me than when he grabbed my hands earlier. A cock is a cock.

"You can fuck anybody," Vincent used to say, "But you can't love everybody."

"Don't mind me, boys. I'll just sit here being superfluous." Sylvia stared hard out of her window.

"Sorry. We're being stupid and messy. Come back," I said and squeezed her hand.

She kissed my cheek.

We pulled up in front of an Italian restaurant on Second Avenue in the fifties. The limo, without instruction, waited at the curb. It was a simple place with a real Italian grandma in a black dress sitting behind the cash register. Rocky, the owner, gave us a prized table in the center of the busy dining room. I was, again, seated between my two new friends. Hassan ordered for everyone: minestrone, arugula salad, veal saltimbocca. We drank two bottles of Pinot Grigio, and Hassan hissed about the party, about how tired he was, between dainty mouthfuls of veal.

"Oh, stop complaining," I said. "You're living the kind of life most people dream about."

"It is work. With no time for love." Hassan rolled his amber eyes at me. Were those contacts?

I poured wine into Sylvia's glass. "Do you have some fabulous thing you do during daylight hours, or do you just sit in the refrigerator like an orchid until the sun goes down?"

"I'm a mind/body practitioner," she chirped.

"You mean massage?"

"That's just one part of what I do. I connect all the dots, physical, emotional, psychic. My husband was a doctor and I worked in his office for a while. I always thought organized medicine wasn't giving us the whole story, so I created my own path. You would be a great challenge. I'm reading so many things from you."

We had tiramisu, espresso, and Sambuca. When the check came, Hassan snatched it, thank God. I caught a glimpse of the total: $317. I pretended to reach into my pocket.

"Nonsense. You are our guest," Hassan said, running his fingers down the columns. "He charged us for the Sambuca!"

"Well, that's only fair," Sylvia said. "We each had several glasses. I know I'm feeling it."

"But we are such good customers!"

"Oh, never mind," she said.

Hassan frowned and gave the check one more examination. "I guess it is all right."

He handed it to Sylvia, who took out her black Amex and handed it with the check to the waiter.

"I have to run. The last bus to Jersey is at midnight, and it's eleven now," I said.

"No. No. Stay with us," Hassan said.

"I can't."

"Don't leave just yet," Sylvia said. "The car will take you home when you're ready."

"All the way back to New Jersey?"

"He goes where I tell him to go," she said.

We walked two blocks to an apartment building on East Fiftieth. The car pulled up in front just as we arrived. It was a white brick building, twelve stories high, with a name, The Afton, written in gold on the awning and the front window. Hassan lived on the fifth floor. His key in the lock activated a screeching alarm system inside the apartment, followed by the sound of someone pounding on the wall.

The lights were on, and Hassan ran to a large, ornate birdcage that held two little parrots. He shushed them in baby talk, and they stopped screeching. The pounding stopped, too. Hassan stuck his hands into the cage, and the two little birds, one green, one gray, hopped onto each hand. Hassan stood in the center of the small room, arms outstretched, as the two birds sidestepped up his arms with muffled squawks.

"These are my babies," he said. "Dolce and Gabbana." The birds reached his neck and nuzzled it. Hassan kissed each one on its beak. "Love you," he said in singsong, "Love you." The birds gargled a two-syllable response.

"Do you hear them?" Hassan asked. "See how they love me? Love you."

Eh aw, the birds said.

"Sounds like Fuck You," I said.

Sylvia laughed. "Oh, you are wicked."

"Come closer," Hassan said. "Hold out your hand. Touch my face."

I stepped toward him and tripped over a sneaker. The birds screeched, jumped into the air, and then settled, squawking, on Hassan's shoulders. He shushed them and took my hand. He guided it up to the green one, which cocked a swiveling eye at me and pecked at it. Satisfied, it hopped on and sidestepped to my elbow, its mean eye scanning my face.

"You see! Dolce likes you too! He knows who my true friends are."

I looked from the bird to the rest of the room. Expensive-looking clothes were scattered everywhere. There was a couch that doubled as a bed, two bookshelves filled with fashion and movie books, a CD player with CDs strewn across it. There was a small table littered with bills, a large bottle of lube with a pump dispenser, and a vase filled with wilted yellow roses, a card still dangling from them. To the right, there was a kitchenette, its counter lined with dirty glasses.

Hassan followed my eyes. "The cleaning lady comes tomorrow."

"Can you put the damn birds back in the cage now?" Sylvia said. She had been standing rigidly near the door, next to a basket filled with dirty laundry. She wasn't smiling.

"Sylvia does not love the babies, but they love her," Hassan said. He gathered the birds and put them back in the cage.

"I hate them, and they hate me," Sylvia said. "All they do is squawk, eat, and shit."

"Are they parrots?" I asked.

"Like parrots," Hassan said. "Conures. From South America. Very expensive."

"Of course."

I went to the window and looked out at the lighted courtyard shared by the identical building next door. I wondered, what am I doing in this scene? I don't know. Their flattery was shameless, and, shamelessly, I liked it.

Without Vincent, I felt lost and shaky. I have been promiscuous since I was a pup. The only thing I ever really owned was the six feet of territory I occupied, and I did with it what I wanted. Vincent knew how much I loved him and let me have my adventures. My father took off early, my mother drank, and I was raised by my put-upon grandmother. Vincent was my family, my rock. Now, without my Vincenzo, I had no context, no safe home. I was just a lonely guy pushing forty at the mercy of the meat market. I had no idea what I was doing in this swank, messy apartment or where it might all go, but—a hot man with a big cock was a good reason to stick around.

"Hello, over there!" Sylvia called from the couch.

I waved at her.

"Come be with us," Sylvia called.

Something about Sylvia was getting to me. She was like the Mona Lisa in Donna Karan. Between one thing and another, my juices were stirring, and I felt, well, *alive!* I didn't know what to do next. Yes, they were exotic and seductive, but something felt off and enticingly dangerous. Whatever the case, this evening was so much more interesting than eating a Subway tuna sandwich in front of the TV.

I decided that Hassan and I were on our first date, and Sylvia was our chaperone. How civilized! But a part of me wondered if they were marinating me for some sordid enterprise. Would it be ritual sex, hallucinogenic drugs, some kind of devil worship? Were they thousand-year-old vampires looking for a new recruit? Would I wind up chopped into bits and left at the curb in a garbage bag? Or just plain sex? My body tingled with anticipation. Or was it dread?

"Really, Hassan," Sylvia said sharply, "you shouldn't invite people over when the place is such a mess."

"Champagne?" Hassan took a bottle of Piper Heidsieck from the refrigerator and pulled three fluted-stem glasses from the cupboard. He gave us each a glass and poured.

"A toast," he said. "May we have everything that we want."

Sylvia held her glass up high. "And we want everything!"

I saw a framed photograph on the table, just behind the wilted roses, and picked it up. Hassan was in the picture, standing between two handsome, brawny men with dense black hair and thick mustaches. Hassan looked very slight between these two. The three men all wore tuxes and surrounded a pretty woman in a wedding dress who looked as if she had just tossed her bouquet. She shared with Hassan those big, sun-struck eyes. She was standing next to a thin blond man with a ponytail who seemed to be squeezed out of the picture, though he was in its center.

Hassan slid behind me and put his hands on my shoulders. "My family. That is my brother Tarek, that is me, my brother Dris, and my sister Suzi. Aren't we beautiful?"

"Hassan, you are shameless!" Sylvia said.

"Suzi lives in New Jersey like you do. She has two babies. Do you know her?"

"No."

Church bells chimed; it was Hassan's mobile's ringtone. He answered it.

"Pablo, my friend." He told Pablo how busy and tired he was. Sylvia sat on the couch sipping champagne, and I joined her. I admired her for not kicking off her tiny red pumps. I wondered what Vincent would have made of this odd pair. He'd have no use for Hassan, too showy, but I think he might have been taken with Sylvia. He liked old-school glamour.

Hassan twirled his fingers through my hair while he chirped to Pablo and made bored faces at us. He put his hand over the phone and whispered, "A millionaire from Buenos Aires. He loves me and wants me to come live with him. Married and very handsome. He gave me the babies."

Sylvia tapped a tiny foot, and I thumbed through *Vanity Fair*. Then she got up abruptly.

"Your glass is smudged!" she said. "And the champagne is flat! Let me remedy that. I must apologize for Hassan. He's being a wretched host." She took my glass and marched into the kitchen. I wondered why she was so impatient. Was this the point where she would slip roofies into my champagne? I didn't care. I felt alive and alert for the first time in months, and I wanted to take the ride, wherever it took me.

I heard the pop of a champagne cork, and Sylvia emerged with two full glasses. Then she went back to retrieve the new bottle of Piper Heidsieck.

I poured more champagne for Sylvia and myself. Hassan snapped his fingers and held out his glass. I ignored him and clinked glasses with Sylvia.

"Get off the phone. You have company," Sylvia said.

Hassan blew loud, wet kisses to Pablo.

"Time to go," I said, giving them their cue to move this along. I downed my champagne. It tasted fine.

"Oh, no. No. Not yet. I want to talk to you," Hassan said.

"Some other time."

Hassan looked to Sylvia. "He wants to go."

"So do I," she said.

Hassan took my hand and, though we were the same size, somehow slumped so that he could look up at me with moist, manipulative eyes. His pupils were dilated. "You can stay here tonight."

"No, thank you," I said.

Sylvia picked up her bag. "Come. Jimmy will drop me off, then I'll have him take you home."

"You're sure?"

"I promised."

Hassan looked mournful and wove his fingers through mine. "You do not like me. After everything I do and say, you do not like me. All I want is for you to like me. I have men all over the world who offer me so many things to be with them, but I think only of you, who gives me *this!*" He snapped his fingers. "Look at the flowers! A very rich man has sent them. He wants me to live with him, and I think only of you, who gives me nothing!"

"Why? We just met. You don't know anything about me."

"I feel you. I know you. I feel like I am already inside you."

"Oh, Hassan, please shut up!" Sylvia said.

I didn't know what to do. I was turned on by Hassan, but I was afraid of being devoured by him. I wanted to see what happened when we didn't have a chaperone.

I turned to Sylvia. "Could you wait for me in the car?"

"Darling, stop babbling and just say good night to the man," Sylvia said, kissing Hassan on both cheeks. The birds began to screech. She put her hands to her ears. "Shut those damn things up!" She threw on her shawl and hurried out.

Someone from the apartment next door pounded on the wall, and Hassan ran to the cage to shush the birds. His baby talk quieted them, and he came to me with his arms outstretched.

"All I want is to be alone with you, but Sylvia is always here with us, and now you are angry," he said.

"Oh, I'm not angry at all. I really like Sylvia. She is fascinating." I said, sounding, I thought, agreeable.

"I am more fascinating." He pressed himself against me. "Hold me. Just hold me. I do so many things for so many people, and I cannot get this simple thing, one man to hold me."

I put my arms around him, and tears sprung to my eyes. I hadn't been this physically close to anyone since Vincent died. I wanted to hold on to something, to someone. I felt the heat and heft in his pants as he dug into me. I was flattered and I shuddered involuntarily.

I looked at Suzi's wedding picture and remembered Vincent preparing his Italian Wedding Soup for the holidays. Skillfully, lovingly, he crafted his delicious, fragrant meatballs, minced his garlic, and chopped his escarole. Vincent's Italian Wedding Soup was a highlight of Bella Italia's menu and not always available. His Ecuadorian cooks made it there. When he made it at home, just for us, it was a special occasion. The fragrant bowls were expressions of his prodigious, sometimes stifling love for me. He liked to wrap his big paw around my hand as we sat at the candle-lit dining room table.

"I feel like I belong to you," Hassan said into my chest, bringing me back to the present.

"No one belongs to anyone," I said, stepping away from him. The words came out in short, clear pops, like gunshots. Hassan absorbed each hit and looked up at me, wounded. He stumbled backward in shock.

"You are a very stupid man," he said, his face contorted with rage.

"No, I am not." He was right, but I could not let him have that.

"You should not say no to me. I do not like that," Hassan said. He picked up the *Vanity Fair* and rolled it into a potential weapon.

"Do you even know my name?" I asked.

Hassan waved away the question as if my name wasn't worth knowing.

Hassan's version of big love felt pinched and puny compared to Vincent's. I didn't belong to anyone anymore and I didn't want to belong to Hassan. The price was too high. It would be a tumultuous month, tops, before I got tossed to the curb.

"I'm sorry." I was sorry for letting myself drift into this situation the way I drifted through life.

The church bells chimed again. Hassan took out his phone and turned his back to me. He waved toward the door, indicating I should show myself out. I tripped over his sneaker again and thought of swatting him over the head with it. We had gotten to the end without the gymnastics, without the jizz and the letdown.

The street air felt good, and I was still conscious. I wanted to keep walking past the big car's open door until I couldn't walk anymore. I was alive. Alive! Was I wrong about the drug, vampire, garbage bag thing, or had I just aborted the mission? Sylvia waved a small, white hand inside the limo, and I slid inside.

"Home, James," she said. "I just love saying that."

"I won't be seeing Hassan again."

"I'm very sorry about that. I hope you and I can still be friends," she said.

"Sure."

"That would be lovely." She seemed distracted, her attention somewhere out there beyond the streets.

"What's going on with you right now? You okay?" I asked.

"Oh, I'm fine. Fine. Just a little tired." She looked out her window. "Hassan is such a fool! You could have been good for him. You don't roll over."

"What's in it for you?"

I saw Jimmy, the driver, smile in the rear-view mirror. His blue eyes glimmered in the light of a bodega on the corner.

Sylvia seemed to be tabulating her answer, weighing something against something else. She arrived at a conclusion but chose not to share it. "You are very sweet," she said and squeezed my hand.

I was still churning inside, my newly awakened senses tumbling over each other. I felt twitchy and restless now.

The car made a left turn off First Avenue onto Ninety-Third Street. There was a faux luxury tower on the corner, but the car passed it and glided down the shabby block. It stopped in front of one of a row of mud-brown five-story tenements. Jimmy got out and opened the car door for Sylvia.

"I'll call you. Safe getting home." She kissed my cheek, started to slide out, but slid back in and kissed me lightly on the lips while Jimmy waited. Over her shoulder, I looked at Jimmy. He was in his thirties, with longish hair that he tucked up into the cap. Tall, beefy, and pleasant-looking, he wore a kind of uniform: short-sleeved white shirt, black jeans, black sneakers. He took Sylvia's arm, escorted her up the steps to the front door, and waited while she dug out her keys. A single bare bulb lit the hallway, and the walls were covered with stained yellow tile. Sylvia leaned against the door, and it opened.

"The lock's still broken!" she said angrily to Jimmy. He shrugged. I wondered if his duties included sex.

She pushed her way in, and Jimmy followed her upstairs. I looked up and saw lights go on in a fourth-floor window. Jimmy came down the stairs and got in the car. He turned and extended his hand over the seat.

"I'm Jimmy Dempsey."

We shook hands. His grip was warm and strong.

"Two down. One to go," he said.

"What?" Did I hear him right?

"Where to, Boss?" he asked.

"I don't know if Sylvia told you, but I'm going to New Jersey."

"Whatever, Boss. Just tell me where."

"Cedar Chips. It's right off Route Forty-Six."

"I know it well, Boss," Jimmy said. "Just tell me which street."

"You've been to Cedar Chips?"

"Oh yeah. This job takes me a lot of places." Our eyes connected in the rear-view mirror. His were sprightly, light, and ironic. Jimmy drove over to Fifth Avenue and took it downtown.

"This is my favorite time to drive in this town," Jimmy said. "I like it after midnight when things get nice and dicey. You know, I used to live in Jersey. I managed a laundromat in West Caldwell. But I was married to the bitch from hell."

I didn't know what to say about that, and he looked hurt as we drove silently down Fifth Avenue. It was soothing to be in a Cadillac again. Its plush back seat felt more relaxing than my no-frills apartment, and Sylvia's intoxicating scent hung in the air like an exotic air freshener.

The car made a right on Fifty-First Street. Jimmy was still pouting.

"Thanks for the ride. I really appreciate it," I said. "You are such a good driver. I feel like I'm in very good hands."

Jimmy smiled.

"And you have dimples!"

He flexed them.

"Now you're showing off," I said. Yes, I was flirting, and it felt good.

Between Eighth and Ninth Avenues, we passed a row of brown tenements. Jimmy pointed at one. "The Homestead," he said. He parked the car. "I got to walk my dog, Gus. You mind?"

He went into the building and came out with a big, black dog. He leaned into the car. "Take the walk with me. It'll just be a minute."

We walked down the block while Gus trotted ahead. "I don't believe in leashes. Nobody tells me and Gus what to do."

"He's a real beauty. What breed?"

"Newfoundland," Jimmy said. "I raised him from a pup."

Gus was the kind of dog you wanted to come home to, the kind that would keep a floundering relationship on life support.

"Yeah, he's in bad shape now, poor old bastard, but he's my good buddy, my only friend. He was great with my kids, but now I got custody of him. The bride got the twins and the house in West Caldwell. That's what happens when you marry into the wrong tribe." Jimmy's eyes shifted toward me for a response. I didn't have one. Gus trotted back and Jimmy took him upstairs. We got back in the car. I was hoping Gus would take the ride.

"You in a hurry, Boss?" Jimmy asked.

"Well, it's after one." If he invited me up to his place, we made out a little, and I could still get the ride home, that would work for me.

"Let me buy you a drink. I know I could use one. I'll have you home in half an hour, I swear."

I did want a drink. "Yeah, but let's make it a short one."

He parked in front of Rudy's on Ninth Avenue. The bartender knew Jimmy and set him up with Irish whiskey and a water chaser. I had the same.

"So, how long you know the Gold Dust twins?" Jimmy asked. "That's what I call them."

"Not long," I said. "And you?"

"Too long," he said. "I used to be married to Hassan's sister, the bitch, but I was banished from the tribe."

My ears rang. *He* was the blond guy being squeezed out of the wedding picture.

"Right!" I blurted, having connected the dots.

"So, one night," he continued, "I was sitting on this very stool, and him and Sylvia breezed in, all in diamonds and furs, and swooped down on me. They bought me drinks and offered me a job. I needed the bucks, so I took it."

"They can be overpowering. What do *you* think of them?" I wanted to unravel the mystery.

"Not much. Alls I know is the money's good. But they expect way too much." Then he imitated Sylvia at her door, "*'The lock's still broken!'* What am I supposed to do about it? She owns the fucking building, but the bitch don't own me!"

He slammed his fist on the bar and his shot glass jumped.

I thought *Sylvia's mind/body hooey must be very profitable.*

"I can't say nothing, because now I'm in the soup." He polished off his drink and the bartender re-filled his glass. Jimmy knocked it back and stood up, patting his pockets.

"Shit. I left my wallet in the car," he said. "You mind?"

Jimmy opened the car's front door. "Boss, why don't you sit up front with me? It makes me feel less like a stooge." He tossed his cap in the back seat and ran his big mitts through his golden hair.

"Okay." I didn't know if he was lonely or hustling me, but I liked being called Boss. He was trying to get up the momentum to tell me something. I looked at his pleasant profile, long eyelashes, and button nose.

Once we were in the Lincoln Tunnel, he cleared his throat. "No offense, Boss, but I hate going back to Jersey. That bitch is sitting in *my* house, yanking my chain long distance. Sometimes, I want to ram this hearse right into a wall. Maybe this wall. Or the back of that bus!" he said, stepping on the accelerator.

"But not tonight, right?" My voice was suicide prevention hotline soothing, but I was braced for impact.

"It's not worth it, is it? It would give them too much satisfaction." He slowed down.

"Exactly. Fuck them."

I imagined him in his high school yearbook, blond, bright-eyed, and smiling. Then I saw him in a family portrait, the picture-perfect husband in his good suit, his rebel ponytail, with his arm around Hassan's tough, pretty sister and the two kids, Erin and Abdul. On Sunday mornings, he washed the car in his driveway, barefoot in cut-off jeans. He was turning to pudding and, in a few years, would be coarse and blurry, but he still had the twinkle of a horny altar boy.

"The old man owns a lot of businesses. I wanted to run the travel agency, but he stuck me managing one of the laundromats; then it was always jump, jump, jump! Well, I got tired of kissing the old man's ass, and I said so. You don't fuck with that tribe. They ran me out of the business. The bride turned on me. I had to get out of town. Everybody warned me, but I didn't listen. Respect, that's what it's all about. Know what I mean?"

"Not exactly."

"I thought I was free of that mob, but now I'm in the soup."

"What soup?"

"How tight are you with the Gold Dust twins?" Jimmy asked.

"I'm through with them."

"Good. They are like carbon monoxide, you know?"

"Huh?"

"You know that poison gas you can't smell, but it kills you?"

"Okay. Gotcha." I thought of Sylvia's intoxicating perfume. It was the kind of scent that could lure you into something. Did Jimmy service her?

He was silent as we cleared the tunnel and drove up the helix, past the deep blue and gold shimmer of the skyline. I remembered this ride so many times with Vincent, coming home from a night in Manhattan in his Cadillac. We always felt solid and connected in the car, had our most intimate conversations within its leather and velour plush. We listened to show tunes and held hands. It was the quiet reward for staying together. God, I missed him.

I gazed out the window and sensed Jimmy looking at me. When I glanced at him, I felt as if he'd read my thoughts. He squeezed my arm. "You okay?"

"Yes. I am okay."

"Good. Listen, I just want to build up a stake and start my own business, then I'll dump those two," Jimmy said.

"What do you want to do?" I asked, trying to lift myself out of my sad reverie.

"My own limo service, but I would, you know, sex it up, see? Everybody remembers getting laid in the back seat of a car, right? Sex and wheels, that's America! So, what if there's this fleet of stretch limos with roomy back seats and mirrored windows? And at your fingertips, you got champagne, rubbers, lotions, Viagra, vibrators, shit like that. So, this limo is cruising all over town, and the customers are getting off in the back seat, and that's part of the rush—getting off in front of the Guggenheim or the Empire State Building or in the middle of Times Square. And the whole thing is being filmed! At the end of the ride, the driver hands you your, you know, recording, or whatever, and you're the star! What do you think?"

"There's probably a market for it," I said.

"You think so?"

"Sure. It just needs a sexy name, something like… Sex Drive."

"Sex Drive! Boss, I like the way you think. Maybe you and me could be partners."

"It's not for me."

Jimmy was looking at me and didn't see the red flashers of a disabled car in the center lane. He slammed on the brakes, and we jolted to a stop. Something slid out from under my seat and nestled between my feet. I imagined it was a pint of whiskey. I looked down and saw a small black gun. Jimmy scooped it up and stuck it in the glove compartment.

"Don't ask. I told you, I'm in the soup."

"I don't know what that means. What soup?" I asked as the car started rolling again.

"Let's just say it has a lot of cabbage in it, and don't ask me again," Jimmy said.

We drove in silence for a while. It felt peaceful and familiar, the gun notwithstanding.

Jimmy cleared his throat. "So, what's your story? Who's waiting for you at home?"

"Nobody. You should get off at the next exit."

"Nobody? A sweetheart like you? That's hard to believe," Jimmy said. "You're very easy to talk to. You know that?" He turned to me, smiled, and slipped his big, warm paw into mine. I felt the thrill of being hustled, lulled by his soft voice, the smooth ride, the whoosh of passing cars.

"Thanks." I felt the fur on his knuckles.

We drove through Cedar Chips hand in hand, and I was happy.

"Make a right at the light, then two blocks up."

We pulled up in front of my building.

"I bet you and me could have a good time. Is there someplace we can get a drink around here?" Jimmy asked.

"I've got a bottle of Jameson's upstairs," I blurted.

"Excellent. You're making me hard. Besides, I got to pee."

He was on the futon. I was hard, too, as I handed him a glass of whiskey. He grabbed my wrist.

"I'm gonna take good care of you," he said. "But first I need a water chaser."

I went to the kitchen and got him a glass of water and heard him switch on the TV. I heard the theme song from *The Golden Girls*.

I handed Jimmy his water. His shirt was unbuttoned, and his black pants unzipped. Hey, you got the wrong idea, I could have said. But a version of this is exactly what I wanted. In the car, his hand felt just right, and I wanted both of them and his brawny arms wrapped around my waist as he rocked me through the night. I turned off the TV. No *Golden Girls* tonight.

"Are you a good boy or a bad boy?" Jimmy asked, pulling my face close to his.

"I can go either way. Depends on the personnel," I said.

He ran his hands through my hair. "You're gonna be a bad boy for me, right?"

"Yes, sir."

He pulled my head toward what I thought would be his lips. I landed south, below his chin, and was led on a furry blond tour to his crotch. I was on my knees and pulled his pants down to his ankles. His cock was fat, soft, and stirring. His pubes crackled and smelled of testosterone and Irish Spring. He was a grower and filled my mouth. Then, too soon, his juice pumped out of him and down my throat. He tasted good.

I sat back on the couch and smiled, then leaned forward to kiss him. He stood and pulled up his pants.

"Hate to run, Boss, but I'm still on the clock. The Gold Dust Twins always want something."

"Of course. We all want something."

He patted my face and headed to the door, then he turned.

"Oh, can you spot me some cash for the toll? A twenty would do it."

"Sure." I handed him the twenty and the bottle of Jameson's. "Here, a parting gift."

"Oh, I will be back, trust me," he said as he walked down the stairs.

"Yes, sir."

Goodbye, Jimmy.

I swigged some Jameson's left in Jimmy's glass. I liked the way it tasted with the traces of his jizz. I didn't turn on the TV for a change but stretched out on the futon, my body trembling, pleasurably, from the night's adventures. As I drifted into sleep, it felt like slipping into warm water. I dreamt I was an ingredient in a simmering pot, a stalk of celery in an exotic soup, boring but essential as I gently tumbled around with the cabbage in the tasty broth.

TIAGO, MY LOVE

Joe Ianuzzi yawned and stretched in this strange, small new bed. He looked at his watch and panicked until he realized that he was on vacation and didn't have to run anywhere or listen to the traffic reports on the radio. He curled back up in the spoon position and cupped his stirring cock and balls. He called them his kittens, and nobody else had touched them in a long time. A few minutes later, he was awake again and padded the few feet from the bed to the pint-sized, bruised-purple bathroom. He splashed water on his face and ran his wet hands through his sparse hair, where salt was overtaking the pepper. He looked in the mirror at the perpetual bags under his droopy brown eyes and said, "You are not a pretty girl, Miss Ianuzzi." Then he saw the merry twinkle in the corners, which he hoped was part of his charm. He smoothed his sliver of a mustache and composed his sleep-blurred face into the alert and amiable one he liked to present to the world. Joe blew a kiss to his mirror image, which, like him, was fifty-six, about five-foot-seven, and, according to his doctor, about twenty pounds overweight.

He was in Lisbon at the Hotel Figueira. Figueira meant fig tree, and fig motifs were on every wall, plate, glass, and cocktail napkin. How he got here was a miracle, one lucky break after another, the cards falling in the *right* direction for a change. Joe sat on the bed and wondered what to do next. It was 5:13 p.m., and Lisbon's sun poured its gold through the window, lightening the figs and fig leaves one shade each.

He was glad not to be in his spotless garden apartment in Moonachie, New Jersey, a sleepy little rectangle of a town with 2,000 people, just off Route Seventeen in the shadow of MetLife Stadium. Refreshed from his two-hour nap, he decided to wander around the neighborhood and play it by ear since he hadn't done any research or bought a guidebook. Joe picked up the business card on the nightstand and read "Tiago Pimentel, LusoCafe" above a phone number and email address. Was it too soon to call Tiago?

The overnight TAP flight from Newark had been filled with Portuguese people. When it arrived at dawn, a good-looking, bearded driver from the hotel met him at the airport, greeted him enthusiastically, and led him to a white Mercedes van. His name was Tiago, and he was tall with curly brown hair and merry eyes. He looked to be in his thirties.

"You are from New York!" Tiago said once they were in the roomy van. "I love New York!" Joe didn't have the heart to tell him that he flew in from Newark, and he only went into New York City occasionally.

"Have you ever been there?" Joe asked.

"No, but I feel like I know it from watching *Home Alone 2: Lost in New York* when I was a boy. I saw it so many times that I know it by heart. Is it anything like that?" His English was good with a slight British accent.

"Pretty much," Joe lied. He'd never seen the movie.

"Are you here for business or pleasure?"

"Pleasure, I guess," Joe said, looking at Tiago's inquisitive green eyes in the rear-view mirror.

"Let us make sure you have some," Tiago said. He winked.

Lisbon whizzed by outside the tinted windows. Joe was so intent on the back of Tiago's curly hair and his eyes in the mirror that the city was a picturesque blur.

Like the good salesman he was, Joe asked a lot of questions because he learned over the years that people like to talk about themselves. Joe didn't. He thought himself the most boring man in the United States, or at least New Jersey.

Tiago was thirty-three, married, with a ten-year-old daughter, Pia, his pride and joy. He didn't talk about his wife. He lived in Lisbon in Lumiar, a neighborhood near the edge of town. Driving the van was his part-time job; his main gig was in the marketing department of LusoCafe, a big coffee company.

When they arrived at Hotel Figueira, Tiago jumped out and carried Joe's bags to the front desk. Joe took two twenty-euro notes out of his wallet to give to Tiago, though the airport ride was offered by the hotel and included in the Booking.com rate.

"Thank you very much," Joe said. "I enjoyed the ride and your company."

"As did I! As did I!" Tiago chirped.

Joe held out his hand to shake Tiago's and slip him the bills, but Tiago surprised him with a big, tight hug, his soft beard grazing Joe's face. Was there a peck on the cheek in there, too?

The hug made slipping him the twenties smoothly impossible, so once they separated, Joe shook Tiago's hand and slipped them into his palm. Tiago pocketed the cash without looking at it and gave Joe another hug. This time, he felt Tiago's soft lips on his cheek.

"If you would like to see Lisboa, call me. If I am free, I would love to show you our beautiful city." With that, Tiago was out on the street and back in the van. Joe's face tingled from its brush with Tiago's beard, and he realized that the hug had left him breathless. His body quivered in an agreeable and unfamiliar way. One hug from a handsome man, the graze of his beard, the brush of his soft lips, and he was undone? Was he really that lonely, really that hungry? Yes, and yes.

As a sales rep for Continental Restaurant Supply, The Ironbound section of Newark with its popular Portuguese restaurants was part of his territory, and Joe was there twice a week. He knew all about glassware, dinnerware, and flatware, but restaurant equipment was his specialty. The stakes were higher and so were the commissions. His clients trusted him and his twenty years in the business. His informed soft sell and reliability made him one of the best restaurant supply salesmen in New Jersey.

Arctic Air had a promotion on its new HC55 Merchandiser, the kind of thing that you reach into at a deli for a Snapple or that a waiter would reach into for a carrot cake. Sell five of them and win a trip to Europe. He didn't expect to win, he never won anything, but he liked the challenge of it.

Thanks to his fact-filled, low-key sales pitch, a heat wave, and a power outage, Joe wound up selling five HC55s, three in Newark alone, in a record three weeks. Arctic Air gave him a week in Lisbon, airfare, hotel, and $1,000 play money. He flew TAP, the Portuguese airline, to keep the vibe Portuguese, and because of his clients, he knew something of the complicated, intriguing language. He enjoyed it in the banter of the robust kitchen crews at their aromatic, communal late-afternoon meals, like music with a gentle, aggrieved undercurrent running through it.

This trip came at just the right time. Joe was stuck. The job was tolerable, and he made a decent living, but there were no surprises. He got up at seven a.m. and was on the road by eight thirty, first stopping by the office/showroom in Hackensack for sales meetings and paperwork. Then he hit the road, seeing ten to fifteen clients a day, and he usually got home by six thirty or seven p.m. His clients and the people at the office constituted his only social life these days. He used to stop at one or another of his clients' restaurants for dinner, but after being told he had to lose weight, he just popped Hot Pockets into the microwave and ate them in front of the TV. Then he watched porn and scrolled the apps, hoping against hope that he could meet someone nice or at least have an adventure. Instead, he felt trapped in a bad video game he couldn't win, so he typed and swiped until he was exhausted. Two glasses of ice-cold Stoli right from the freezer, and then it was bedtime.

But not tonight—Lisbon was waiting for him.

He took a shower and got dressed, a baby blue Tasso Elba short-sleeve shirt, cotton pants, and a Tasso Elba tan linen blazer. As he was packing, he'd googled "What to wear in

Lisbon" and got "Smart, casual, understated. And wear nice shoes." Perfect. That was his summer salesman uniform. Joe took the fig-leaf-filled elevator three floors down to the lobby, then he was on the street in the middle of a crowd waiting for one of the quaint yellow street cars. He looked to the left and to the right. To the right, the lines for the streetcars clogged the pavement with tourists, and there was a hill with an imposing castle on top of it. A castle!

There was more light and air to the left, and the balmy air carried a promising maritime tang. He walked toward the light, passing bakeries with creamy pastries front and center and those deceptively simple, addictive pasteis de nata, Portuguese custard tarts that he bought in Newark and used to eat by the dozen. He passed spotless, upscale pharmacies staffed by what looked like models in dazzling white lab coats. He heard the insistent but benevolent sound of rushing water. Was there a waterfall in the middle of the city?

One more block and the street opened onto a massive, brightly lit square, Rossio. Its size and unexpected beauty took his breath away. Coming from the clogged roads and tight spaces of New Jersey, he wasn't used to such an expanse. The waterfall turned out to be two massive, ornate fountains at each end of the square, green with age and algae, occupied by bronze mermaids, cherubs, gods, and goddesses either spouting the water or basking in its spray.

The pavement of Rossio Square, black and white tile in a zig-zag pattern, looked like a disorienting optical illusion: a yellow brick road on a black-and-white TV. Entranced, Joe walked around the perimeter of the fountain, admiring its striking green inhabitants.

In the center of the square sat an imposing white marble monument, topped by a dashing soldier who gazed sternly over his domain, a book in one hand. He was King Pedro IV, the plaque said. He looked like Tiago, his new friend. They both had curly hair and beards. Joe would ask Tiago about this king when next they met.

"It's lovely," an elderly British woman in a straw hat said to her elderly male companion. "But you did *not* want to be here in the fifteen hundreds. This is where they burned heretics at the stake!"

"Heavens!" the old gentleman exclaimed and fanned himself with his boater.

The woman continued, "Auto-da-fe is a Portuguese word, you know."

"The savages!" he replied. "Now I should like one of those scrummy custard tarts."

Joe had a vague idea of what the Inquisition was. Wasn't Joan of Arc caught up in it? He stood in the middle of Rossio Square, drank in its historic splendor, and wondered what to do next. He turned to the right, and there was a wide street, Rua Augusta. It was a promenade, closed off to traffic, with a black and cream tiled sidewalk in a soothing geometric pattern, and it was crowded on this Saturday evening. At its entrance was a life-sized green statue of a woman in a full-skirted dress on a small pedestal that turned ever so slowly. Who was she supposed to be, the Joan of Arc of Portugal? On her turning platform, she was a foot taller than him, and Joe stared up at her passive, mysterious face. Suddenly, she moved her arms into another static position. Oh! She was a puppet. She opened her eyes and winked at him. Oh! He jumped. He'd never seen anything like her before. She had a green hat near the pedestal, and Joe instinctively dug in his pockets but remembered he had no change, just three twenty-euro notes, and he'd have to catch her on the way back to the hotel.

After that, Joe encountered living statues every few feet: ballerinas, monks, knights, and he loved them—what dedication and technique! You would never see *them* at the Willowbrook Mall back home. Musicians held court every fifty feet or so: three young men in black capes playing guitars; a tall tan man pounding on a conga drum while his short, dark female partner played the marimba and sang a sprightly, hypnotic tune in a language he didn't recognize; and the most energetic, a wiry African man with bongos and a boom box who had strollers clapping along and dancing with him. A block away, an over-mic'd and amped rock band with flowing blond hair looked like they stepped off a 1987 album cover.

Four-story pastel buildings with mini balconies on their second floors lined Rua Augusta. Every kind of shop took up the first floors: jewelry stores, aromatic bakeries, stylish pharmacies, a Zara, and an H&M. There were several cafes smack in the middle of the promenade with dapper waiters who beckoned you to have a seat. A fragrant gravitational pull lured strollers westward, where the last rays of light beamed over an enormous, glistening white arch.

The pedestrian traffic thickened as he approached the majestic white archway at the end of Rua Augusta, with the promise of something grand and gleaming on the other side.

He waited for a light to change behind a beautiful Scandinavian family: a tall, lean father with sandy hair; a tall, lean, pretty mother with golden hair; a ten-year-old boy who looked just like his father; and a seven-year-old girl who looked just like her mother. He gazed at the father's beautifully shaped little ears and wanted to nuzzle them. With a resigned sigh, he took in the rest of the crowd at the curb. They were all families and couples, in glowing spirits and holding hands. On this beautiful street on this golden evening, all these happy people were coupled up, and only he was alone. The thought zinged into his heart like a poison arrow. How had he wound up so alone for so long?

He grew up in Clifton, New Jersey, an only child in a small ranch house. His terse, unpleasant father wasn't around much and walked out one day after a shouting match on his wife's forty-sixth birthday. A teenager, Joe was left with his mother, Connie, a squat, tart-tongued hypochondriac. To protest her husband's departure, she refused to drive anymore, so Joe became her chauffeur: once a week to Stop and Shop, once a week to CVS for her meds, twice a week to various doctors for a variety of ailments. Her singsong lament of a voice leaked out of her like carbon monoxide; after a few hours, you were nearly unconscious. Joe developed immunity over time. Each time Connie barked, he imagined the kindly face and melodious voice of his fifth-grade teacher, Mrs. Feingold. He wasn't a good student, but she was patient with him, and when she came to his desk, she rested a hand gently on his shoulder. It thrilled him.

"I hope that stupid doctor takes me right away. That waiting room is so dingy."

Yes, ma.

"Are you listening to me?"

"Yes, Ma. Yes, Ma." Twenty, thirty times a day or more.

"Pay attention when I talk to you!"

She liked to grab his wrist and twist it for emphasis with her surprisingly powerful claws. He longed for Mrs. Feingold's lovely touch.

Connie and Joe were always side by side at home on the couch, at the kitchen table, in the car, or in a doctor's waiting room, sharing twice-chewed information about television shows, their neighbors, the family, and Connie's health in high, plaintive voices. Connie had given up cooking, too, so Joe learned how from an old *Fanny Farmer* and newer *Nella Cucina*.

They needed money, so, while still in high school, Joe got a job as a busboy at Il Marinello, a big barn of an Italian restaurant on Route Forty-Six. He enjoyed the hectic pace and friendly racket of the restaurant, refreshingly different from life with Connie. When a coked-up waiter had a meltdown in the kitchen one night, Joe was pushed onto the floor to take over his tables. He did a good job and graduated to waiter.

The manager pulled him aside one busy evening and said, "You sound like a pussy. You need to work on your voice, and you'll make more money," Joe was mortified and went to the library, where he found a book: *How to Improve Your Speaking Voice*. He listened carefully to news anchors and Jeopardy's Alex Trebek and cobbled together his own *Ianuzzi Process*: slow down, breathe, talk from your diaphragm, and warm up with a mooing rumble that sounded like a buffalo stuck in the mud. He found a phrase that he liked and used it as a mantra and a diction warm-up; *I'm sending you a bottle of wonderful fundamentals*. His tips doubled, and when that manager quit, Joe took over.

His salesman from Continental Supply was a short, sexy Cuban, Julio, who breezed in and out once a week to take Joe's order. Joe envied Julio's freedom. As a restaurant manager, he had to contend with drug-addled kitchen staff, flaky servers, sticky-fingered bartenders, lengthy, unconvincing excuses, and long hours. Julio pointed out that as a salesman, he could leave all that behind and show up in a nice suit, write stuff down, and be home for dinner every night. He already knew the gritty, grunt end of the business, so why not try the glamour side?

Joe couldn't afford to take chances; Connie needed him, and this schedule worked for them. Pulled into Connie's sour undertow, Joe's days stumbled into years, and his youth evaporated. He came home from the restaurant one afternoon between shifts and found Connie on the couch, staring bug-eyed at *Oprah!* She was dead, and Joe, at age thirty-seven, was free.

Continental hired him, and after a slow start, he became a good salesman, using all the skills he learned on the restaurant floor: reading people and giving them what they want. His *Ianuzzi Process* voice didn't hurt either.

While Connie was alive, there was the tacit understanding that if he had any social life whatsoever—it would kill her. She never asked him what he was up to or how he felt, so his sexual orientation was lost in the mist of her narcissism. He found a few outlets for quickies: adult bookstores, rest stops, some cruisy sections of parks, but now with Connie gone, he could finally go to a gay bar and stay out all night if he wanted. He had heard about Feathers, a famous gay club from prehistoric times, so he chugged some Stolichnaya courage straight from the bottle and went one Tuesday night. The crowd was a mix of very young guys and guys older than him. The blasting music made his heart pound, and he found a seat at the bar and took in the exotic sights. Joe liked the look of the thin, attractive young guy next to him. He had red hair and freckles, and when he spoke, he sounded just like a woman. Joe didn't care; he imagined the boy's pug-nosed profile on the pillow next to him. Joe's elbow accidentally touched his, and the boy glanced at him, then glanced through him, scooped up his money from the bar, and walked away. Wounded, Joe looked across the bar and saw his own unhappy face in a mirror there.

But—it wasn't a mirror. A guy on the other side of the bar had the same round face, the same little mustache, and a halo of brown hair. His shirt was red, and Joe had to make sure that his shirt was blue, and he wasn't seeing his own troubled reflection. His doppelganger held up a glass and toasted Joe. Then he waved for Joe to come over and occupy the empty stool next to him. He introduced himself, Angelo Fiore, and bought Joe a drink. He was about thirty-five years old with prominent black eyes and a blunt nose, and he looked a bit like a bulldog terrier. There was a perpetual frown around his mouth, and his voice was sharp and scolding even in banter. When Joe got ready to leave, Angelo put his hand on Joe's knee and squeezed it. They went back to Joe's house. Angelo had a nice big ass. He moved in the next day.

Joe slogged through ten rocky years with Angelo. He was a hairdresser, and a good one, but he kept losing jobs because of his terrible temper. Over time, his voice got more scolding, and he lost the terrier and just looked like a bulldog. After the first couple of years, they didn't have that much to say to each other, but Joe felt better being part of a couple, even an unhappy one. So what if Angelo lied about everything? So what if he thought everybody was stupid? So what if he didn't pay his share of the expenses and snuck money from Joe's sock drawer and wallet? Even though Angelo cheated on him regularly and blatantly, Joe vowed to stick it out.

One night, Angelo picked a fight about a misplaced remote, stormed out, and took off for Jersey City to live with his sidepiece, a chubby Venezuelan masseur. Joe was relieved. To get away from the lingering exhaust of both Connie and Angelo, he sold the house and bought the condo in Moonachie, three miles away. That was twelve years ago. There were a few dates after Angelo's departure, then a bunch of hookups, and then a lot of nothing for a long, long time. Instead, he fell instantly in love with every attractive man he saw and imagined romantic adventures with them that evaporated in a moment or two.

A horn honked, there was movement around him at the curb, and Joe dropped back into his body and the present. The light had changed, and he followed the delicate ears of the young Scandinavian father toward the magnificent white archway. It was a balmy evening in beautiful Lisbon, and he was alone, yes, but he was free to explore. There was a plaque on the arch: Arco da Rua Augusta. The clock at the top said it was seven twenty.

He walked through the arch onto another enormous, glorious square, Praça do Comércio. In its center stood another huge bronze statue of a man on a steed while churning white bodies on the marble base below tried to reach him. Beyond the statue, the square ended with a body of rugged blue water.

But before that azure horizon, the massive plaza was generously sprinkled with booths sprouting rainbow flags. Some of the booths represented civic organizations, but most repped gay bars from across the city, and they offered beer, wine, cocktails, sausages, and grilled sardines. Joe had stumbled onto Lisbon's Gay Pride celebration, and the square was filling up with an army of excited, vibrant gay people of every color and shape. Beautiful boys sashayed by him in tank tops and short shorts, glamorous lesbians clustered in rings, butch dykes strolled hand in hand beside burly drag queens and slender trans teens. Every few feet, Joe saw nondescript middle-aged men just like himself. No, like his former pre-Lisbon self. And, so far, he was the best conventionally dressed man on the square. Joe took a deep breath and remembered his mission to have fun and leave his boring old self behind.

There was a small stage up by the waterfront, and a DJ in a skintight purple body suit spun mostly American dance tunes. Joe stopped at a booth from the bar Shelter, and a beefy, bearded boy with glasses served him a gin and tonic in a plastic cup. He smiled a gap-toothed smile as he handed it over. The smile from the beefy boy, the good music, the crowd's high spirits, and the first few sips of gin put Joe in a happy daze. Finally, for the first time in his life, this was exactly the right place to be, and he stood, happily, right in its joyous center. Yes, time for another drink; he wanted to see that smile again, and he got it.

Five people got up on the stage behind the DJ: a young woman dressed as a nurse, a young man done up as a sailor, a young woman as a nun, another boy as a priest, and a slightly older, dark-haired man with a goatee dressed as a cop. He seemed to be the leader and looked like Johnny Depp in *Pirates of the Caribbean*. The quintet started a sweet, synchronized dance routine to "Pump Up the Volume" by M/A/R/R/S. The Johnny Depp guy looked about thirty-five, and his dancing was looser and more confident than the others. Joe got another drink and another smile from the beefy boy.

People were dancing in front of the bandstand, and in the center was a knot of pretty trans people with heavy mascara and spiky rainbow hair wearing identical pink tee shirts. The square filled, nudging Joe closer to the bandstand. He wanted to get a better look at the short and wiry Johnny Depp, who danced ecstatically: was he *in* ecstasy or *on* ecstasy? The sun set in an orange sky, bathing the crowd in its glow, and Joe decided that Johnny Depp would be his next boyfriend. He waved at the stage as his body rocked side to side to the hot dance music. Johnny led the onstage ensemble down a few steps, and they snaked themselves into a space right in front of the bandstand, ten or so feet from him.

Joe stopped dancing years ago after Angelo told him he looked like a gimpy elephant on the dance floor. But, right now, in this lovely, joyful crowd bathed in sunset and high spirits, this, *whatever he was doing,* felt good. The music had infiltrated his body, and maybe he did look like an elephant, but he felt like a gazelle. He edged closer to Johnny, who was just within reach. Joe just wanted to be face to face with him, and he hoped, like the rest of this enchanted night in this enchanted city, something good would happen. One more step.

His left foot landed on a piece of pineapple from a spilled pina colada, and he skidded into the hairy back of a burly leather bear who spun around, glared, then smiled at him, his teeth gleaming through his black beard. Joe realized he was drunk and that he was hungry, too. Johnny had disappeared into the crowd.

Praça do Comércio was mobbed now, and he wanted air, so he squeezed his way back toward the arch where there were some food stands. He got a delightfully greasy sausage sandwich and washed it down with a refreshing bottle of orange Sumol. There was a comparatively quiet spot with an empty table, and Joe sat there watching more excited people entering the Praça. So, he didn't wind up with Johnny Depp, but he was finally surrounded by his own tribe, and in its rousing midst, his belly and heart were full.

He woke up with a hangover, and he wanted coffee, lots of it, so he headed to Rua Augusta, where he found a congenial, uncrowded spot under an umbrella and took a seat. A dapper, older waiter was immediately at his side with an ornate menu. The waiter spoke English and suggested a galao and torradas. Why not?

The waiter returned with the galao, a blend of espresso and steamed milk in a glass container, and two large pieces of buttery golden toast, the torradas, on a bone china plate, his salesman's eye noted. Perfect. A word popped into his head: *civilized.* Everything here was so civilized.

He called Tiago. Uh oh. His voicemail message was in Portuguese. Wait. Then it switched to English. Joe left a message and got a text in response.

Good to hear from you, my friend. I will call you later.

My friend!

Joe strolled down Rua Augusta, back to the splendid Praça do Comércio, where a cleanup crew was efficiently dealing with the aftermath of last night's celebration. He walked to the water's edge and googled his location, ah, the Tagus River, Rio Tejo, with the Atlantic and the magnificent Golden Gate Bridge tantalizingly within view. Wait. The Golden Gate was in San Francisco, right? He knew that much. He googled the bridge: "It is traditional for poets to refer to the entwining Tagus as Lisbon's lover," the Google entry read. "The 25th of April Bridge was named after the date of the Carnation Revolution in 1974." It was the longest suspension bridge in Europe and built by the same company that built the Golden Gate.

As he gazed at the ocean, Joe felt the tug Portuguese explorers like Vasco da Gama must have felt, that you were at the edge of the world, and a powerful magnet, like horizontal gravity, summoned you westward toward adventure—whether you could swim or not. He couldn't.

Tiago called. Today he was with his family, but he could give Joe a tour on Monday, and maybe Tuesday, if that suited him. They settled on 200 Euros a day. While Tiago spoke, Joe could hear a young girl's voice in the background, piping for her daddy's attention.

Joe went back toward the hotel and saw hop-on/off tour buses leaving from Figueira Square. He got on one with a female driver, who was, alas, not in a good mood. The bus trundled up a particularly wide, stately boulevard, Avenida de Libertad, and then wove all over town to the majestic Belém Tower and back again. The driver brusquely announced locations in Portuguese but didn't explain them, and her mike cut out after every other word. Joe had not been on a bus in years and felt nauseous, so he couldn't wait to disembark when it got back to Figueira Square. Between the bus and the hotel was a lively market with fragrant food stalls. Feeling better, he got a bowl of delicious shrimp and garlic and washed it down with a couple of bottles of good Portuguese beer, then he shuffled back to the hotel and took a long nap.

The Gay Pride celebration the night before whetted his appetite for more of gay Lisbon. He tried to remember the name on the booth where the boy smiled at him... Shutter? Sh-something. Shelter!

He googled it, "Cozy and friendly bear bar in a relaxed atmosphere." He took a shower, got dressed, and stepped outside, where he hailed a cab and gave the gaunt driver the address.

It seemed a long and twisty uphill route through narrow streets before they pulled into a tiny square surrounded by ancient buildings, and there, tucked in the corner, was Shelter.

It was comfy and intimate inside on this late Sunday afternoon. Four patrons at the bar all looked to be bearish and in their forties. They sat separately and looked at their phones while they nursed the beers in front of them.

There was no bartender to be seen, so Joe stood awkwardly at the bar, instantly invisible to the quartet, who glanced at and away from him when he entered. He heard clumping from a back room, someone coming upstairs. It was his young dreamboat from the day before wearing a lime green tank top from which his furry pecs and big arms bulged. He smiled as if he might have recognized Joe and said, "Ola."

"Um. Gin?" Joe cleared his throat and asked. He saw a bottle of Hendricks behind the bar. "Hendricks. And can I have some cucumber with that?"

The bartender nodded. Under his scruff and muscles, he looked like an altar boy, with big dark eyes beneath his rimless specs. He disappeared into the back, and Joe took a seat at the bar, a couple of stools away from the nearest patron. There was a stack of gay pocket guides on the bar, and Joe flipped through one: bars, baths, masseurs, escorts, and parties. Was Lisbon the center of the gay universe?

The boy returned with his Hendrick's and tonic. It was so full of thinly sliced cucumbers that it looked like an appetizer. How thoughtful! Now, he loved the boy even more.

"This is gorgeous," Joe said. He held out his hand. "My name is Joe."

The boy gripped his hand with a big, warm paw. "I am Duarte."

Joe tried to think of something to say but was stumped.

"I hope you enjoy," Duarte said and went to the opposite end of the bar.

Joe smiled amiably into the empty space where Duarte had been, just in case he returned momentarily. He sipped his drink and munched on the thin, crisp cucumber slices. He looked at the TV with its mismatched sound and video and looked down the bar at the other patrons who didn't look up. How could he judge them? He wanted to hide in his phone, too, but this trip, this captivating city, was an opportunity for him to change. But without Duarte in front of him, giving him a context and something to look at, he was just a chubby and lonely fifty-six-year-old man.

No, none of that sad sack stuff tonight. The smooth gin seeped into and soothed his nervous system, and the crunch of the cucumbers kept him alert. There were so many! His drink was now a glass full of invigorating cucumber slices, and he happily crunched on them. When he got home, he would patent and promote these gin-soaked cucumber slices as an alternative to potato chips, refreshing and good for you.

Duarte set another gin and cucumber appetizer in front of him. Joe sipped happily, his chin comfortably in his hand in his new home away from home, and he spaced out for a spell. Another drink magically appeared.

"Oh boy!" Joe blurted, startling the guy next to him, who looked up and then right back down again.

"Buenos dias!" Joe said to him. He was drunk. What time was it anyway? He looked at his watch. There was no watch. Did he lose it or forget to wear it? What is time anyway? And who cares about it?

Duarte's face swam before him. He looked so serious! How adorable. Duarte tapped his shoulder. "My friend. You are very tired. Let me get you a taxi."

Joe nodded. Duarte took his hand and led him out the door, where a taxi was waiting.

"Where do you live?" he asked.

"Moonachie," Joe said.

Duarte eased him into the cab, shielding the top of Joe's head against a bump. Joe woke up at eight the next morning. He didn't have a hangover, which he attributed to all those nutritious cucumbers.

Tiago called at nine and said he would be at the hotel by ten. Perfect! He knocked on the door at exactly ten, and his frame filled the doorway. Joe had forgotten that Tiago was over six feet tall. He had on a white polo shirt and jeans and a fresh, citrusy scent, which Joe smelled in the crook of his neck when Tiago hugged him. Joe recognized that it was Hermes Eau d'Orange Verte, a fragrance he'd sampled, but it didn't smell good on him. On Tiago, it was intoxicating.

"What would you like to do today?"

"You take charge," Joe said.

"Have you had breakfast yet?"

Joe shook his head.

The van was parked in front of the hotel, and they hopped in and drove a short distance uphill past posh stores, shops, and cafes that gleamed in the misty sunlight. Tiago parked on the street, and it was a short walk to their destination, a café called a Brasileira, with bright white tables and chairs shaded by yellow umbrellas outside. In front of its ornate, Art Deco exterior sat one of those living statues, a serious bronze gentleman in a hat, his leg crossed, one arm resting on a small table, a vacant chair nearby. If the hat was on his head, Joe wondered, where did he expect people to put donations? This city loved its statues, living and otherwise.

"That is Fernando Pessoa, Portugal's greatest poet," Tiago declared.

Poor guy, Joe thought. A famous poet, and he still had to perform on the street for money. Joe had some change but wasn't sure where to put it. Tiago rested his hand on the poet's head, and he didn't flinch. This Pessoa guy was the best living statue he'd seen yet.

Tiago cleared his throat and recited:

Nao seu nada

Nunca serei nada

Nao posso querer ser nada

Aparte isso, tenho em mim todos os sonos do mundo.

Tiago knocked on the poet's head, and there was a soft metal clank.

Oh, it was a real bronze statue.

"What did you just say?" Joe asked.

"Oh, that is one of my favorite Pessoa poems. It translates:

I am nothing

I shall never be anything

I cannot even wish to be anything

Apart from this, I have within me all the dreams of the world.

"I don't read much," Joe said, "but that is interesting."

"A Brasileira began in 1905, and Pessoa came here sometimes, as did other artists. Pessoa had a quiet and sad little life, and his writing is simple and strong."

A quiet and sad little life, like me, Joe thought. *I am nothing… Stop that!*

Tiago squeezed Joe's bicep. Did he read his mind? Was that for reassurance?

"Let us go inside," Tiago said. "It is like stepping into history."

The striking interior was like an expensive jewel box. The floor was composed of black and white tiles with a long bar on one side, wooden tables against mirrored walls, and rich ochre wooden panels. Imposing brass lamps hung from the ceiling, which, like most of the room, was ablaze in red and gold with mahogany accents.

A waiter rushed up to Tiago, hugged him, and kissed both his cheeks, and they were led to a table in the back.

"I am glad this worked out for us today," Tiago said. "I enjoyed our ride from the airport."

"Me too!" Joe said.

"Are you very hungry?" Tiago asked, glancing at the rococo menu.

"I know what I want," Joe said. "A galao and torradas. I had them yesterday."

"Esplendido!" Tiago exclaimed. "Now you are one of us!"

Tiago ordered the same thing.

"I would like to know more about you," Tiago said. "Your surname is Ianuzzi, right? I remember from the pickup sheet. And you are Joseph?"

"Everybody... People call me Joe."

"Ianuzzi? That is Italian, right? Does it mean anything?"

"Don't think so."

"May I just call you Joe?

"Sure."

"My surname is Pimentel. It comes from pimienta, the word for pepper, so my people must have been spice traders."

"Tiago Pimentel. I like it," Joe said.

"Tell me about yourself, Jose."

No one had ever asked him that before, and Joe was flummoxed. He haltingly talked about his job and the contest that got him here. The words squeezed out slowly, and Joe was embarrassed by relating his small life in front of this lovely man. *I am nothing. I shall never be anything.* He was quiet.

"What happened?" Tiago asked.

I am the most boring man in the world, Joe thought. And then the words slipped out of his mouth.

"Oh, I thought that was my father-in-law," Tiago responded, unfazed, his eyes twinkling. "But if you won a contest, you must be a very good salesman, so you cannot be *that* boring."

"Yes. I guess so." Joe blushed. "This is a beautiful place. This is a beautiful city."

"I like what you are wearing. You look sophisticated and comfortable," Tiago said. "Not like the usual tourist."

"Thanks!" Joe said. *Sophisticated!* No one had ever said that to him before. "It's all Tasso Elba. They have a good range, stuff in my size, and it holds up. They're Macy's private label."

"Macy's!" Tiago exclaimed, and he was instantly a little boy watching *Home Alone 2* again. "I would love to visit Manhattan and stay at the Plaza Hotel! I would wander in Central Park, walk on Fifth Avenue, and go to Duncan's Toy Chest. It must be very exciting." His face glowed, and Joe had never seen that kind of happiness in a real person, only on TV commercials.

"Yes," Joe said. He saw the Plaza once when he and Angelo went to see the tree at Rockefeller Center. He wasn't sure about Duncan's Toy Chest, though. Was that a real place?

"I'm gay," Joe blurted.

"Wonderful. Do you have someone?" Tiago asked as their eyes met momentarily.

Joe shook his head.

"I am surprised. You seem like a very warm and domestic person."

Tiago's phone rang. His ringtone was the theme from *Star Wars*. "I am a nerd," he said with a shrug. He glanced at his phone and frowned.

"You can take that," Joe said.

"No," Tiago said. "It will only..." Tiago changed gears abruptly. "I would like to take you to Sintra today, a nice drive a few miles out of the city on the Portuguese Riviera. It is filled with palaces and castles. It is *over the top*, as you guys say."

"Okay."

The phone rang again, and Tiago glared at it. His *Home Alone 2* joy had evaporated. He didn't take the call and signaled for the check.

Tiago was quiet as they walked the colorful, crowded street to get to the van.

Once they were inside it, Tiago looked at his phone, read a text, and spluttered some Portuguese profanity.

"Are you okay?" Joe asked.

Tiago was quiet and stared out onto the street.

"I am sorry," he said.

"No worries."

"Sometimes being alone, as you are, is better than being with the wrong person, I think," Tiago said. "My marriage is very… desafiador…"

"Huh?"

"It is very, um, problematic."

"Oh." Joe didn't know what to say. His conversations were all business-related small talk, and nobody had ever said such a thing to him. They were on the road now, quiet as they drove along the coastline with the sparkling Atlantic Ocean on their left.

"It's like it's alive," Joe said, nodding his head toward the roiling blue expanse.

"Yes!" Tiago said. "You are a poet at heart."

"Me? You mean like that statue guy? Nah."

"Yes. Pessoa has a poem about the sea. Um, something, something…

There are no more reasons for loving, hating, doing one's duty

There are only the Abstract Departure and the water's movement

The movement of pulling away, the sound

Of the waves lulling the prow

And a large, skittish peace that softly enters the soul.

"We could all use that large, skittish peace, yes?"

Joe could only nod. He'd only been in Portugal two days, and he felt like he was on another planet, in another dimension. This gorgeous view, this charming, civilized country, this adorable, poetry-spouting man with his problematic marriage, compared with Joe's mingy life back home. Suddenly, his eyes burned. He never cried.

He felt Tiago's warm hand on his.

"Are you okay over there, my friend?" he asked.

Joe nodded out the window.

"This is your holiday. I do not want you to be sad."

Joe nodded again and rubbed his burning eyes. This lovely man was holding his hand and comforting him in his soothing voice. It was too much. He wanted to run back to his safe apartment, plant himself on the couch, watch TV, eat a hot pocket, and zone out into his cozy, benumbed Moonachie stupor.

No. Not today.

Joe composed himself. "I am okay. I'm sorry you are having a hard time."

"Let us forget it. I am sorry it came up," Tiago said with a shrug. "Cada pe dolorito, ha um chinelo rasgado."

"Huh?"

"Something that my grandmother used to say, it means for every sore foot there is a torn slipper."

They drove in silence, still holding hands, until the landscape got rockier and twistier, requiring both Tiago's hands on the wheel. Joe drifted into a cozy nap as they navigated rugged, dun-colored hills. Tiago pulled into a parking area, and not far away, a large white cross jutted out onto the mountainside while fierce waves crashed way down below. They walked a winding path filled with a busload of exuberant Polish tourists, the wind whipping them while the ocean frothed to their right.

In the distance, the sea and sky melted together into a slate-blue horizon that suggested infinity and that there just *might* be a God and a heaven.

"Where are we?" Joe asked.

"Cabo da Roca. It is the westernmost point in all of Europe." Tiago spread both arms as if he needed to supplement its grandeur. "Centuries ago, people thought that this was the edge of the earth."

Joe shivered a bit and wished he had a windbreaker.

"Oh, you are cold." Tiago put his warm, furry arm across Joe's shoulders and pulled him close. Its weight and temperature felt just right, and Tiago seemed his merry self again.

"I am sorry about earlier," Tiago said. "I want you to have a good time. No more saudades."

"No more... what?" Joe asked.

"Saudades. It is, um, a feeling of sadness, of, let's see, missing something. It is very common in Portugal. We invented it!"

Tiago pulled out his phone, entered some text, and then read: "Saudade or saudades is a deep emotional state of nostalgic or profound melancholic longing for an absent something or someone that one cares for and/or loves. Blah, blah, blah... Ah, here we go... One English translation of the word could be *missingness*."

"Oh, ok," Joe said, beginning to understand. *If* he didn't keep himself busy. *If* he didn't numb his feelings with TV and porn, there was an overwhelming ache at his core that he dare not explore.

"Yearning," Tiago said. "I think that is a good word for it. Everyone has it, but we Portuguese have perfected it. There is the story of the old lady who complains, *I am so thirsty, so thirsty. Oh, how thirsty I am.* A stranger gives her water, and she gulps it down. She does not thank him. Instead, she says, *I was so thirsty, so thirsty. Oh, how thirsty I was!* That is being Portuguese!"

"I get it," Joe said and meant.

"Just listen to our music. Have you ever heard fado? It is never good news," Tiago said as they stopped walking. "We Portuguese are good at three things: complaining, teasing, and singing."

"Do you sing?" Joe asked.

"I love to sing but am not very good," Tiago answered. "I suck, as you guys say. Come, my friend; we should go. You are cold, and we need to get away from the end of the earth and into its warm center."

They drove on to Sintra and visited the Pena Palace while Tiago acted as the tour guide and recited valuable information that Joe had a hard time absorbing. Tiago knew the staff at the palaces and was greeted warmly with double-cheeked kisses by men and women.

Who *were* the Moors exactly, and why were they so important? Joe wished he read more. Whatever he was saying, Tiago looked and sounded good saying it, and Joe was touched that he was trying to give him his money's worth. He had something that Joe had never experienced before. What was it?

Charm! It was his first time seeing charm in action up close and the effect it had on people, on him. There had been a drought of it most of his life, and now its effects were disorienting and overwhelming—but most welcome. After just a few hours with him, Joe felt closer to this lovely man than he'd felt to anyone. They had even held hands, which Joe had never done with anyone except maybe Connie when he was small, and they crossed a street.

They entered an airy room with walls covered in gleaming white and blue tile that pictured elaborate stories from history. Joe thought the tile, without all the stories, would work in his bathroom back home. Then he imagined shaving at the sink while he listened to Tiago singing in his shower as he rinsed Joe's favorite shower gel, Cremo All Season No. 4, off his lean, furry body. *Tiago, my love,* Joe whispered to himself.

"What do you think?" he heard Tiago ask over the sound of imaginary running water.

Joe was startled. "Um. Nice," he said. "I've seen this blue tile all around Lisbon."

"Azulejos," Tiago said. "Another thing we got from the Moors."

They found themselves alone in an opulent bedroom, its gold-flecked walls absorbed and then reflected the sun pouring in through a large window draped in silk curtains. In its center stood a massive burgundy four-poster, the kind of bed fit for a king, with matching, ponderous festoons dripping off its ebony bedposts. With the bed so close, Joe felt very, very tired and imagined lying down on it with Tiago, the two of them in a tender embrace as they drifted into sleep. They drove back along the coast to Lisbon in relaxed, intimate silence and parked on Rua Nova da Almada. They walked down the narrow street and passed an old bookstore that looked like it belonged on a movie set.

"We are back in Chiado, not far from the café we went to, a Brasileira," Tiago said. "This bookstore, Livraria Ferin, began in 1840. Do you read very much?"

"No. Just trade magazines," Joe said.

"Oh. I love this place. I had a reading here last year."

"Nice," Joe said. What was a reading?

Tiago looked disappointed, then recovered.

"Let us have a drink."

They strolled a block or so south of the bookstore to Nova, a sleek wine bar. The door was open, but the place was empty. The interior was woodsy, cool industrial chic with long blond plank tables and dark walnut shelves filled with hundreds of wine bottles. A short, sexy blond man with a goatee and a bodybuilder's frame came out of the back and hugged Tiago, kissed his cheeks. Jeez, this guy knew *everybody*.

Tiago introduced him to the owner and chef, whose name was Pedro. He ordered a bottle of alvarinho and some tapas. Pedro and Tiago chatted intimately in Portuguese like old friends, and the chef giggled like a schoolgirl several times until he headed back to the kitchen to prep for the dinner crowd.

"So, my friend, I hope you are feeling better," Tiago said.

"Oh, yes. Thank you."

"You know, you are very relaxing to be with. You are very simpatico," Tiago said.

"I think I know what simpatico means, and it's good, right? I feel the same."

"You are in sales, yes? Like me. Remind me, what exactly do you sell?"

"Restaurant supplies, refrigerators, ovens, plates, glasses, well, everything in this place."

"I suspect that you are good."

"I am the best restaurant supply salesman in New Jersey," Joe said, echoing what the Arctic Air sales manager said when he handed him the prize check. It felt good to say it out loud. "Tell me about your work. What do you do at LusoCafe?"

"Sales and distribution to wholesalers. It is very boring, but it pays well enough."

"Do you like it?"

"Do you like *your* job?" Tiago asked.

"Yes. I do. I really do," Joe was happy to say.

"I do not feel the same way. I was, what is the word? Yes. *Conscripted* into service by my father-in-law."

"Oh."

"Yes. His daughter was pregnant, and they wanted to make sure the princess would not go hungry, so we were married, and I went to work." A cloud crossed Tiago's face.

"Oh."

"I love my daughter, Pia. She is ten years old and is the apple in my eye. The rest is not so good."

"I'm sorry to hear that," Joe said, not sure if he was, but he sensed Tiago's distress.

"I am a writer, but now I am too busy to write. Her family thinks I am crazy. Que tenho macaquinhos na cabeça." He made the international finger twirl sign for crazy. "They think that I have monkeys in my head."

"What do you write?"

"I write plays. Some of them have been produced. I like to write historical dramas. I would like to be on the West End and on Broadway. Do you go Broadway?"

"Yes." He and Angelo went to *Les Misérables* years ago. Angelo skipped out at intermission and didn't come home that night.

"My play, *A Death in Coimbra,* is about the murder of Ines, the mistress of Pedro the First."

Joe lit up. "Oh, Pedro, the statue in the square." He finally knew something!

"No. That is Pedro the Fourth. The first Pedro fell in love with his wife's lady-in-waiting, Ines de Castro, and even after his wife died, he was not allowed to marry her. His father had her killed. The legend is that Pedro had her body placed on the throne. It is one of the great Portuguese love stories." Tiago was his merry self again. His eyes really did sparkle.

"That sounds great," Joe said.

"I can only imagine and write about such a grand passion, but I have never felt it. Have you?"

"No."

"I feel it for life, for art, for people in general, for my daughter, but not in that grand, romantic way for someone. I have had many romances but no great love." Tiago took a sip of his wine and sighed. "My job is very tedious, but sou preso, I am, um, trapped. Pia is in private school, and it is expensive. I want to be independent, so I work with the hotel and do tours."

"I understand."

"That way, I get to meet interesting people. Like you!"

"Thank you," Joe said and blushed.

"*The value of things is not the time they last, but the intensity with which they occur. That is why there are unforgettable moments and unique people!* That is from Pessoa too."

"I like it," Joe said.

"My wife and her father want me to quit writing. They say, 'tira o cavalinho da chuva.' But no, I am just taking a break for the moment."

"What was that thing you just said?"

"Oh, sorry. Tira o cavalinho da chuva means take your little horse out of the rain. To stop dreaming." He took a swig of wine and brought his palm down hard on the table. "But I will not!"

Joe instinctively reached for Tiago's hand, then withdrew it.

"I am talking much too much. I am sorry."

"I like listening to you," Joe said.

Tiago smiled. "You are sweet, Joe." He looked at his watch. "I will take you to another of my favorite places, and then I must go home."

They got in the van, drove through narrow, twisty streets up steep hills, and parked near a small park where a walkway led to a spectacular view of Lisbon.

"Miradouro de Sao Tiago de Alcantara," Tiago said, waving his arm over the view. Lisbon sparkled below. "Sao Tiago. I am named after him. Saint Tiago. He was one of the Apostles, and he came to Spain to spread the word."

Tiago draped his arm over Joe's shoulder.

"You see why I love my Lisboa so much?" Tiago said. "You probably feel the same way about New York, yes?"

"Almost," Joe said. All this beauty, he thought, just because I did my job and sold a few refrigerators. Without the HC55 Merchandiser, he would not have met this sweet man and felt the warmth of his lean body, the sensation of his furry arm across his shoulder, and the pain that tinged his charm and good spirits. Joe gasped as he realized that he had never felt this way before. *This* was love, and *this* is what it felt like. Finally! His spirits soared and plummeted in a dizzying and terrifying freefall.

They got in the van and drove through a few more twisty streets and wound up in a quaint, tiny square that looked familiar.

"One of my favorite places," Tiago said. It was Shelter.

"I know this place," Joe said.

"Yes?" Tiago placed his hand on the small of Joe's back. It felt like it belonged there, and going through life without it from now on was unthinkable. Once they parted, once he got back to Moonachie, he would go back to being that cavalinho, the sad little horse in the rain. How terrible love is!

Shelter was busier tonight, the music louder, and there were two bartenders, a sexy bear with gray hair and a goatee in a red tank top, and there was Duarte, the sweet boy of all those cucumbers. Both bartenders lit up at the sight of Tiago, and he hugged each of them and kissed them on the lips.

Joe was startled. Back in the States, he would have been shocked that this married man kissed men at a gay bar—but this was a new world, a better world, and he was immersed in it, for now.

"Would you like the Hendrick's and cucumber again?" Duarte asked.

"You remember?"

"That is my job!" Duarte said with a smile.

"I will have the same," Tiago said. They sat at the bar.

"Thank you for today," Tiago said. "You are very relaxing to be with. You do not say much, but I feel your good heart. Your voice is very soothing."

"Thank you," Joe sputtered. *Yes, the Ianuzzi Process!*

"You are like vitamin B to me, good for the nerve endings. You can be sad, but your eyes have a cintalacao… a twinkle."

Joe's ears rang. No one had ever said anything like that to him before. He always felt, believed that there was a twinkle inside him, and it kept him going, hoping for the best. No one had ever noticed it before. Tears welled in his eyes, then instantly dried up. He couldn't think of anything to say.

"Have you made plans for tomorrow?" Tiago asked.

"No."

"I can be available if you would like."

"Yes! I would like that very much!"

"Formidavel!" Tiago said. "There is so much more to show you. And tomorrow there will be no tears. No saudades."

Joe had polished off his gin and munched on the cucumbers left behind. Duarte set another drink in front of him. Tiago downed his and got another too. Shelter was cozy and inviting tonight, a pleasant mix of younger and older men involved in intimate conversations. Joe sipped his drink and smiled at it all—Duarte, the rest of the patrons, all of glorious Lisbon and its surprises. He was agreeably tired and agreeably buzzed.

"There is a free table by the window," Tiago said. He took Joe's arm and, with his hand on the small of Joe's back, guided him to it. They sat and smiled at each other goofily.

"We have had a busy day," Tiago said. "I hope you are happy."

"Very," Joe said. "Very, very. Oh, before I forget," he took an envelope out of his jacket pocket and handed it to Tiago. It was the two hundred euros, plus an extra one hundred.

"Obrigadinho!" Tiago said and stuffed it, unopened, in his pants.

Joe looked at the placemat on the table, a picture of a man with a big black hat, Henry the Navigator, whoever he was. That made him happy, too.

"I must leave soon. I want to get home in time to kiss Pia good night," Tiago said. "I will take you to the hotel if you like."

"Great!" Joe said. He tried to remember who Pia was. The murmur of Portuguese men's voices blended perfectly with the old-timey disco tunes from the sound system. Tiago shifted in his chair and put his hands on the table.

"Well, my friend," he said.

Joe leaned forward. "I know this is crazy… but… but I love you, and I want you to come back to the US and live with me." He took a breath and kept going. "Being with you makes me happy, and I think I can make you happy. You said that thing about Vitamin B."

Tiago's eyes widened, and he took a deep breath. "But you know I am married and that I have a daughter, yes?"

"Yes, I do."

Tiago set his drink on the table and looked down at the Henry the Navigator placement as if his answer was going to come from it.

Joe knew that this was the end of them, that he had gone too far for the first time in his life. His body vibrated with anticipation and dread.

Tiago looked up and gazed into Joe's face. He clasped both of Joe's hands in his. He spoke slowly.

"Joe, you are a wonderful man, and I am flattered by your offer. I am sorry to say I cannot honor it. You understand."

"Yes." He did understand, but everything he had ever wanted, dreamed of in his life was before him right now. The thought of going back to his lonely, spotless condo, sitting in traffic on the Garden State Parkway, was unbearable.

Tiago released Joe's hands and stood up. Joe braced himself for something: a scolding, a slap, or just the sight of Tiago walking out of the bar and out of his life. That's okay, he thought. I did it. I said what I wanted to say, and it's not for him.

Tiago came to Joe and motioned for him to stand up. He did.

He took Joe's face in his hands and kissed him on the lips, a warm, wet, gin and cucumber-flavored kiss. Their mustaches were perfectly aligned, and their combined bristles felt like they made sparks.

Tiago ran his hand through Joe's thin hair. "Now, sit back down, my friend. Let us have one more quick drink before I go home. I hope we are still on for tomorrow, yes?"

"Yes." Joe sat back on the rickety chair. He looked at Tiago and smiled. Tomorrow, he would really lay on the—what was it? The cintalacao, the twinkle. He could extend his stay in Lisbon or—why not move here and get a job? There were so many restaurants in this beautiful city, and he *was* called the best restaurant supply salesman, after all. He would learn Portuguese and, if he played his cards right, he and Tiago would be together every day. This idea made him very, very happy.

LOVEY

I was driving the recycling truck for the Bloomfield Department of Public Works in June 1981 when I found her. Her pale face was exquisite: a perfect oval shape with high cheekbones and cool blue eyes. The arch of her pale eyebrows suggested she was thinking, *I should be surprised—but I'm not.* Those red lips were parted in the hint of a smile, daring you to say something clever. Her small head was tilted to the right, quizzical but encouraging. Like Jane Fonda in *Barbarella*, her magnificent breasts were just the right size, in the sweet spot between what my co-workers called squeakers and honkers. She was bald, which only added to her allure, and, oh, she had no arms.

She was stuffed head-first into a garbage can on Watsessing Avenue, not far from my apartment in Bloomfield, New Jersey. She was half a mannequin someone didn't want anymore. I was thirty, tall and scrawny, and had a ten-year-old son who lived with his mother. I felt as displaced as the mannequin. I brought her into the truck's cab and stuck her between my truck mates, Schatzie and Chad. Chad named her Lovey after Mrs. Howell on *Gilligan's Island*.

Our truck was 607, a dinged-up canary yellow, four-ton dump truck. There was the vague promise of a new recycling truck on the horizon, but we had to make 607 work for us until it arrived. Our assignment was to drive through town, in different neighborhoods on different days, and pick up the residents' curbside newspapers, bottles, and aluminum cans. Chad was the youngest and smallest of our crew. With his long, golden hair, golden mustache, and wide-eyed expression, he looked like a combination of a rock star and Tweety Bird. He was a good-natured boy with a cowboy swagger, a booming voice, and an abrupt, hearty laugh. It was easy to make him laugh.

Schatzie was full-bodied, dark-haired, and ruddy. He had soulful brown eyes, a permanent five o'clock shadow, and a pretty mouth that lisped like a baby's. His specialty was sound effects: sirens, airplanes, car crashes, animals (especially monkeys and elephants), and the tribal war chants he learned from Tarzan movies. Schatzie's real name was Robert. He was twenty-eight and lived with his parents, the Schatzingers.

Chad, Schatzie, and I were all hired at the same time two years ago, and we each spent those two years bouncing from department to department. Our randomly tossed-together boy band was, luckily, a harmonious one. Though we were always covered in grime and slightly behind schedule, we laughed most of the day.

We were a little shy around Lovey at first; we just stared at this beautiful creature tucked between us. Then we looked at each other and burst out laughing. As we drove, I got an idea:

I took off my blue denim shirt and put it on Lovey. I sat at the passenger window and put Lovey in my lap. I poked her head out the window while I stared straight ahead. I turned Lovey's perfect little head slowly from side to side so that she looked like a queen who was curious about her subjects. If she had arms, she would have waved. We drove through the center of town several times just to make sure people got a good look at her. About three out of five noticed her, and the reactions varied: a shout, a wave, a whistle, a hoot, a honk. Somebody threw a donut at us. I had to keep a straight face because I was, you know, used to a beautiful bald woman in my lap, in my truck.

After an hour of Lovey's Grand Tour, we pulled in front of Buff's Diner and howled for fifteen minutes. We put Lovey under wraps, locked the truck, and went inside for our usual monster breakfast: pancakes, bacon, fried eggs, and home fries served by Rose, our scowling but tender-hearted waitress. Thinking of Lovey's Grand Tour, we howled again. And then again.

"You ain't laughing at me, are you?" Rose asked as she squirted whipped cream on Chad's blueberry pancakes.

"No, baby. Never."

"Then I don't give fuck," she said and shook her copper-red head.

On the way back to the yard, we stopped by my place so I could drop Lovey off at her new home. I wouldn't bring something so beautiful back to the maintenance yard. Those animals would destroy her.

When we got back to the yard, we were called into the management office. Our foreman, Richie Rastiello, waited with his arms folded.

"Are you ladies done playing with your dollies?"

There were reports from all over town about the beautiful bald passenger incident. He tried to make it a general accusation, but his focus kept drifting back to me. All I could do was shrug. "It won't happen again." Though I couldn't guarantee it.

Richie was short and dark with lustrous chocolate eyes and a glorious, towering pompadour. Even when he was stern, his eyes sparkled. He looked like a heroic mouse from a fairy tale, and some of the guys called him Mouse or Ratso to his face. Though he got the job because he was Chubby Venello's son-in-law, he was a by-the-book professional, and I appreciated that.

Lovey had an exalted place in my spare and sunny apartment, where she sat between my two other prize possessions, a mimosa bush and a little maple tree, both of which I had found as saplings in the park. My apartment, furnished with stuff I found on my route, was above a barber shop on Watsessing, a block away from the train station. The barber, Willie Feather, was also the super of the building. He was a wiry little bird of a man who looked like he'd fit right into the ensemble of a Preston Sturges movie. The barber shop didn't do much business. It was mostly a hangout for the remaining older white men in the neighborhood. Though Willie was pleasant enough, he always called me Randy, which wasn't my name. He was a little deaf.

The Watsessing section of Bloomfield was in the town's funkier South End, on the border with even funkier East Orange, and it was in rapid decline. The halfway-decent diner down the street closed suddenly, and the bar across the street from it went topless and got shut down. Half of the storefronts were vacant. The Watsessing train station was just a gloomy, forbidding platform that a handful of commuters used to get to Newark, New York, or Hoboken. I assumed the name Watsessing came from some Hessian who helped us out in the Revolutionary War—General Gunter Watsessing! While we walked through Watsessing Park, my son told me the word Watsessing came from the gentle Lenni Lenape tribe, the area's original inhabitants, and it meant crooked. The crooked thing it referred to was the Third River, which may have been a real river once but now was just a sluggish creek that zigzagged through the neighborhood and collected shopping carts along the way.

Lovey was the perfect roommate. She was quiet, for one thing, easy on the eyes, and very soothing for the nerves. Like me, she enjoyed listening to the radio, WNCN, the classical station and funky, listener-sponsored WBAI. Her perpetual sidelong glance was non-judgmental, no matter how foolishly I acted when I was with someone or alone. Though my days were loud and lively, most nights were solitary and sleepless. A few times when I was really drunk and lonely, I brought her into my lumpy fold-out sofa bed for a chaste cuddle. I just wanted something to hold on to. While I held Lovey's hard body, I thought, *this is really, really sad,* and that realization, along with the gin, acted like a sedative.

I felt like a failure. There were a million reasons why I could not stay married, but I missed being a full-time dad, and I especially loved the bedtime stories part.

Chad usually brought his mini boom box to the truck, and we had it cranked up to the two best rock stations most of the day. Schatzie loved Rush. Chad and I weren't crazy about them, but the way Schatzie sang along with Geddy Lee on "Limelight" so impressed us that we shut up and listened to him. Chad's theme song was AC/DC's "Dirty Deed Done Dirt Cheap." We all joined in the chorus, with Chad's rock star gravelly pipes taking the lead. My band for that year was Foreigner. I could hit the high notes on "Waiting for a Girl Like You," and no matter what the situation, I always had to dance to "Urgent."

It came on the radio one late summer morning while we were on a quiet street near the Glen Ridge border. I was on the truck stacking the piles of newspaper in a crisscross pattern based on a crochet double stitch I learned when I tried to quit smoking. It really did keep the papers from tumbling over. I started my "Urgent" dance, which included a lot of fist-pumping, kicks, and jumping up and down. I imagined that my long hair looked like David Lee Roth's when I tossed it. It didn't. When it got to Junior Walker's scorching sax solo, I ripped my shirt off and waved it in the air like a flag, and as the song powered down, I jumped off the back of the truck into a perfect dismount, landing on my feet. Chad and Schatzie cheered, and I put my shirt back on. When we got back to the yard, Richie called us into the office.

"What the fuck! When you ladies ain't playing with dollies, you're stripping. Nobody wants to see your bony ass, Ribs." (One of my nicknames was Rack o' Ribs.) "Can you keep your fucking clothes on and pick up some fucking newspapers for a fucking change?" His tone was withering, his delivery spot on, but his big brown eyes were merry. "And P.S., Ribs, your blouse is on backwards and inside out."

We also went through patches where we said everything with exaggerated English accents. Chad had to stop at home to pick up his radio. He'd told us his mother had been born in England and that his full name was Chadwick. I saw his mom waving at him from the window. I loved the movie *The Lady Vanishes*, and when we pulled up, I did my Dame May Whitty impersonation as Chad's mother, "Oh look, it's Chadwick, stopping in for a spot of tea. I *do* hope he likes the crumpets and watercress sandwiches."

Our fantasy was that people would put out their newspapers in bundles neatly tied with twine, but they rarely did. They liked to stuff them in brown paper shopping bags, which were not recyclable. The shopping bags were like ornery brown life forms, hard to fold and hard to tear. No matter how skillfully we crumpled and crammed them into every available inch of the truck, they always sprang back to spiteful life and defeated us. When I talked to Richie about it, he smiled as he listened and gave us permission to put the bags into garbage cans *if* we were ahead of the garbage trucks. Our brilliant new system lasted only three glorious days. On the morning of the fourth day, as I stuffed shopping bags into a couple of cans at the curb, I heard a scratchy female voice behind me.

"Hey, you, Get away from my garbage can! Get away from my can!"

I turned and saw a scrawny old white woman in a faded pink robe and pink slippers, with pink curlers in her hair, a cigarette dangling from her mouth, defiantly standing on her lawn.

"It's OK, ma'am. We're from the town's recycling department. We got permission from the town to put the paper bags in garbage cans if we were ahead of the garbage trucks,"

I said, feeling and sounding reasonable. The poor woman just didn't understand how important this system was to us. Not yet, anyway.

"Get the hell away from my garbage can, or I'll call the cops!"

"It's OK, ma'am, the garbage truck is a block or so behind us, and they'll take it all away. I promise," I cupped my hand to my ear. "Listen. You can hear them."

"Get away from my house, you! I'm calling the cops!"

I started walking toward her. "Ma'am, you don't understand. We work for the town. See our truck and the town insignia?" *And can't you see how smart and presentable I am?*

"Get away from me, you! Get your ass off my lawn. I'm calling the cops right now!"

I lost my temper. I pointed at her. "Get back in the house!"

"Fuck you!" she said, backing up.

"Get back in the house right now!" I kept pointing and advancing like an overgrown toy soldier. My voice was big and filled the block. She backed up toward her door, still yapping.

"Get back in the house! Get back in the house!" I kept jabbing my finger toward her until she was back in her house, yipping at me from behind her screen door. She held her pink Princess phone in her hand and was talking to someone. I heard a distant siren and braced myself for a big scene.

As I approached 607, the siren got louder and then sputtered into a raspberry. It was one of Schatzie's sound effects. He and Chad were howling.

When we got back to the yard, Richie was aware of the dust-up and was surprisingly mellow about it. Apparently, the woman called the cops all the time about something. But because of her, we lost the paper bag/garbage can option.

Besides paper bags, some creative town folk used duct tape or pantyhose to bind their newspaper bundles. One family used pet droppings as glue to keep their bundles intact. We came across a big pile of these waste product monstrosities and, as I sifted through them, I did the Dame May Whitty voice, "I say, Chadwick. Look at these bundles! How *bizarre!*"

"Bizarre!" became our word for soiled, unrecyclable newspapers that went into their own pile of shame. The glass and aluminum we picked up were kept in barrels on the truck, which we tied together to keep from tipping over. We had three bays in the maintenance yard, a small one for garbage (*bizarre!),* and two bigger ones where we dumped the aluminum and the glass at the end of the day.

We took the newspapers to Garden State Paper, one of the first newspaper recycling plants in the country and the last vestige of the late great *Newark Evening News*, which had patented the process. It was nice to get out of town and a pleasant ride on Route Forty-Six along the Passaic River to get to the recycling plant in Garfield. Garden State Paper was a sprawling white complex that took up sixteen acres. We had to check in at the front office, where the smiling ladies always offered us cookies. Then, with our paperwork squared away, we lined up behind other trucks to get onto the ramp. We turned the truck around and backed onto the ramp, making sure we were lined up properly with the restraints that kept the truck from sliding off it.

We got out and watched the ramp lift our truck and dump its newspapers into a giant vat, the size of a generous backyard swimming pool, full of swirling soapy water. An enormous, jagged wire arm stirred and swooped through the water, snagging and scooping out any debris like string, staples, or glue. The washed paper was funneled into another big vat, where it mixed with water to create a slurry, the base component from which new paper was formed. It was thrilling and somehow soothing to watch the flowing, swirling process.

This satisfying tail end of the operation was efficiently overseen by a tall, wiry Polish man whose name tag had a lot of consonants on it. As a joke, I referred to him as Lazslo Pierogi. He was always remarkably pleasant, as were the rest of the guys in the plant and the women in the office. You knew they believed what they did was important, and as a result, the whole place hummed with purpose, like a working-class Oz.

One day, after a couple of puffs on a joint, Chad slipped and called our Polish friend Laszlo Pierogi to his face.

"Hello, Laszlo Pierogi!" he said in his booming voice.

"Laszlo Pierogi? Laszlo Pierogi!" our Polish friend repeated, making sure he heard it right, and then he let loose with a wonderful cackle. Every week after that, we always boomed out, "Laszlo Pierogi!" as he approached us. This tickled all four of us immensely, and we wound up laughing too much. Then Laszlo had to say, with a smile, "OK. Knock it out, you guys. Knock it out, and let's get back to work."

Garden State Paper was later bought by Enron, yes that Enron, and when they went belly up, they shut down Garden State Paper in 2001, and 750 people lost their jobs. The blue-collar magic of the place lingers on a Facebook page where former employees reminisce about the good old days and plan reunions where I imagine Lazlo is the DJ and unleashes his joyous cackle.

Before I got the DPW job, I worked for the Erie Lackawanna Railroad as a carpenter. We rarely built anything. Instead, we knocked things down before they collapsed and killed somebody. I was there for five years and watched the railroad die a slow, gasping death before I got laid off. Then, I was out of work for six months with no job prospects as the economy tanked even deeper. I was the sole support of my wife and son then, and for a while, we were on food stamps.

Things changed when Jimmy Carter initiated the CETA program (Comprehensive Employment and Training Act). I was one of a dozen or so men, including Chad and Schatzie, hired by the DPW under it. We were all of diverse ethnicities and ages because diversity was part of the mandate. For all of us, the program and the job were lifesavers, and the goal was to do well and be hired by the town as a permanent employee. The pay and benefits were decent, the hours were easy, and you didn't have to commute.

Before CETA, most of the guys got their jobs through nepotism, and most of them were from the *connected* Italian families in town. Everybody had nicknames, sometimes more than one. Chubby Venello was the Director of Public Works, and Chubby Tortola was in charge of street signs. There were two guys named Junior and one Tiny, who, of course, weighed three hundred pounds. Stinkweed and Useless were the nicknames for the pair who drove the "honey dipper," the truck dispatched to handle sewer backups. There was Binky, Blinky, Shakey Jake,

Tony the Horse and Ray the Horse, and Twitchy Guglilotta, to name a few. Twitchy sometimes came to work in his pajama tops and left them on all day.

The DPW was the repository for the less-than-stellar relative who'd have a hard time keeping any other kind of job. A prime example was Lucius Castelli, the nephew of a councilman. He was thirty-five with the mind of a twelve-year-old, a short, solid body, a jack-o-lantern head with wide-set saucer eyes, and a sweet grin. His mother ironed his impeccable work shirts and pants every day and filled his gleaming stainless steel lunch box with fragrant, homemade calzones and sausage and pepper sandwiches that he ate very, very slowly. We worked together for one week picking up bulky waste, and all day long, he asked me the same two questions in his strangled little voice.

"What's your name?" and "How many girlfriends you have?"

I tried to come up with a new exotic name every time, as I would with a child.

What's your name? Pinchus Marinkus.

How many girlfriends do you have? Twenty-seven.

What's your name? Shlomo Nostromo.

How many girlfriends do you have? Nine and a half.

What's your name? Larry Caligari.

How many girlfriends do you have? None.

That last answer was accurate. I was gay. Lucius giggled every single time, so it was hard to be mad at him.

Lucius had a huge dick, according to Mugsy (Neil) McGinty, who was the grandson of an ex-fire chief. Mugsy was short and talked like a Lollipop Kid from *The Wizard of*

Oz. There were big flakes in his greasy dark hair, and his glasses were taped at the bridge. The grimy, ripe blue jumpsuit he wore every day was covered with cat hair. After punching in, he took a swipe at his assignment and then went to the house cleaning service he owned.

He was married to a woman who looked just like him (Mrs. Mugsy) and their son (Mugsy Jr.), which completed the Munchkin family portrait. Even though he talked about eating pussy all the time, Chief Inspector Mugsy knew what every guy was packing and reported on it, like an FBI of the urinal.

"Chubby Tortola needs a compass and a map to find his teeny-weeny scaloppini."

"Mike Tonzola's piece got a big head with dents in it."

"Lucius the Doofus is number one. It's like an elephant trunk—and Nicky Nardone is number two. His is like a sword—and it glows!"

"You mean like Excalibur?"

"Who's that?"

"How do you know all this stuff?" I asked him.

"Don't worry, you ain't doing so bad," he answered.

There were a few Polish guys who were distant relatives of the Polish mayor. The three black men on the roster were Lawrence, in his fifties, tall, quiet, and dignified (and number three on Mugsy's list), and Lenny, close to retirement, and, for protection, he chose to play the shuffling fool. The other was a gigantic young black man with an afro and beard who bristled with attitude, Bartlett Lee Ruffridge. He was treated like a star because he drove the street sweeper and handled all the heavy equipment like the front loader, backhoe, forklift, and bulldozer. He had a deep, booming voice and looked like he could snap any guy in two, though his wide-open face looked like a happy baby's when he smiled. He was referred to as Big Black Bart, and I was warned not to mess with him.

At the end of the workday, the break room was like a black-hearted social club with poker and gin games and darts that were sometimes aimed at your head. It took me a long time to adjust to the brutal gossip. Nothing was off limits: wives, kids, or mothers. I didn't know men talked that way. The railroad's locker room was no tea party, but it seemed like a country club compared to this slugfest. For the first year, I kept my trap shut after Shaky Jake Fiore listened to me talk to Richie in the break room one day and announced to everybody, "Ribs, when you talk, it's like, it's like... fucking *Masterpiece Theater*!"

I was with a crew chowing down at Buff's Diner on a blizzard night. Rose scolded them. "My God, yous eat like animals. Why can't you be dainty—like my boyfriend here?" She patted my head. The dainty thing took a while to die down.

I was weird. I was different. I was gay. I kept my trap shut and felt the buzz all around me until Twitchy Gugliotta broke through. Twitchy was a little cross-eyed, and I'd pegged him as dangerous. He marched up to me while I played gin with some summer college kids.

"So, what are you, Cuban or Puerto Rican or what?" The whole room waited. I took a beat.

"None of the above."

It kept them at bay for a while, but I had been breached.

A few months later, Twitchy came up to me again.

"So, what's your name again? Is it Garcia or Jimenez or Rodriguez?"

"None of the above."

It didn't work as well this time, and I became Rodriguez, then Regis, then Ribs.

Twitchy and I almost came to blows shortly after that. I was still married when his daughter and his two bratty grandsons moved onto our block. My son was seven then, smart and mellow with a wicked sense of humor and an iron will. Twitchy's mutant offspring started to pick on him. He was no pushover and could handle himself. One Sunday afternoon, I looked out the window and saw Twitchy's brats sneak up behind him and knock my son off his bike. I bolted down the stairs and chased them down the street and all the way up to their kitchen, where their grandmother, Mrs. Twitchy, was at the oven, stirring Sunday gravy in a pot while they hid under her apron.

"Keep those brats away from my son!" I shouted and left.

The next day, Twitchy confronted me in the break room.

"Stay away from my family, you spic. I can have you rubbed out for a measly hundred dollars."

"Go ahead," I said. I felt so righteous that I wasn't spooked at all. Besides, I knew Twitchy would never spend $100 on anything.

I was still married those first two years before I got on the recycling truck. After one last scorched earth argument, I stormed out of the house and left everything behind. I bounced around, sometimes sleeping in my car, until I found the apartment on Watsessing Avenue. I was raggedy and raw and taking it one day at a time. The day Lovey and I found each other was a good day.

I bounced around the DPW, too, going from department to department. In the spring, I was assigned to pothole repair and street paving. In the summer, I got assigned to the Tree Crew, the rock stars of the DPW, and their truck was The Magic Bus. The same dinged-up yellow as the rest of the trucks, it had a hollow, covered wagon body and a long, thick arm with a bucket big enough for one man. When its long, graceful arm was extended, the truck looked like a dinosaur, the Diplodocus, as it grazed among the treetops. It often trailed a baby Diplodocus behind it: the woodchipper. I liked working on Linden trees the best. Their branches sailed easily through the woodchipper and gave off a sweet spray. When you sawed them, the wood was soft and tasty looking, like fresh turkey breast. Best of all, in the summer, the Lindens sprouted fragrant yellow blossoms.

The tree crew was headed by volatile, charismatic Nick Nardone, number two on the Mugsy list. Short, wiry with black hair and coal-black eyes, he sported a snappy Clark Gable mustache that he used like a prop. When he stroked it, you braced for impact. Most of us had mustaches, but nobody used his for punctuation like Nick. He was married and had two young sons. When there were three men in the truck, Nick insisted I sit next to him because he liked the way I smelled and the sound of my voice. We were usually elbow to elbow, and when he shifted gears, the silky graze of soft hairs on our forearms gave me jolts of manly pleasure.

Lenny, the old black fool, wore the same khaki flak suit every day and may have worn it on duty in Korea way back when. His long, convoluted stories usually included some reference to Korea and were meant to assure the white assembly that he was harmless—and a patriot. If he went on too long, I noticed Big Black Bart groaned and left the room.

One morning, Lenny walked into the break room and announced, "Hey, Ribs. I was driving by your building last night, and I saw you. You had on your little short-shorts, and you was skipping across the street with your little boyfriend."

I did not see it coming—from that direction.

Everybody stared at me. I huffed and puffed but had nothing to say.

I considered, *that wasn't my boyfriend, just some guy I met at a bar.*

Just in time, Richie came out of the office.

"Okay, ladies. Time to get on the road. Move your asses out!"

Some guys heard Lenny; some didn't. Some understood what he meant; some didn't. I was big and strong and worked hard, *but* I was weird. Wasn't I married? Wasn't I seen around town with my wife and kid? How could I be gay? I didn't proclaim it. I didn't hide it. I didn't back down from it. I gave up a lot to be a gay man, and there was no turning back. Lenny's proclamation nudged the gay fact forward again. Some of the guys didn't care. And some did.

I was on the tree truck with Nick that day. When we got to our first stop, he turned off the engine and stared at me.

"So. Are you gay or what?"

"Yes." I braced for a fistfight.

"I knew you were fucked up. Now you're even more fucked up than I thought you were."

Now when it was just the two of us in the truck, Nicky often took his big dick out "to give it some air." It did glow like Excalibur, golden in the sunlight.

"Look at this, Ribs. Look, but don't touch," Nick said.

"Okay."

"For a fag like you, this is a fucking banquet, huh?"

"Oh, yes. For all us fags, you know, everywhere."

"Okay," he said as he waved it back and forth. "I was just checking to see how much of a fag you are." Then he put it away.

A storm blew through town and knocked over more than fifty trees. We were out all day and into the night, cutting them up and pushing them through the woodchipper. I was tearing through a juicy sycamore with a power saw. Its spray choked me and made my eyes water, and I was pouring sweat. Nick came up behind me and pressed up against my butt.

"If only your little friends on Christopher Street could see you now," he whispered in my ear. I wished I had little friends on Christopher Street who could see me.

One morning, he had to go up in the extended arm of the bucket to reach some upper branches.

"Come with me," he said, holding open the little hinged door.

"There's only room for one," I said.

"It'll be OK."

I squeezed in, in front of him, and we rose, shakily, into the upper reaches of a Norway maple. I used the pole pruner with the extended arm to trim the lighter branches while Nick tore through the sturdy ones with a power saw. He was pressed up against me with his hot, Chesterfield breath on my neck. His own pole pruner was extended, and I felt it nudging my butt.

"This is nice, ain't it, you and me way up here alone?" he whispered.

"Yes." It was wonderful.

"I bet you're thinking about what it would be like to be in bed with me, huh?"

"I certainly think that would be, um, interesting." We laughed, but with the wood and the sweat, one twitch and he would have been inside me.

They came in waves, the airings, the unsheathings, and the whispers. Always when it was just the two of us. Yes, it was a big, beautiful cock. And yes, I was gay, but two and two did not have to make four this time. Nick had a hair-trigger temper. His mighty sword waved, but it was attached to a stick of dynamite.

One otherwise pokey afternoon, I watched him play gin with a couple of new CETA hires in the break room. Suddenly, he whipped out a switchblade and sliced the wrist of the guy opposite him because he thought he'd cheated. Another CETA hire, a scrawny Latin guy with a bad attitude, was assigned to the tree truck before me. Nick was in the truck; the guy was yapping outside of it. Nick jumped out, punched him in the face, and pushed him to the ground. The guy went home bleeding and never came back. In the DPW yard, Nick Nardone was the boss.

Nick did what he did, and I smiled. He was playing me, and I was playing him. This mating dance was just sexy enough for me as it was. Anything else was too dangerous and not worth it. So that was that.

And then it wasn't.

Nick and I were at the Preakness Pub for lunch. We all loved Kitty, the pretty blond barmaid. Some of the guys asked her out, but she turned them down. She had plans: she was working her way through business school and wanted to open a chain of nail salons. Her voice was tuneful and perky, and her dazzling smile was genuine. I had a bit of a crush on her myself and always asked her about school.

Nick worked her over from the minute they met. He flattered her, built her up, and then knocked her down. He tantalized her, then demeaned her, rotating his weapon array so that she was always off balance. After a few months of Nick's toxic attention, Kitty smiled less, gained a little weight, and seemed scattered and anxious. He had her where he wanted her. I was sure Nick was fucking her because he never bragged about Kitty the way he did about all the others.

It was payday, so Nick and I split a Preakness Pizza with the works and drank boilermakers. He told Kitty her hair looked pretty, "all loose hanging."

"But I better not find one of them bleached blond hairs in the pie."

When Kitty turned to get us more whiskey shots, Nick said, "Oh yeah. That's my favorite view. And it looks like you went up a pant size, Mama. More to love."

Kitty looked crushed, and she spilled some of the whiskey.

I went to the bathroom and was at a urinal doing the final shimmy shake when Nick came in. He stood at the next urinal.

"Look at this, Ribs. Look at this thing."

I looked. It throbbed and glowed even in the dreary bathroom light. Was that for me or for Kitty? How many birds can you kill with one big dick?

"You want this, right?" He shook it.

"Yep." I was tired of it and him.

"You want to suck on this, don't you?"

"More than anything in the fucking world."

"I bet you *dream* about sucking on this, right?"

I was drunk. I was pissed off. I didn't like the way he treated Kitty. She was a good kid. And—most important—never tell me what I dream about.

I zipped up and stepped toward him.

"Yeah. I want it. I want it right now. I want you to give it to me right now."

He looked scared. His cock got soft.

"It's just you and me here right now. Nobody has to know." I blocked the door.

I held out my hand and beckoned him, beckoned *it*.

Nick backed up and wound up against the toilet stall door.

"Yeah, that's good, baby. I can do you in there. More privacy," I said.

I locked the bathroom door, stepped toward him, and growled.

"I want it. Give it to me, now. Give it to me. Come on. Give it to me."

He screamed like Jamie Lee Curtis in *Halloween*, squeezed past me, unlocked the bathroom door, and ran out. When I came out, he was gone. I paid the check and found him in the truck. "Let's get back to work," he said, and we were quiet for the rest of the day. That was the end of our mating dance. Now and then, a few sparks went off and fizzled out.

Nick, of course, was the one who developed the system for rating breasts. The big ones were called Honkers, and the small ones were Squeakers. Nicky and crew felt it was their duty to let women know how their racks rated. They would lean on the horn and yell out, "Nice honkers, sweetheart!" or "Show me those squeakers!"

On the way to a fallen tree one morning, we saw a pretty, well-dressed woman in her thirties crossing Broad Street just in front of us. I got the feeling this was a big day for her, a new job, a new dress—something was up. Nick blasted the horn and shouted, "Gorgeous honkers, sweetheart!"

The pretty woman jumped. She was startled and upset. You could see she lost her momentum. Nick started to honk again.

I grabbed his arm. "Let her live, Nick. Let her live."

He stopped, stared at me with his blunt black eyes, and shook his head at my strangeness. Later that day, we passed another good-looking woman, and Louie (Rags) Ragazzi reached past me for the horn. Nick stopped him.

"No, Rags. We can't do that no more. *Let her live!* Right, Ribs? *Let her live!*" he said in a whiny, singsong voice.

In the fall, all power was deployed to leaf removal, and Richie was like a general leading his balky troops in battle against the forces of nature. The bright green leaves of summer were now the crispy, red, brown, and gold enemy, clogging streets and drains. With his walkie-talkie glued to his ear, Richie seemed to be commandingly, adorably everywhere. Some of the guys called him *Mouse-o-lini*, but if it weren't for him, the town would have been smothered in leaves that were dangerous when wet and even more deadly if they froze.

Don't mess with Bart. I learned why one golden autumn afternoon. I was one of Mouse-o-lini's army of peons raking leaves into piles. Leaf blowers had not been invented yet. Bart was working the front loader. He scooped up the piles of leaves in his bucket and dumped them into a fleet of waiting trucks. We rakers decided to take a break, but Bart wanted to finish for the day. He singled me out of the crowd and shouted in his booming voice, "Move your bony ass, Ribs!" I didn't look up or turn around; I just leaned on my rake and gave him the finger. I didn't see him jump out of the loader. I was six foot two and 180 pounds. Bart was about six foot three and packing around 300. He grabbed me, picked me up like I was a sack of dirty laundry, and tossed me into a truck, where I landed on a bed of fragrant, crunchy leaves. It was fun to fly through the air and land safely. I should have been pissed, but I wasn't. Bart and I nodded at each other in a guarded, friendly way after that.

A month later, there was a blizzard. We got the word a few hours earlier and were sent home to prepare. I knew that I might be on duty for twenty-four hours or more, so I laid out my thermal long johns, fleece ear warmers, a bulky sweater, and two pairs of heavy socks. I slathered my work boots in mink oil and set a small bottle of sambuca on my kitchen counter. Then

I lay down with Lovey and tried to sleep while I waited for the call from Richie. I never used an alarm clock. I would set my mind to the time I needed to wake up, and that system worked for me. Now that I had Lovey, I placed her within view so I could wake up looking at her sidelong glance.

Richie had me on his short list of first responders because I was dependable and good at the prep part of a blizzard, getting the trucks ready by attaching the plows and putting chains on the tires. It was a tough, cold, and sometimes dangerous job, but it was important and made me feel valuable. I didn't mind getting dirty.

The trucks, lined up in the garage bays side by side, were shuddering, slobbering behemoths. We jacked up their rear ends and wrapped the cold, coarse chains around the massive wet tires, sliding under the truck to make sure the chains were securely connected on all sides. It was disgusting and sexy to be underneath the truck, our faces intimate with its greasy, aromatic rear end. We worked quickly just in case the heavy-duty jack decided to collapse under the truck's grunting, shivering tonnage. After a couple of hours, the rest of the crew showed up and took the trucks out. There was a pair to every truck, plow guy and wingman, since not everyone was proficient in plowing. I usually got stuck with the peons with shovels, sometimes with Schatzie and Chad. We would often be out all night and came up with a rule: you could only complain about the cold three times. Anytime you let it slip after that, you got a face full of snow.

Don't mess with Bart, Lesson Number Two came when I was part of a crew clearing out a municipal parking lot. Bart was working the front loader, and I had a shovel. I was cleaning snow around a parking meter, and Bart wanted me out of the way so he could scoop out the whole lane. I held up my hand, wait, and he blasted the front loader's obscene "Fanfare for Satan" horn. I jumped out of my skin and shouted, "Fuck you, you fat bastard!" I wanted to say, "You fat *Black* bastard," but luckily something stopped me. On his throne way up high, Bart stared at me and leaned on the horn again. I knew he hated the cold and wouldn't get out of the warm cab, so I was safe. I stood my ground and held my shovel in front of me like a lance, the village idiot squaring off against a dragon. In one graceful swoop, Bart scooped me up in a bucket full of snow and dumped me and the snow into the body of a dump truck. It was big, bad, and wrong, just like Bart, but so bold and brilliantly executed that I was exhilarated.

The next big snow, he slipped on ice getting off the front loader and sprained his ankle. I was there when it happened and drove him to the emergency room at Columbus Hospital. I stayed with him through the waiting room and treatment, and we talked the whole time. He said my two brave, stupid stands with the rake and the shovel tickled him, and he thought: *Who the fuck is this guy?* He didn't know whether to kill me or kiss me, so instead, he just tossed me. Bart was a year younger than me and unhappily married to his tough high school sweetheart, Kayla. They had a beautiful two-year-old daughter, Kenya, who looked just like Bart. Instead of going back to his tense apartment, Bart began to stop by my quiet pad with beer and pizza or a bucket of Kentucky Fried Chicken to hang out. He often didn't show up when planned but would pop by unexpectedly at other times.

"What's up with that?" I asked.

"It's a Black thing," he said.

Bart had a crush on Lovey. One night, he picked her up and held her in the air in front of him. "She's the perfect woman," he said. "She's beautiful—with no voice for nagging, no hair for shedding, and no arms for grabbing." Then he kissed her on the lips, and I thought I saw a blush on her alabaster cheek.

One snowy night, we were assigned plow detail. I had never operated the plow and wanted to learn how, but Bart only let me be his wingman. It wasn't a big snow, and we were just cruising around, racking up overtime, until Richie told us to stop. We listened to the jingle bell chant of the truck's chains, talked trash, and got buzzed on my trusty little bottle of sambuca. The truck was running smoothly, but we kept hearing a strange, rhythmic whirring sound. We were near the Animal Shelter and pulled into its quiet, dead-end street. Bart turned off the engine, and we still heard the sound. He turned it back on, and we still heard the sound. Bart was a gifted amateur mechanic, and tinkering with cars was fun for him. On/off. On/off.

In the quiet of the cold night, I thought the whirr sounded like a shy little flying saucer looking for a safe place to land, and I said so.

"No, it's not that. I know this sound," Bart said. "Let me think."

He stroked his goatee and announced:

"The belt has slipped off the alternator, and now it's just a motor."

"What?" I asked him to repeat it.

"The belt has slipped off the alternator, and now it's just a motor."

We were completely buzzed on the sambuca now.

"Say that again."

"The belt has slipped off the alternator, and now it's just a motor."

I took his hand.

"I think that is one of the most beautiful sentences I have ever heard," I said.

He blushed, completely taken by surprise. He stared at me, then smiled. There was so much love in his eyes that it took me by surprise. We started making out, and I wound up blowing him in the truck while the possible little flying saucer hovered around us, sending photos of us back to Mars. It felt just right, and when we were done, we both laughed uncontrollably. When we stepped out of the truck to pee, I noticed that the flashing red beacon light on top of the cab was out. It was still turning, which explained the sound, but the light was dead. We laughed hysterically. When we got back into the truck, Bart flipped a switch above his head. The whirring sound stopped, and the Martian invasion was averted.

One Saturday night, he wanted to go out, but he didn't have any money. That's OK, I said, I have money. I had twenty dollars. When he showed up, it turned out his idea of no money was twenty dollars, so between us, we had forty, just enough to make some noise. We drove into New York and wound up at The River Club, a big gay dance warehouse in the far West Village. It was Bart's first time in a gay bar, and he was nervous. A pack of sweet guys who said they were from Staten Island thought we were a cute couple, offered us coke, and bought us drinks. "It's Raining Men" was blasting through the club, and I didn't want to spook Bart by leaving him to go dance, but our Staten Island friends came and dragged us onto the floor. Bart was a good, showy dancer. At one point, he picked up the smallest Staten Island guy, tossed him in the air—and caught him! I suspect it caused several involuntary ejaculations throughout the club.

We got cranked and hammered and danced all night long, crawling through the Holland Tunnel at ten a.m. I wondered how he squared this with Kayla, who was no pushover. All I had waiting for me was Lovey, sitting propped by the window like a beautiful Mrs. Bates, you know, Norman's mom. She didn't have to be apologized to, walked, or fed, and her shapely shadow at the window kept burglars at bay.

Bart and I fucked around a couple of more times, but it wasn't about sex at all. We had great chemistry and lots of mutual nerve. I was in freefall. Bart chose to tag along for the ride. It could *seem* like fun sailing through the air, but the direction was down, down, down, and the landing wasn't soft.

Hanging with Bart fueled the hothouse gossip of the break room. We came in together from a job, and Nick stood up, smoothed his mustache, and announced, "Well, well. Here comes Mr. and Mrs. Ruffridge." All eyes were on us. He pointed at us and said, "I don't wanna say nothing... *but* I'm not sure who's fucking who here. One always got a hole in the front of his pants, and the other one always got a hole in the back."

In response, Bart kissed my hand, and I curtsied.

Whenever you heard that phrase, "I don't wanna say nothing," it was always followed by a big *but* and something hateful being said.

Chester (Binky) Binkowski was the supervisor of the Water and Sewage Department. He was a notch above Richie in seniority and a sour little Humpty Dumpty with a crew cut, who always had a Parliament dangling from his frown. Binky's wife was a big shot in the Board of Education. Binky cruised around town on personal errands in his pickup and showed up at job sites where he watched, hands on his hips, and barked out a few orders. Nick called him Meat Byproduct.

Binky got sick, was out for a while. It was cancer. He came back to work for a bit and looked terrible. One afternoon, he was in the full break room, talking, and then he left. For some reason, he didn't go all the way outside. I could see his shadow in the doorway.

"I don't wanna say nothing," Nick said, touching his upper lip, "*but* who wants to get in on my pool?"

"What pool?" Twitchy asked.

"Pick the month that Binky dies."

I looked at the shadow in the doorway. It shuddered.

"RECYCLING PROGRAM REPORTS PROGRESS" was the headline in *Bloomfield Life*, below which was a picture of us loading the truck. "In an average week, the Bloomfield Recycling Department picks up between sixteen and twenty tons of newspaper, glass, and aluminum. The program has brought $25,000 into the town treasury in less than a year."

Hot on the heels of that headline, a black cloud descended on our glorious, well-reviewed Camelot of Refuse, and his name was Fausto Farina. He had been appointed Recycling Supervisor to oversee the operation. Fausto was the aluminum siding czar of Bloomfield. Just about every house in town was covered in aluminum siding and posted a sign with his name on it. His wife, Albertina Farina, was the town administrator's secretary, a powerful position.

Fausto wore black all the time, including a black trench coat and a black fedora. He was short and dark with slicked-back, thinning hair, a broken nose, and dazzling white caps that accentuated the cheerlessness of his infrequent smile. Tinted shades always covered his bulbous eyes. The rumor was that he knew the whereabouts of an entire truckload of Montebello Extra Virgin Olive Oil that "fell" off a truck that was parked outside Buff's Diner while the driver had lunch.

We hadn't heard we were getting a new boss, so we were surprised when Richie introduced Fausto to us one morning as we were getting the truck ready to pull out.

"You guys have been doing an OK job so far, but now that I'm in charge, I want one hundred percent performance one hundred percent of the time," Fausto said. "We are on the shortlist for a brand-new recycling truck, and I want to make sure we get it. If you got a problem with any of this, better speak up now so you can kiss this job goodbye." Then he added, "Capiche?"

"Nice to meet you, too," I said.

We were off to a bad start. A brand-new prototype recycling truck had been designed in Canada. Thanks to our work and the aggressive recycling program, Bloomfield was on the shortlist to try it for three months. If that test went well, we *might* even get to keep it. Fausto, with his greasy combination of skills and connections, was brought on to ensure that we got a shot at this miracle truck.

We had to be on our best behavior because we were often trailed by a mini fleet of state officials and reps from the recycling truck company to gauge if we were worthy of this sexy, whispering miracle truck. They all dressed in black, just like Fausto, and followed us in official black cars. And, like Fausto, they even wore silly little black fedoras. Schatzie called them The Black Hat Brigade.

For us, it was like Lent. We had to give up singing, dancing, weed, and monster breakfasts at Buff's. The Black Hat Brigade sometimes got out of their cars and watched us at particular stops. They talked about us like we were lab rats but never directly to us. If they did have a question, they asked Fausto, who had to ask us since he didn't know anything about the job. All this trailing and stopping and starting, in addition to the daily reports we had to fill out, put us consistently behind schedule.

Fausto sucked up to the Black Hats and, when they were gone, tore into us. He started at a growling sneer and worked himself into something like a scream. His rage was so out of proportion that it stunned us into silence at first. He used the word *sabotage* a lot. I was surprised that he knew it. We were just doing our job as usual, so I didn't know who the saboteurs were. I had never seen someone froth at the mouth before. His fits sucked all the joy out of our merry band.

When I got the DPW yard one morning, I saw a big, beautiful green entity through the chain-link fence. There was a small crowd around it. At first glance, it looked like a jolly Disney-fied stegosaurus without the bony plates on its back. It was our gorgeous new recycling truck: twenty feet long, eight feet wide, almost nine feet high. It had two axles,

200 horsepower, and a five-speed manual transmission, and it weighed over 30,000 pounds. Schatzie, Chad, and I all got to it at the same time and jumped up and down, clapping our hands.

"Don't touch nothing," Richie said. "They're gonna give you a demonstration."

While Fausto, Chubby, and the Canadian reps were having breakfast at Buff's, we crawled all over the gigantic yet fragile, beautiful green monster. Its snub nose and two big windows gave it a merry face and personality, and the complicated dashboard, loaded with dials, buttons, gauges, and levers, was like a boy's wet dream. Bart jumped into the cab and instantly figured it all out, then he explained it to us.

When the truck reps and Fausto showed up, they were accompanied by a television crew and some reporters. The jolly Canadian rep gave us a very cursory tutorial on the truck's operation, playing to the cameras the whole time. A state senator breezed into the yard and, after a quick huddle with the Canadian rep, went on camera to say, "This is a wonderful day in the history of recycling." Then he left.

The truck's cavernous rear end had a giant auger in it that leisurely turned and massaged the papers into its gaping maw. A TV reporter wanted a demo, and Fausto barked at me to throw some paper in there. All we had on hand were a couple of filthy bundles from the *bizarre* bin that were tied with pantyhose. The cameraman gave me the cue, and I tossed the bundles into the maw, pulled the lever, and watched as they were spun and drawn deeper into the truck's black hole. Later that night, I watched the segment on the News at Seven. I saw my bony arms toss the bundle in, and then the camera pulled back and showed me unhappily staring into the truck's big ass as if I were going to throw myself in too.

That camera captured me looking at my immediate future. The truck was beautiful, that was true, but our honeymoon with it was short. Yes, the cab's cool, sleek, lime-green interior had a new baby/new car smell. Yes, the luminous dashboard looked like it belonged on the *Starship Enterprise*. Unfortunately, the truck's handsome head didn't match its enormous, clunky rear end. And, in operation, the truck had the technical and emotional problems (its ignition didn't like rain) of a French sports car. The leisurely auger in its big ass turned clockwise in a circular motion, like a washing machine. Papers tended to get jammed unless you inserted them carefully, a few at a time. When it jammed, we had to open up the back and manually remove the paper.

There were two jaunty square containers on the passenger side designed to hold glass and aluminum. When they were full, we pulled an equally jaunty lever, and the containers rose shakily like little elevators in pre-war buildings. When they reached the top, arms attached to their sides stretched out, tipped them over, and dumped their clinking, clanking passengers into the truck's hollow body. The containers often got stuck in the tipping position, which meant one of us had to climb up there, bang on them, and help tip them all the way over.

At some point every day, Fausto's car screeched into our path. He jumped out and charged at us, screaming, "What the fuck! What the fuck! What the fuck!" He was in over his head, and it was going to be our fault.

I dreaded coming to work now. We were always off balance and felt stupid. Chad and Schatzie launched into long, soaring anti-Fausto arias in the safety of the truck but trembled under the assault of his foul, foaming mouth. I tried to keep my trap shut because when I piped up, it usually got me in trouble.

We were behind schedule at a stop on East Passaic Avenue that had called in with a complaint about their piled-up recycling. We sorted through their *bizarre* newspapers and wet boxes overflowing with empty bottles of Old Crow bourbon. The auger was jammed, and the jaunty containers were stuck in mid-air. Since the bottles hadn't been rinsed, I was getting a nice buzz from whiffs of cheap booze. It was a cold day in early November.

We heard the screech and there was Fausto.

"What the fuck! Why are you still here? What's taking so long?"

We pointed to the jammed auger and the suspended containers.

"Fix it!" he screamed. "I'm tired of getting crap because of your lousy work, you bunch of retards."

I saw Chad and Schatzie wince and shrink.

"You can't talk to us like that!" I shouted.

Fausto's eyes bugged out behind his shades. The spit bubbled around his shit-crack lips. He was right in my face, well, in my chin since I was a foot taller than him.

"Who do you think you're talking to, asshole?"

"I'm talking to you." My voice was bigger than his.

"You just made the biggest mistake of your life!"

The Biggest Mistake of My Life! I was thinking hard about what that would be when the radio in Fausto's car crackled.

"Attention all supervisors and foremen. We just got word that Binky, uh, passed away. Please return to the yard."

The miracle truck went back to Quebec for repairs, never to be seen again. Instead of assigning us our trusty old dump truck, 607, Fausto rented us vans from Rent-a-Wreck. We never knew the reason why. I didn't understand, and I didn't like it. Wasn't the program a success that brought in new revenue? It said so in the paper! Couldn't we at least get our old truck back? We knew how to stack and pack a dump truck, but the Rent-a-Wreck vans were something junkies used to move their soiled futons from one shooting gallery to another.

Everything was so clear before Fausto; our work was sunny and wide open, but now we dreaded every day, and the days were filled with shadows and secrets. Along the way, the spirit of our merry band had been broken, a lot less laughter, no singing and dancing. Whenever Fausto scolded us now, he ignored me and talked to Schatzie in a somewhat gentler tone. Schatzie did very few sound effects, and Chad's hearty laugh was seldom heard.

The first week of December was cold. We were now days behind schedule, chugging around town in a succession of Rent-a-Wrecks that kept breaking down. One afternoon, as we turned the corner on a busy street, the strap holding the barrel full of aluminum cans snapped in the cold. They can fell off the truck and rolled into the middle of the intersection, scattering cans in every direction. Once we got it cleaned up, we got back in the truck. It wouldn't start. We sat in the dirty cab, tired and defeated, and radioed the yard to get a jump start. We got the tire screech and Fausto.

"What the fuck is it *now?*" He started at a scream this time.

"You're kidding, right?" I said.

"I ain't talking to you, asshole."

"Well, I'm talking to you!" I started pointing, usually a bad sign. "This is all *your* fault. We lost the new truck. We lost 607. We are going backwards, not forwards, since you showed up. You're no manager."

"You're a dead man," he said. His eyes bulged, and the mouth foam flew into my face.

I kept pointing and he started backing up.

"You're pathetic!" I shouted. "You fucked up somewhere, and now we're stuck with this stupid truck, and nothing works anymore. We were doing great until you showed up with your lies and your shady—"

"Shady? What are you talking about, you stupid spic?" He looked scared. I hadn't meant to say shady. To me, he was now the same as the yapping old lady. I kept pointing and advancing.

"You're pathetic! Get the fuck out of here. Get the fuck out of here!"

He got in his car, wild-eyed, and screeched away. Chad, Schatzie, and I were quiet until we got a jump and drove the truck back to the yard. I thought I was defending us, defending them. Did I go too far? Probably. I *was* a stupid spic—and crazy too.

The next morning, in the break room, we were told that Fausto had a heart attack that night and was in intensive care at Columbus Hospital. Everybody looked at me and then looked away. The *looking away* took root because nobody really looked at me again after that. Fausto was right. I was a dead man. I was right there in front of them, but I was not to be seen for any reason. Except for the end of that day, when we assembled in the break room, Nicky stroked his furry upper lip.

"I don't want to say nothing," he said, "*but*—Ribs, you gave that man a heart attack."

Was I supposed to feel bad? I didn't. I was a wild animal like the rest of them now, and it was him or me. I was braced for a big, ugly payback.

Richie gave us trusty old 607 back, but Schatzie and Chad were quiet and glum now. The bond was broken. Schatzie started to give orders in a new voice with the same lisp. Chad's girlfriend was pregnant, and he was getting unhappily married. The job limped along, drama-free and joyless. Fausto was making a recovery, damn it. Christmas was around the corner, and the CETA guys were supposed to get a bump in pay. I was a dead man walking, except to Bart. He said it would all blow over.

The morning of December 23rd, I went to punch my timecard. It wasn't there, but in its place was a handwritten note: *Report to the office.* Chubby Vennello handed me an envelope and said, "Sorry."

Richie, the beautiful mouse, shook my hand and squeezed it. I wanted to kiss him. I was terminated with two weeks' severance. I walked out, went to my car. My ears were ringing. I drove to my apartment. I turned on the classical music station and lay on the couch with Lovey next to me—with her quizzical look, *what happened?* My head was spinning. Me and my big mouth. I asked Lovey: Was *this* the biggest mistake of my life? I thought she turned her beautiful head a millimeter and lowered her eyes infinitesimally, which I intuited as *ask again later.*

I had been fired for misconduct, and my unemployment claim was denied. I appealed it.

An appeal tribunal was scheduled. The town had a long list of complaints: lewd behavior, foul language, terrorizing a senior citizen, and insubordination (*insubordination!*), among other crimes. The hearing took place in a windowless back room in the unemployment office. I was flattered that so many high-ranking *officials* were assembled to testify against me. The arbitrator was a well-dressed young woman, Miss Silvestri.

I wore a jacket and tie to each hearing and brought one of my favorite books with me, Grace Paley's *Enormous Changes at the Last Minute.* Her bracing prose helped me focus. I borrowed Lovey's cool, steady gaze and felt rooted in what I knew to be true. Whenever a charge was leveled against me, I channeled Lovey. I tilted my head, raised an eyebrow, suggesting, *I should be surprised, but I'm not.* The magic word was *inscrutability.*

"You punched in late one hundred fifty days in a row," the attorney said. They had doctored my timecards. He waved a fist full of them in my face. They were out for blood.

"That's not true," I said, my voice low and calm. It seemed to stop everybody in their tracks.

"He drove around town with a naked dummy!"

"That's not true." She was wearing my shirt, and she was no dummy.

"He attacked his boss and almost killed him."

"That's not true." It was just luck that he had a heart attack.

"Nothing personal," the angry villagers said to me as they walked by after lying about me.

"Nothing personal," I said after I calmly testified that this witch hunt was created to cover Fausto's incompetence and some shady deal that lost us the new recycling truck.

My Lovey-inspired inscrutability spooked them. There were three hearings. After the third hearing, when the angry townsfolk left with their pitchforks, Miss Silvestri squeezed my hand.

"You're right and they're wrong. There's something fishy here," she said.

I didn't win the appeal, but by then, the six-week penalty period was over, and I was able to collect unemployment benefits.

I fell behind in the rent. I told Willie about getting fired and the unemployment thing.

"That's a tough break," he said, looking at the ground. "I don't know what to tell you, Randy," (which still wasn't my name). "The landlord wants you out of the building."

A day later, someone banged on my door. I was doing pushups and opened the door with no shirt. Fuck it all.

It was the landlord, a waspy, handsome man in his fifties. He was startled.

"Nothing personal," he said, "but you can't live here without paying rent. You're going to have to leave."

I was struck by a thunderbolt of courage and logic. My back was against the wall, and I had nowhere to run. I would not run. Enough was enough. I felt calm and strong. I was Excalibur, and I glowed with righteousness.

"I understand. I'm not going to give you a long, sad story. I lost my job, and I'm not collecting unemployment yet, so I have no money," I said in my steady, appeal-tribunal voice.

He was startled. He started to walk away and then turned back. "Can you give me *something?*"

"I can't promise that right now," I said. I took a beat. "So, you do what you have to do, and I'll do what I have to do."

Those words rang out loud and true like my own private Liberty Bell. They sounded so good, made me feel so good, I said them again.

"You do what you have to do, and I'll do what I have to do." I smiled this time.

"I understand," the landlord said. He smiled, too. He was impressed (phew!) "Keep me posted." He shook my hand.

"I will," I said.

"Thank you!" He was still smiling.

I was shaking after I shut the door. I picked Lovey up and lay down on the couch with her.

I held her above me, and there was a glow in her cheeks. Was it the sunlight, or was she, could she be, proud of me? I kissed her and lay with her cheek to cheek. She felt warm. I thought I felt a tremble in her cheek. Was she smiling? Was I? We fell into a deep, happy sleep even though, technically, things were still really fucked up.

INSIDE
CHATEAU ARBOGAST

When I worked for the Bloomfield DPW, I could walk to work, so I didn't need a car every day. When I got fired, I needed wheels again, so I bought a used red VW Beetle in good condition.

My wife divorced me and had a boyfriend, so there was less tension between us. I would see my son a few days a week. We'd go hiking on weekends, and he would sleep over sometimes. Lovey, my half of a mannequin I rescued from a garbage can, stuck by me. But where could she go?

I took her for a spin in my new car. Feeling frisky, I propped her with no shirt on the passenger seat and had her looking out the window. I'd only gone a few miles on the Garden State Parkway when a massive, blond State Trooper pulled me over. After the license and registration step out of the car routine, he examined Lovey and the car's interior.

"What's up?" he said, suppressing a smile.

You and me, right here. Right now, I wisely did not say.

"I'm taking her to a friend who is a dressmaker," I did say.

This Viking shook his head and squinted at me. He was square-jawed and tanned. I saw myself looking foolish in his sexy tinted shades.

"We got some complaints from drivers that you had a topless woman in the car. Cover her up and toss her in the back seat." He took off, and Lovey stayed home after that.

I was on unemployment, so to be able to pay for the Bug and to catch up on my massive debt, I applied for a job as a bartender at The Chateau, a catering hall about a mile away. The ad in the *Newark Star-Ledger* said experience preferred but not necessary. I'd driven past it many times, part palazzo, part fortress, its gleaming mock limestone exterior combined columns, cherubs, gargoyles, wood beams, and turrets.

What was it like inside?

Frosted gold mirrors lined the halls, and white spiral staircases led to upstairs and downstairs rooms. The banquet rooms were all color-coded, and the Gold Room was the biggest and most expensive. Then there was Silver, Rose, and Blue.

I was interviewed in a small, cluttered office off the main ballroom by Marty Arbogast, who inherited the business from his mother, Yetta. He was thirtyish, scrawny, dark, and intense, like a chain-smoking muskrat that had just crawled out of the sewer.

"You got any bartending experience?" His voice was raspy, and his tone was serious, but there was a gleam in his haunted, dark eyes.

"No."

"What's in a gin and tonic?" he spat.

"Gin and tonic?"

"Scotch and soda?"

"Scotch and soda?"

"What's in a screwdriver?"

"Vodka and orange juice?"

"See? Look how much you know already," Marty said. "We are in the party business. I want party people. No zombies."

I almost said, *oh, I'm not a zombie,* but I kept my trap shut.

I was hired.

After ten years of manual labor, five with the railroad and five with the DPW, and being covered in grime, it was nice to get dressed up to go to work for a change. I channeled John Travolta in *Saturday Night Fever* and hummed the tune as I slid on my tight black pants and buttoned my white shirt. I finger fucked my curly hair to get it just right, then put on the silly, shiny black polyester vest with the Chateau crest on the breast pocket and stuck my fat clip-on bow tie in that pocket. After years of clunky steel-toed work boots, it was a treat to shine my one good pair of shoes, which, luckily, were black. In them, I felt like I could fly if I flapped my arms hard enough.

The Chateau staff vibe was part Catskills and part keg party with some elderly bartenders and waitresses who started when Marty's mom, Yetta, ran the business out of her kitchen in

Newark. They were balanced by a squad of juicy young students bursting out of their dreary polyester uniforms. At thirty, I was ten important years older than them, the cool, patient, older brother to some of them; to others, the suave, older man from the glamorous adult world who could teach them a thing or two. A dozen or so of these boys and girls haunted my steps and poured out their adorable tales of woe about mean parents and cheating boyfriends or girlfriends. We all usually worked Friday nights and double shifts on Saturdays and Sundays, and in the heat and frantic pace of catering, we formed a shorthand that bonded us. Because I'd had much tougher jobs, I could seem comparatively wise and mellow. My young friends didn't have to know I shared my Spartan apartment with a beautiful, bald upper half of a mannequin.

The bemused arch of Lovey's pale eyebrows reminded me of the great noir actress Jane Greer in *Out of the Past*, and her small head was always tilted to the right, quizzical but encouraging. Her small, hard breasts were like upturned vanilla cupcakes. Non-threatening, non-judgmental, non-human, her quiet, constant presence was a great comfort to me. When I went out at night, I propped her near the window so her silhouette would deter burglars and trick me into thinking she was waiting up for me.

I was often drunk and wired after working a party and had to go places to blow off steam. One of them was Doops, a new and glamorous bar in East Orange with a big dance floor and hot bartenders. Wearing my bartender uniform gave me extra balls, and before I walked into the club, I psyched myself into believing that I was the owner of the joint and was just checking on my investment. It got me a lot of action. When I stumbled home with somebody, there was Lovey, patiently waiting. Most guys commented on her, but nobody said anything memorable. One guy got up out of my foldout bed and, naked, went over to Lovey and put his crotch in her face. To me, that was sacrilege, so I threw him out. I probably became a story he tells to this day (if he's still alive): the weird guy with the dummy. When I was feeling particularly raggedy and lonely, I brought Lovey into bed with me, and her cool, hard form was cold comfort but beat nothing and no one at all.

What did I want? To meet a handsome, witty man in his late forties or early fifties who was a painter and played the viola with a local string quartet. Someone calm and wise with a deep, mellifluous voice who could fill in the blanks of my checkered education and teach me about abstract expressionism. We'd go to museums and concerts, and I would learn the difference between adagio and andante movements in music. In his spacious, book-lined, sandalwood-scented bedroom, he would teach me how to really make love to another man and soothe my frazzled nerves. His name would be something waspy, like Malcolm, and his goatee would tickle me in all the right places.

I didn't meet Malcolm. Instead, I was a magnet for cute boys who needed a daddy. I was a daddy who missed his son. I met them all at Doops, where I could always flirt with Frank, the sexy Italian bartender. With his dark curly hair, dark eyes, and mustache, he looked like a lot of the gay porn stars of the day. With his big brown eyes and soft voice, every conversation he had with me and just about every other customer at the bar suggested an amiable bottom's availability. No great fireworks but a lovely cuddle. If you didn't get a date, you felt like Frank was your date, and you weren't invisible. It worked out for Frank; his tips were colossal.

I was a good club dancer, and if I started moving on the dance floor on my own, I could always snag somebody. I loved to dance since I was a little kid when we went to the Portuguese Club dances, and I instinctively wandered onto the dance floor and just started moving. In high school, I was one of the few white boys who could dance the fast dances. The other one was my best friend, Joe Gargani, and everybody knew he was gay. Joe, yes. Me? Nah! Like being gay, good dancing affects one out of ten boys, sometimes simultaneously.

One of my lost-boy playmates was Zeke, who was in school in California and visiting his Jersey parents. He was small and delicate with a beautiful profile, curly brown hair, and the taut body of a modern dancer. He was clever and literary and read me his favorite passages from *Swann's Way* as a kind of foreplay that connected mind and body. He taught me the correct pronunciation of Marcel's last name, which I'd assumed was *Prowst*.

I met John at Doops, too. A beefy Italian boy with fluffy blond hair and a deep, sexy voice that rumbled through my body when we lay together. He was a sweet, soft, snuggle bear. John had a lot of money or acted like he did. He drove a snazzy 380Z and always had a big wad of cash, which he spent on fancy dinners with me. I wanted to object. I was thirty, he was twenty; *I* was supposed to be the sugar daddy in this situation, but hey, I was poor and hungry, and a guy's gotta eat.

One night I was at Doops, flirting with Frank. A young guy with long chestnut hair and a wide-open face came to the bar. Everything about him was unlikely and arresting, his green eyes, a noble Roman honker, scraggly mustache, and wide, generous mouth. His red shirt had several buttons open, exposing his tawny chest fur and a puka necklace. His name was Bruno, and he was that most prized of all Jersey tomatoes, Italian. Frank liked both of us and decided to play matchmaker, giving us free drinks and telling us what a cute couple we made. Bruno told us he was twenty-five. We believed him, and after last call, he and I stumbled back to my place.

He was a good kisser, and when we got naked, he confessed to being eighteen. Uh oh. I paused but didn't stop. He was too adorable to resist, and he seemed to know the ropes. Though he was young, his previous dates must have been huge or plentiful because his passageway was generous. He was my favorite combination, a bottom with a big dick. We fell in love, of course.

I got married when I was twenty to a girl I met at eighteen, so this was my first romance in a long time. Bruno and I had a lovely time together. He had a puppy's amiability and growl, and when he thought hard, his tongue popped out. We were both good dancers, which helped keep our love alive. Sylvester's "You Make Me Feel Mighty Real" was our theme song.

One shockingly warm Palm Sunday, we decided to drive to the Island Beach in his big old Chevy Monte Carlo. On the entry road to the beach parking, there was some congestion, and the car in front of us stopped short at a red light. It caused a chain reaction of dents and crumpled bumpers. Six cars pulled over to the side of the road to await the police. The passengers of every car were teenagers.

"My mom is gonna kill me!" They all wailed, just about in unison. I shrugged and puffed on a Marlboro. I was thirty. My mom was satisfied with a phone call every few weeks. What was I doing in this scene?

It lasted six months, and then Bruno said, "I can't do this anymore." I understood but was devastated. The thing about dating younger guys is they really want what they want—they think. And then they don't. If you willingly get into the playpen, you can't cry when you get poked in the eye with a rattle.

I was lonely and heartbroken again. I wanted to take a break from bars. Working at parties, I was getting flirted with, stimulated, and then I drove home alone to trusty Lovey. Was there some other way to connect with men?

I'd read about bathhouses, saw their ads in gay rags, and was curious about them. I imagined them as gay snake pits churning with drug-fueled orgies. There was one in Newark. I did some recon missions, scoping out its nondescript entrance tucked into a busy, gaudy block of bodegas and cheapo furniture stores at the edge of Newark's downtown.

I left a party completely buzzed one night and drove there in my Chateau uniform. I pressed a button and got buzzed in through two sets of doors into a cool, clean gray lobby with a small snack bar to the left and a small check-in counter to the right. A handsome, muscular man with gray hair and a gray muscle tee stood behind it, blending in perfectly with the décor.

"How can I help you?" he asked in a soft, deep voice.

"I would like to, um, come in," I said.

He looked quizzical.

"You know what this is, right?"

"Yes."

"You don't expect to find women here, right?"

"Right."

A thin, comely younger guy with red hair folded towels in the small room behind the front desk. He wore a black tee. The scent of fabric softener filled the lobby.

The manager's name was Russ. He shook my hand and welcomed me. He introduced the towel boy, Tommy, his boyfriend. Tommy handed Russ two fresh, clean towels right out of the dryer. Russ handed them to me with a key to a room. Tommy gave me a brief tour of the first floor: the locker room, the steam room, the showers and sauna, and the TV/orgy room, and he escorted me to a small room on the first floor that would be mine for the night.

"Have fun!" he said brightly. "If you need something, sing out."

The charming welcome from two handsome men and the clean, mellow interior put me completely at ease. It was all so… so… wholesome!

I took a shower and wandered around the two floors. There were ten rooms on each floor. I was more curious than horny. The rest of the place continued the hushed gray motif and smelled clean and inviting, with a nice whiff of man funk drifting among the grunts and whispers. On the top floor at the end of the hall was a big dormitory/orgy room. I heard sounds first, then made out six men in different combos—I reached out and touched the smooth marble haunch of a fucker, and my cold hand made him flinch. I wandered around in a happy daze, past rooms where men sat in near darkness or displayed themselves proudly in bright light. It was all a little too much, so I went back to my little room and sat on the cot, not sure what to do next.

Tommy popped his head in. "You doing OK?"

"Yes. My first time here so, you know, getting adjusted."

"You take your time, baby." He sat next to me and kissed me on the cheek.

I turned and met his lips. He closed the door. I had a boner. He pulled off my towel and went down on me. There are few things finer than getting head from a handsome man. It feels so good *and* looks good, too.

The Club Baths became a regular stop after a job. You could stay for eight hours and sleep it off if that's what you wanted to do. The variety of men made it fun, and I met some spectacular ones. If I wasn't interested, I tried to find ways to discourage them politely. One older guy stormed away from my door and hissed, "Today's trade is tomorrow's competition." A brilliant passage from the gay bible: the Old Queen Testament. The first time I got turned down was like a punch in the face.

I met Kenny at the Club Baths. He was in his fifties and had a face like a bulldog, a thick, squat body, and a soft Carolina drawl. His dark rug looked cheap up close, but his mustache was real. We messed around a couple of times, but then I kept him at bay and just chatted with him. He was an engineer with a major corporation and traveled the world. For whatever reason, he was tongue-tied around me but liked to hear my voice, which he said reminded him of wind chimes. When he traveled, he sent me postcards from exotic places, *thinking of you in Jakarta, Montevideo*, or *Rotterdam* in a swirling hand. What he really wanted was a real date with me. I thought, why not?

Kenny picked me up in his electric-blue Oldsmobile Toronado, the most luxurious car I'd ever seen, and I thought about moving into it as I settled into its velvety, baby-blue passenger seat. He took me to dinner at Le Perigord, a beautiful

French restaurant, and then to see the Broadway play *Crimes of the Heart.* It was all very nice, but Kenny had nothing to say, and when I asked him about his travels, he changed the subject back to me. We drove back to my place in silence. Lovey was by the window. Kenny never noticed her. I poured two glasses of wine, and then he did me. As he got ready to go, he pulled a box of Godiva chocolates out of his coat and left it on my kitchen table with a card on it. When he left, I opened the box of chocolates and the envelope with a Hallmark card in it. *With Love to My Special Friend.* Inside the card was a check for $500. Now *that's* a good date.

I unfolded the lumpy sofa bed and picked up Lovey. When I looked at her, it seemed as if she were biting her lip, and her eyes were gazing in the opposite direction, trying to avoid mine. Okay. But I didn't *ask* Kenny for the money. Lovey and I slept apart that night, and the next morning, she forgot the whole thing… I think.

Fade out, fade in: December 22, 1981, the night before the night before the night before Christmas. The annual holiday party for Saint Mary's Hospital. I was now a seasoned bartender, and there was still the senior brigade and the college kids, with only a few people in my age range. One of them was Betsy, who was thin, waspy, and slightly older than me, and it was a relief to talk to an adult. Smart and frazzled, she seemed out of place among the burly older waitresses and the dewy college girls. She used to live in Manhattan, where she had a career in advertising. Her husband worked on Wall Street. They lived in a big old house in Montclair with their two kids. Why was she working as a waitress? Her husband was a cokehead in rehab, and their house was in foreclosure. She was at her wit's end, doing whatever she could to keep a roof over their heads. Using their car always caused an argument. Since she lived nearby, and so her husband could have the car in case of emergencies, I usually picked her up on the way to The Chateau and took her back home again. We gossiped about the job, and she complained about her troubled husband. Having been a troubled husband, it was interesting to hear an unhappy wife's perspective. Betsy called me a man without a country. I was happy to be a man without an unhappy wife.

She was worried about me, she said. I seemed so lost. She chain-smoked, usually downed a couple of glasses of Seagram's 7 before every job, and drank all the way through if she could get it. I felt sorry for her. She had her demons. I had mine.

Though it was against the rules, I always drank on the job, and when the coast was clear, I snuck drinks to the staff, including Marty, the boss. After cocktail hour, we had to go out on the floor and take drink orders. I got pinched a lot. A very drunk older woman insisted I was the newscaster John Stossel and dragged me onto the dance floor. It happened that the band was good, The River Street Cheaters, and they were doing a hot version of Rick James' "Give It to Me, Baby," one of my favorite tunes. I was able to escape the drunk woman's damp, apricot-sour-infused embrace and do some solo moves. A very pretty girl guest who was a good dancer joined me, and a cheering circle formed around us. After that, if the music was right, especially when The Cheaters were on duty, and the vibe was right, I could wander out to the dance floor and start to move on my own, and a girl guest usually joined me. I would look at Marty frowning on the sidelines. He usually gave me a thumbs up. Thumbs down—I stopped.

The night of Saint Mary's party, I picked Betsy up at her big old Victorian house. She was in the driveway, smoking and shaking. She had just had a big fight with her husband.

I had a half pint of Old Bushmills in the glove compartment and handed it to her. She took a deep swig and was still shaking. We pulled into The Chateau's parking lot and saw the red van that belonged to the River Street Cheaters. Phew! At least the music would be good.

Gavin, the soulful, mellow guitar player, was leaning against the van, puffing on a joint. Though the band was great at rocking out on dance music, I particularly liked it when Gavin soloed on the "One Note Samba" during cocktail hour, singing along with his deep, velvety voice. At the dinner break, when the rest of the band chowed down in the kitchen or shot up in the parking lot, Gavin stayed on the floor and played. He said he liked the way I danced, and I said I liked the way he sang. He asked me what my favorite song was. I told him: "The Closer I Get to You," sung by Roberta Flack and Donny Hathaway. He sang it whenever he played the dinner break just for me, and it made the hectic nights much more palatable. Someday, I would be ready for a good guy like Gavin, but for now, it was Lovey and an assortment of drive-byes.

I slipped Betsy the bottle of whiskey, and she stuck it in her bag. "See you inside."

I went up to Gavin. "Good to see you, sir."

"Good to see *you,* sir." He handed me the joint.

After a couple of puffs, I said, "Tonight's the night, man," thinking, *for you and me.*

"Oh yeah," Gavin responded, probably not thinking what I was thinking.

I grabbed his bicep. "See you inside."

"Oh yeah," he said as he exhaled. I heard it as seductive.

When I got inside, I stood at the top of the winding gold staircase for a moment and looked down at the pendulous, glowing chandelier and my bustling co-workers in their penguin outfits. The older women expertly wrapped skirts around the buffet tables while the younger ones put water in the chafing dishes. I was happy to see that Wesley was the other bartender on duty. He was a good-natured, church-going family man and the only black person on the banquet floor, though the kitchen was filled with Haitians that year. Wesley saw me and called out, "There he is!"

Everybody looked up and, with a staircase to dramatically descend, I was compelled to say, "Fasten your seat belts. It's going to be a bumpy night."

And it was a bumpy night. Holiday parties were always the rowdiest. Saint Mary's Hospital was a crumbling old landmark in a distressed neighborhood and was scheduled to close, so this was their last Christmas together. Before the party started, I knocked back a few gin and tonics until I had drunk myself into a state of nerveless, boneless functionality that kept my demons at bay. I wanted to get to the point where I was just liquid. I did my trick, you know, where I made three drinks at once and never spilled a drop. I kept up a snappy patter. Betsy kept checking on me because I was heading... somewhere. Her belligerent compassion got on my nerves.

"I'm *so* worried about you." She was drunk.

When it was time to clear the heavy brass service plates off the tables, the guys always pitched in and carried the loaded trays into the kitchen. Because I was drunk, the tray full of brass plates didn't seem so heavy this time. As I crossed the dance floor, I stepped on a piece of cantaloupe from the intermezzo. I started to skid and could have wound up under a pile of brass. In my next-best-thing-to-liquid state, I turned the slide into a skip-and-hop. Gavin saw it and alerted the Cheater's drummer, who added some drumbeats, cymbals, and a cowbell. I straightened up and made up a step that was a little march and slide that got me to the entrance to the kitchen. There was a drum roll. People cheered and I took a bow.

A short, sassy young woman with a pixie cut and tight red dress kept coming to the bar. She said she danced with me at another party, and she wasn't going to leave without dancing with me again. She said her name was Darlene.

"Are you a Darlene Love?" I asked.

"You asked me that the last time!" She beckoned me to lean forward. When I did, she kissed me. Her lips felt good.

"What do you do at the hospital?"

"Admonitions," I thought she said. I imagined her at work. *"You should cut down on your drinking."*

"Huh?"

"Admissions! Admissions!"

My eyes followed her to the dance floor. She was in the middle of a circle of young beef, grinding her voluptuous little body up against most of them.

"You can definitely tap that," said Church Deacon Wesley.

The River Street Cheaters were cranking up the music before the dinner course was served, one great tune after another to work up people's appetites. They started with "Weekend" by Loverboy, then "Tainted Love," then The Cars' "Shake It Up." Darlene came and got me, and I stayed on the dance floor while poor Wesley covered for me. When I looked over at him, I shrugged, and he, shaking it up, waved back, *keep going*, while he danced in place. I was getting to that sweet spot where I was pure fluid, and my feet weren't really touching the ground. When I looked over at the bar again, nobody was behind it, and guests were pouring themselves drinks. Wesley was on the dance floor now, and Marty, the manager, was dancing in a corner with Patti, the whorey waitress with the big ass.

The music stopped.

It was time for the dinner course. We all came to our senses and went back to work.

Wesley and I repaired the damage to the bar and met the rush. This was a hard-drinking crowd, and the wine course with dinner was of little interest to them.

"I bet you never saw a bunch of party animals like us, huh?" a burly young guy said as he grabbed ten bottles of Heineken to take back to his table.

"You guys really know how to party," I said for the hundredth time. It was my standard pitch for a tip. Gavin was alone on the platform stage. He was singing "Masquerade" by George Benson while the guests dug into their prime rib and The Cheaters were on break.

Betsy was the last one out of the kitchen with her dinner tray. She was wobbling, and I remembered that she took the pint of Irish whiskey. She could usually drink anybody under the table, but she was in bad shape tonight. I eased up behind her, tapped her on the shoulder, and took the tray from her. We went to her table together, and she served the food English style with two large utensils while I held onto the tray.

Gavin sang "The Closer I Get to You." He smiled at me, and I imagined he was, as always, dedicating the song to me. If I didn't pass out, I was going to ask him out for a late bite or back to my place. I just wanted to lay down with his pleasing form, velvety voice, and gentle soul after this long, ugly day. I wanted to run my fingers through his long, thick chestnut hair. While I was transmitting my intentions to him with my eyes, Betsy came up to me and turned my face toward hers. "I'm *so* worried about you. You know that?"

Yeah, yeah. I waved her away. I didn't want Gavin to get the wrong idea. But, oh yeah, I had to take her home after the party. The Cheaters took the stage again. It was time to crank up the music and get this party done. Wesley and I worked the tables, hoping to snag some tips, but everybody was too toasted. We were operating on the flip side of *my pleasure to serve you:* get drunk, get sick, and go home.

But—

I didn't really want this party to end. As long as I was here with these people, I had a context: The Dancing Bartender. Outside of The Chateau, after this party, I was nobody. I wanted to keep drinking until I was barely conscious, then jump in my car and drive toward the horizon and hope that I would fly off a cliff or just evaporate.

The Cheaters were in high gear, cranking out one great tune after another. The entire staff of the hospital was on the dance floor; doctors danced with the cleaning staff, and there was a lot of dry humping going on. Wesley was bumping with Patti, the whorey waitress. I was winded and started to clean up the bar.

Darlene came and said, "No, no, no, no."

She pulled me onto the floor, and she didn't have to tug too hard. Being this drunk and dancing this hard was the best form of oblivion. Darlene's firm body was pressed up against me in all the right places. She had her legs wrapped around one of mine and sent me hot labial Morse code. D Train's "You're the One for Me," Cameo's "Word Up," Lime's "Your Love." While I was in the Darlene pretzel, I watched Gavin wailing on the rhythm guitar and using his deep pipes to drive the tunes forward. His jacket was off, and his shirt was open. My vest was off, and my shirt was open. The River Street Cheaters were pros, and they were reading this party right: it was the night before the night before Christmas, the hospital was closing, and more than half the people in the room wanted oblivion.

They launched into "Abacab," the Genesis tune, which I didn't think of as dance music. Gavin was on bass for this one. They extended the instrumental break and poured on the bass. The whole room of tired hospital and catering staff turned into one sinuous, writhing serpent undulating across the dance floor. The music got inside all of us and told us what to do next. Oh yeah, this is exactly the way I want to evaporate.

Darlene and I wound up in the belly of the beast. She opened my shirt all the way and put her little head on my chest, then slid slowly down my body. There was a chanting circle around us: *Go! Go! Go!* I slid to my knees and leaned back.

The music stopped. I fell backward on my ass. Wesley had to give me a hand getting off the floor. The Cheaters started playing Donna Summer's "Last Dance," the musical equivalent of a bitch slap and the signal to The Chateau staff to get it together and shut the party down, a long, messy process.

Betsy came up to me. She had been crying. "You're a disaster. You know that? I'm really worried about you. How are you going to get home tonight?" Her face looked like a crumpled tissue.

"I'm OK, really. Don't worry about me. Just take care of yourself," I said, though I knew I was in bad shape. Thank God my little red VW ladybug knew the way.

"You should know that your girlfriend with the big tits is in the ladies' room, puking her guts out," Betsy said in that snappy voice, the one she probably used on her husband.

"Poor Darlene," I said, though I didn't care one way or another.

"She's a tramp!

When we got out to the parking lot, The Cheaters were long gone, and Gavin, of course, was not waiting for me.

I saw Patti and Wesley making out in her car in the back of the parking lot.

It was 2:15 a.m.

"We need to get you coffee," Betsy said.

"I don't want coffee."

"Then we need to get *me* coffee. If I go home like this, I will wake that bastard up, scream my head off, and stab him in the chest."

There was no place open nearby at this hour.

"What about your place? I just need some coffee and a few minutes to compose myself."

"Um." I wanted to get rid of her.

"Please!"

So, I brought her back to my place. It felt wrong. She was just a woman I gave a lift now and then. Now, she was a drunk and angry woman in my home.

"Oh, my," Betsy said when I turned on the lights. "You poor thing."

"Works for me," I said.

She sat on the couch next to Lovey. "Oh my!"

"That's two *Oh mys*. You reached the limit."

"What is this thing? It's creepy!"

"That's Lovey. I rescued her from a garbage can." I was in the kitchen making coffee.

"Send her back!" Betsy said. "And what's with you and tits? Is this some kind of fetish?"

I thought I didn't hear it right and popped my head into the living room. Some kind of radish?

"Is what some kind of what?"

"Fetish!" She said in her steely voice.

"Coffee will be ready in a minute," I said and sat on the couch with her.

"Move that... that thing!" She pointed at Lovey.

I picked Lovey up and put her near the window, looking out. I didn't want her to see whatever came next. She had been subjected to too many ridiculous scenes.

"Fuck the coffee," Betsy started to clumsily unbutton my shirt. "You like the way *I* do this? Am I as good as the tramp with the big tits?"

"Huh? Wait. Stop."

She tore off her vest and started to tear at the buttons on her blouse.

"Wait!" I said.

"You do it! You fucking do it!"

I unbuttoned her blouse. She tore off her bra. She lay back on the couch.

She grabbed her breasts. "How do you like these, big boy? How do they compare to that tramp you were dancing with? Huh? *Huh?* Are they as nice as the fucking robot's?"

She was kissing my neck now and pulling me on top of her.

"What robot?"

"That creepy bald thing over there. What about *my* tits? Huh?"

They were the perfectly fine breasts of a drunken woman I didn't like anymore.

I was on top of her and, alas, I had a boner.

"Yeah, that's nice. Give it to me. I'll show that bastard!"

She pulled my cock out and guided it to her center. Where were her panties?

I hesitated, pulled back.

"What's the matter? Can't you fuck another man's wife?" Her voice was like a guillotine.

"No." I got up, zipped up. "You have to go."

"What? Okay. I'm sorry. I'm very, very sorry." She was crying now.

"Yeah. Whatever. Get your stuff together." I stepped over her panties and then pointed at them. "Don't forget those."

"I'm sorry. I'm so so sorry."

"No more talking."

I drove her home in silence. No goodbye.

When I got back home, Lovey had turned from the window and was staring at me. Her expression was new to me: her eyebrows were raised, and her mouth was open as if she were saying, *what the fuck was that?*

"I don't know either," I sighed. I picked her up, stroked her cool, smooth head, and sat her next to me on the couch.

I turned on the little black and white television I found on the curb before I found Lovey. It was on Channel Five, and one of my favorite movies, *Swing Time* with Ginger Rogers and Fred Astaire, had just started. Perfect. I put my arm around Lovey's small shoulders and pulled her closer to me. She didn't feel the same; she was hard and cold—a mannequin, and I just didn't have the juice to imagine her as anything else. Betsy's visit had soiled our happy home. I put Lovey back at her post, looking out the window, and wondered what to do next.

I imagined myself sitting there with my imaginary boyfriend, my Malcolm. He would look at me with wise, patient, sparkling eyes. I would run my hands through his thick salt-and-pepper hair, and when we kissed, my eyes rolled back in my head.

I propped up a pillow and leaned against it, pretending it was Malcolm's strong shoulder, and watched Ginger Rogers sing "Pick Yourself Up" to Fred. I let their talent and grace pick me up and carry me away from all things insignificant, messy, and human—mortal or not—and drifted into a contented sleep. On the night before the night before Christmas, life was good.

THE LITTLE TROOPER

DECEMBER 25, 1978

T he Male Box in East Orange was packed on Christmas night. The parking lot was full, and Frank had to park on the street. Frank scanned the bar and saw men much like himself, decent guys in their thirties who could stand to lose a few pounds, men who had fled the arms of familial bliss for arms less familiar and more particular. He didn't want to wind up sitting on the couch with his mother watching the Perry Como Christmas Special after his sisters and their families left.

What he wanted was to connect with someone lean and mean tonight, to work off all that tryptophan and family feeling he could only take in small doses. That man hadn't shown yet, and when he did, he was sure to be pounced on by the other goodwill wishers in the joint. If Lean and Mean never showed, some would turn to each other and eventually stumble out together. They would drive to a spotless apartment with a tiny, blinking tree. In good faith, they would tend to each other's bodies, warding off disappointment until the last possible moment, and parting amicably, they would break the dinner date set for the following week.

John, the night attendant, buzzed him into The Tubs, the bathhouse on the edge of downtown Newark.

"Merry Christmas, honey. The gang's all here tonight, so if you don't get laid, it's your own damn fault." The lobby looked warm and homey, with a beautifully decorated silver tree next to the cigarette machine. Just past the lobby, a handful of men in towels sprawled across carpeted tiers and watched *It's a Wonderful Life* while keeping their eyes out for new meat. Frank walked past them to the back, and the film's stringy soundtrack gave way to a soft, thumping disco track. The place was hopping. Men darted from the orgy room to the steam room, from the showers to the video room, and the door of every cubicle was open. He walked past trim shadowy forms and toweled Buddhas. He took a shower and stood next to a short, curly-haired boy with a tiny, sleeping cock and a big ass. The boy gave him wide, blank eyes as he rinsed, then followed him to his room. Frank positioned him every conceivable way, gobbling up the blankness as the kid watched impassively. After twenty minutes, he released his silent partner and sat in his room, unsated, swigging cognac and sniffing poppers. He felt like an unassembled robot, his parts scattered across the cot.

Frank closed his door, lay back, and listened until someone next door came to a thumping, cursing climax. He fell asleep.

An hour later, he opened his door, and a well-built man with dark hair walked by, giving Frank the barest nod. He waited fifteen minutes for the man to return, then went out to look for him. He found the dark-haired man downstairs, watching the tail end of *It's a Wonderful Life*, smiling to himself. He looked slick and well-put-together, like the young dad in a television commercial. He was probably married, but so what? This is the man I want, Frank thought and went back to his room and waited for him. The man walked by and nodded. The next time around, he smiled, and his teeth looked perfect. The next time, he stopped.

"Come in." Frank's voice, strong and clear, startled them both. The dark-haired man entered, and Frank jumped him. The session was long, satisfying, and silent. They parted with a sweet kiss and met again a few minutes later at the front desk as they checked out. Frank said, "How about coffee?"

They sat in a booth at the Crescent Diner. Frank learned that his new friend, Ed Webster, had just moved to New Jersey from Ohio. He used to be a gym teacher back home, but now he sold menswear at the NBO outlet on Route Forty-Six.

"I need some new clothes," Frank said.

"I like you without them," Ed said, "but stop by anytime. What do *you* do?"

"Um… traffic… management."

Frank studied Ed's face. He was good-looking with a strong jawline, and Frank couldn't stop looking at the dimple in his chin. His eyes were dark and lively with a melancholy down slant to them that the liveliness sought to overcome. Looking at him gave Frank a beneficent boner.

"I don't want to talk anymore. I want to fuck," he said.

Frank liked Ed's Spartan, spotless apartment, everything brown and white, including the sheets and pillowcases. It looked like a setting for upscale porn. He wanted an apartment of his own just like it. Frank had never been with anyone so delighted in his own skin, who used his body so well. He was a skillful, accommodating bottom and could arch his body so that his pretty cock just about grazed his face. He looked very good doing it. Ed fell asleep, and Frank stayed up, listening to hail hitting the frosted windows, wondering about the beautiful man next to him.

Frank Antolino was a cop in Cedar Chips, New Jersey. He didn't usually tell guys he was a cop because there was always some kind of reaction that stopped the progress of him getting laid. He was thirty-four, tall and beefy, with green eyes and a trim mustache. He kept his thinning brown hair short. With his size and his sweet, amiable face, he was often called a teddy bear. Frank was a cop because his father, Big Frank, had been a cop. Big Frank was a popular figure around town, pear-shaped and merry. He knew everybody's name and told terrible corny jokes. At Christmas, he was the designated Santa at most church and school holiday parties. Big Frank had a heart attack and died while he snoozed in his squad car parked outside of the Municipal Building on Election Day, 1975.

Frank Jr. had to take the initial Law Enforcement Examination three times before he passed it, but after that, he aced the training and was surprised at how well he handled firearms. His beat was days in Cedar Center, where he filed reports on fender benders, nabbed shoplifters at the Dollar

Store, and helped senior citizens and moms with strollers negotiate the busy intersection. He liked to blow his whistle and hold up his hand to stop traffic.

Frank lived with his mother in the big old family house on the north end of Cedar Chips. He had been a middle linebacker at Cedar High, then worked as a landscaper before he joined the force, but in the last few years, his body had gotten soft. It didn't help that Mrs. Antolino was a great cook, and there was always something delicious in the house. She taught him her recipe for lasagna.

Frank's snoring woke Ed up. He didn't mind and watched Frank's broad back, with tufts of hair on his shoulders, as he snorted and snuffled. It felt good to have this big, warm body in his bed after so many solitary nights. For a few hours, this sweet, sexy man had kept him from thinking about his breakup with Nick.

Ed sat up in bed and thought about how different he felt from the night before. He had dutifully called his mother in Columbus, Ohio, on Christmas Eve and tried to keep the despair out of his voice. He didn't want to worry her. She was a single mother, a nurse who raised him in a small house in Columbus. They were devoted to each other, and Ed was the perfect latchkey kid. He excelled in gymnastics and helped his team take the state championship in his senior year. He became a phys ed teacher in the Columbus school system. He loved kids and was sad he would never have any of his own.

He had "Jingle Bell Rock" on the radio, and a *Cheers* repeat was on the television for some faux-festive background noise.

"Do you have company, dear?" she asked.

"Yes, some friends stopped by," he lied as he took a swig of vodka straight from the bottle.

"You sound like you have a cold, sweetheart."

"I'm fine, Mom, fine." He cleared his throat.

"And Nick?"

"Nick's fine, too." He was losing it. "Gotta go, Mom. Merry Christmas I love you."

He was out of vodka. He stared at the television, switched channels, and found a glitzy remake of *Miracle on 34th Street*. He stared at the screen through the bottom of his glass, holding it up like a monocle.

"This is very sad," he said to himself.

He drove to the McDonald's off the Parkway. His friend Randy, another Ohio transplant, first took him there in the summer, right after Nick split. They had a one-night stand that Ed tried to forget, but Randy could not. Randy taught at the middle school and was trying to get Ed hired there.

It was a steamy night, and the parking lot was full, with men draped around their sparkling cars.

"See?" Randy said. "There's a whole world of men out here waiting to be had. In Jersey, the parking lot is ground zero for hookups."

"I did all this stuff years ago. All I want is Nick back. Once he gets this kid out of his system, he'll be back. I'll give him a month. It hurts now, but we'll be stronger for it."

Randy kissed him on the cheek. "You're dreaming, honey."

"I don't want this. Please take me home," Ed said, striding to the car.

He went back twice. Once, he came home with a stacked little football player who wouldn't look him in the eye. The kid popped his load out of sheer terror and was gone in fifteen minutes. The next time was a rainy, killer Sunday afternoon. The rain made it hard to decipher the action in the parking lot, so he went to the tearoom. The stalls had doors hung so low anyone over five foot nine could look into them. Two guys sat in adjoining stalls, stroking and giving any passersby the bright eye.

While Ed washed and re-washed his hands, a father and son hurried in. The daddy, about Ed's age, took his son, who was about seven, to the only free stall. The kid tinkled leisurely, asking if he could get a strawberry shake. The daddy did not answer and zoomed the kid out without washing his hands, glancing at Ed as he passed. The hysterical glint in the man's eye made Ed feel like a lowlife child molester. He vowed he would never go there again.

Until tonight. Only one car in the lot. He saw a shiny bald pate, glasses.

"Blow job?" the occupant asked.

Ed shook his head and got in his car. He drove down deserted Cedar Boulevard. He imagined the whole world was huddled in cozy clusters tonight, drinking eggnog.

He had a drink at Rah Rah's, a cozy little gay bar in Orange. There were seven other people there, including Carol, the bartender, and a straight, drunken Hispanic couple. And there was Al, who was everywhere, with his lumpy body, bulldog face, and insinuating voice. He was like the ghost of homos past and present and, one hoped, not future. Ed wondered: do we all wind up like Al?

Ed sat at the opposite end of the bar, but Al joined him anyway, bought him drinks unasked, and told unbelievable stories of tricks with delivery boys, plumbers, toll collectors. The punchline always wound-up being Al's hand on your knee, no matter how many times you said no.

Ed drove to New York to Trilogy in the West Village, his favorite bar. Its tables were empty, and the bar was lined with pale, thin, leather queens with busy, silver hair; they were all deaf and part of a club, the Deftones. This was their holiday party. They all turned, waved at him, and blew him kisses. One of them mimed jerking Ed off, then taking his load on his face and smearing it around like a moisturizer. It made Ed smile.

He weaved uptown to the trusty Everard Baths with its endless, non-denominational marchers. A small, beefy blond man wearing a jock strap sat in the next room. Ed started to enter his room. The blond stood and held up his hand.

"You are a beautiful man, but no, please."

Ed was too drunk to care. He went to his room, lay down, and passed out. He woke at seven forty the next morning and drove shakily home.

At four thirty that afternoon, the phone rang and woke him up. "What's up?"

It was Nick.

Ed was immediately alert. "Go fuck yourself," he said.

"Come on, Ed. I just want to check in with you. I still care about you, you know."

"If you care about me, then you get your ass over here and live with me again. I don't want you caring about me and fucking somebody else. Look, why are you calling me? Where is your little boyfriend?"

"I'm talking to you now."

"So, where is he?"

"At his folks."

"How is the little darling?" Ed burst into tears. "I don't want this. I don't want it like this, Nicky! I mean, nothing makes sense. I thought you would get that kid out of your system, and we'd be back together like we're supposed to be. Why did this happen? I'll never understand it. Never!"

"Please, Eddie…"

"What did I do wrong, Nick? What? It's Christmas and you are not here! It just keeps getting worse and worse…"

"Shhh. You'll pull through. I know you will. You're my little trooper."

"I am? Still?"

"Always, always, always."

Ed blew his nose on the bedspread. "Let me get off the phone before I make an even bigger fool of myself."

He hung up and roamed around the apartment, looking for a place to settle, and eventually curled up on the cool, clean, uncomplicated bathroom floor.

From the night they met at The Manhole in Chicago during Gay Pride 1975, there was something electric about their connection. Short, wiry, half Spanish and half Algerian, with a wolfish gleam in his eyes, Nick was adopted when he was four years old by a kindly older couple who ran a soybean farm in rural Fayette County between Cincinnati and Columbus. Nick appreciated them but hated the farm and its chores and ran away a few times, once to Cincinnati and three times to Columbus.

Nick disrupted Ed's ecosystem like an invasive species. Ed welcomed the invasion, a change from his perfect little gentleman upbringing and temperament. Nick appreciated Ed's all-American good looks and amiability, and the dimple in his chin was intoxicating. Nick's gaze was molten, hungry, and penetrating. Nick planned to be a pharmacist but learned that the real money was as a pharmaceutical sales rep. He was a good one.

Their first night together, Nick pounced on him and drilled him in every position three times. This one-night stand turned into a six-year living arrangement. Their opposite personalities blended well, and their domestic life was peaceful, with only minor disruptions along the way. Then Nick was transferred to New Jersey, an offer he couldn't refuse, and Ed joined him. That's when everything fell apart. Ed couldn't find a teaching job, but in Nick's first year, he had his team's highest sales rate. A new salesman, Danny, a pretty, young Italian boy, was assigned to trail Nick and learn the ropes. After a month, they made regular stops at the Pine Brook Motel on Route Forty-Six, where Nick taught him new kinds of ropes—and they were in love.

Ed showed up drunk and a couple of hours late for Randy's Christmas bash and downed everything handed to him, including half a Quaalude. Randy kept pulling him into the bedroom for long, touchy/feely pep talks.

Ed left without saying goodbye and drove down the highway with all the windows down. Something loomed in his back seat. It was dark and hooded and had arms that Ed felt would strangle him any minute. He stepped on the gas, hoping the evil spirit would be sucked out the window, but it was caught on something, a hook or seat buckle. He floored the accelerator, and the dark thing struggled and eventually was sucked out onto the highway, where it bounced along before getting hit by a van. It was the black hoodie he wore for his morning runs.

He didn't want to go home just yet.

He was sitting in The Tubs, watching an old movie, surrounded by men in towels. He avoided looking at anyone and removed any hands placed upon him. He felt better. Christmas was just about over, and this old movie had never seemed so interesting before. I am just going to sit here. It's better than sitting home alone. A beefy Italian gave him the once over, and his cock stirred. He decided it was time to walk around.

After their hot and satisfying one-night stand, Ed and Frank started dating. Once a week at first, then it went to three times. The sexual chemistry was intense and addictive, and when they were done, the dismount was cozy and drama-free.

Frank got tired of his mother asking where he was all night, so he got an apartment in Newark, a twelfth-floor studio in one of a row of high rises on a once prestigious street. The neighborhood was in transition: well-to-do old white ladies, young Hispanic families, and white gay professionals stood in the checkout line at the Foodtown. He wasn't used to living alone yet. He missed his mother's cooking but not her endless chatter. The apartment was furnished with his sisters' leftovers. When he wasn't working or with Ed, he ate takeout, watched

TV, and looked out the window. In the morning, he could see Boys Town on the hill across the Passaic River and, beyond it, Manhattan's silver steeples. After dark, the squatty hills looked like a backyard barbecue's haphazardly strung lights, while beyond them, Manhattan glowed like some great, unquenchable fire.

The apartment rang with the hollow sounds of his slow movements. An empty glass placed on the kitchen counter reverberated for minutes after with no sound to take its place. When the phone rang, it startled him the way an alarm might, and when he answered, he heard his earnest voice bounce off the shiny white walls. When Ed wasn't there, he usually fell asleep on the couch.

Ed asked him to go to a Valentine's Day party. They were both nervous and silent on the way down to Randy's Garden apartment. Frank wondered about Ed's twitchy mood and wondered if the ex-boyfriend, the famous Nick, would be there. Whenever Ed mentioned him, it was in hushed tones, as if Nick were a messiah of sex.

"I don't want to talk about Nick anymore," Ed said the last time he came up.

"Good. I don't want to hear about him," Frank said. He had never before cared about anybody enough to be jealous, and he didn't like the feeling.

They walked into a crowded, noisy room decorated in silver and black with pink trim. A tall, bearded man with frizzy beige hair ran up to Ed and gave him a big kiss. He gave Frank a withering look, then squeezed his hand.

"Frank, Randy. Randy, Frank. Where's the booze?" Ed said.

Jennifer Holliday wailed from four speakers. Ed got swallowed up in a kissy circle, but Frank pushed ahead to the kitchen counter, which was set up with half gallons of Shop Rite booze and mixers. Some guys sat around a pink modular couch in the living room doing lines of coke on a black marble coffee table. Frank, surrounded by strangers, downed three stiff gin and tonics. He thought of announcing, I'm a cop, and showing his badge, just to shake things up.

"Is this your private stock, or can anybody get to it?" a voice growled at his shoulder.

"Sorry," Frank said and stepped aside for the squat, swarthy man who pressed against him. The growler wore a lumpy yellow velour pullover and tight designer jeans with a big, swirly label on the rear end.

"Could you slide it over a bit, tiger?" the man said, pinning Frank against the counter. "Oh, did I say tiger? I meant bear. You look like a big, grouchy bear. I'm Al." He held out his right hand while his left hand rested on Frank's shoulder, and his knee grazed his groin. Al's bloodshot, feral eyes glittered and widened in Frank's momentary gaze. His wet hair had the purple tinge of a home dye job. Upon closer inspection, it was a rug.

"I have to tell you this," Al said. "I'm not the kind of person who throws himself at another person, but I am sincerely attracted to you and hope you will consider corning home with me tonight."

"Um, I have a ride. I mean a date."

"Oh, forgive me. But I have to tell you, I wouldn't mind being smothered by you, if you know what I mean." Tufts of wiry hair crawled out of his pullover.

Frank said. "Are you in some kind of new religion or something?"

"No, my darling. Why?"

"It's just hard to believe somebody could be so obnoxious on their own."

"Oh, you're a vicious bear," Al said. "So, who's your date?"

"The guy in the red shirt. By the couch."

Al's face flattened. "Oh, Edwina, that tired old trash? You can do better. Take me, for example."

"No thanks."

"Believe me, honey, beneath those pectorals beats the heart of a dizzy queen."

"Shut the fuck up!" Frank blurted, startling everyone within earshot. He pushed past Al and headed toward the bathroom, where a line had formed. He went into an all-white bedroom. A poodle-haired blond was sprawled across the enormous bed, giggling into the phone. Frank walked onto the terrace and shivered. He went back to the living room and saw that Ed was part of a little circle formed around two men who had just made an entrance.

He was introduced to Nick and Danny. Nick was short and dark with a bushy mustache and sleek black hair streaked with gray. Danny was young, a little taller, tawny-haired. He looked pretty and pampered, his full lips stuck in a nervous centerfold pout. The two men conspired to look as if they had just come from the gym, muscles pumped and bursting out of identical black tees that read THE WORKS and might have said across the back, WE'RE LOVERS. Ed seemed determined to make small talk with these two, though nobody made eye contact. Having summoned him, Ed appeared to have lost his nerve and didn't include Frank in the stilted, forced conversation.

So, this was the famous Nick who broke his heart? The guy was a midget. Frank had never seen this skittish, chatty, and fake version of Ed, and he didn't like it. Is this what happened if you cared about another guy? You turned into a silly queen?

He saw that the bathroom was free and went to it. Then he went to the bar.

"A little drink to ease the pain?" It was Al. "Are you jealous, my darling?"

"Get lost."

"They tell me you're a cop."

"Yeah." It wasn't something Frank advertised since it sometimes scared guys away.

"Fabulous. Did you ever kill anybody?"

"Not yet."

He didn't see Ed anywhere and he wanted to get out of there. If he had to, he would call a cab. He went back to the bedroom and stood on the terrace, shivering. The poodle-haired blond came out and offered him a toke of his joint. His name was Kip, a respiratory therapist from Oregon.

Frank zoned out while Kip talked about his miserable childhood. His father was a junkie, and his mother was an alcoholic, or vice versa. "All my life, I've been an enabler."

Frank yawned. "Huh? A neighbor of who?"

"Am I boring you?"

"A little."

"I love it." He slipped Frank his card with his mother's phone number penciled in.

Frank went back to the living room. Ed and Nick were in an intense huddle, and young Danny had been pounced on by Al. Frank stood behind Nick and made a *let's go* gesture with his thumb cocked toward the door. Ten minutes, Ed mouthed.

Randy made coffee. Frank helped him set out Styrofoam cups and bring out a sheet cake. He finished off the rest of the chicken wings and ate about ten deviled eggs.

"Are you having fun?" Randy asked.

"Oh, I'm having a fucking blast," Frank said, his mouth full.

Randy turned to him with a pained, earnest face. "Look, you seem like a nice guy," he licked pink frosting off his fingers, "but you are not what Ed needs right now."

"Thanks," Frank said. "What you mean is that you hope he needs you." He realized he sounded like a character in a soap opera. "Look, me and Ed are big boys, and what goes on between us is our own business."

They were silent on the drive home.

Nick still loves me, Ed thought. This thing with Danny won't last.

He's still hung up on that midget, Frank thought.

THE LITTLE TROOPER | 173

Ed pulled in front of his building. Frank got out of the car without saying a word. He walked around an elderly woman who led two ancient tottering poodles. When he got inside his apartment, the buzzer sounded.

"Look, I'm sorry," Ed said.

Frank yanked him into the bedroom. Later, Frank pulled up behind him and held onto him. "I don't care where you came from or what you did. All I want is when you're with me, you're with me. Do you understand?"

"Yes."

"You can do what you want on your own time, but I don't want to hear about Nick... or anybody else."

"Yes, sir."

Their romance was back on track. Frank was a consistent, thoughtful top. Ed wasn't in love with him and didn't think he would be, but he felt very comfortable and safe with Frank. His sweet face, satisfying bulk, and calm temperament were soothing. Every couple of weeks, Frank made his lasagna, and that sweetened the deal.

They spent a weekend in New Hope. Frank hated it but kept his mouth shut. They drove to Provincetown for four hectic days. As they approached their hotel, they saw Wayland Flowers and his puppet, Madam, sitting on the veranda. Madam said, "Hi boys!"

The next day, they went to Herring Cove Beach, where all the men were naked, and some were hooking up. Ed stripped right away and pulled down Frank's trunks. Frank was scared at first and jumped into the frigid bay to hide his junk and get his bearings. When he stepped out, his chubby cock was shriveled by the cold, and he was embarrassed to have his furry, meaty ass exposed. When he got back their blanket, Ed had a boner. The heat in Ed's gaze when he looked up at him made Frank hard. Frank knelt, lifted Ed's taut legs, and they fucked while a few onlookers beat off. One of them came on Frank's back, his jizz sizzling in the sun. Later, they walked along the shore as the sun set.

"Watch this!" Ed shouted. He ran along the beach, his perfect buttocks bouncing like volleyballs, and launched into a cartwheel. Frank thought his heart would burst with love.

They went running in Branch Brook Park in Newark, which was green and lush in mid-summer. Ed was in a good mood. He was teaching again and back in shape.

"Are you still with me?" he called.

"Right behind you," Frank said. "Stop showing off." Frank caught up with him. "You do this every fucking day?"

"Just about."

"Christ!"

"Come on. It's good for you. Besides, you're a public servant. You should be able to chase down a bad guy."

"Hell, I'll just shoot him."

"Stop complaining. You could stand to lose a few pounds."

Frank stopped. Ed turned and saw his unhappy face, jogged back to him. "What's the matter?"

"You think I'm fat," Frank mumbled.

"No, I don't. You're always complaining about your weight."
Ed sighed. "Listen to me. I just want you to be happy. As happy
as I am. With you, I mean." He swatted Frank on the ass. "Come
on. Don't mope. Be my little trooper."

"I really hate it when you say that," Frank said. "You mean
like a state trooper? I'm just a cop. What does little trooper
mean, anyway?"

"It means… you're brave and beautiful, just the way you are."

That night Ed lay in Frank's bed, covered in his own jizz.
The way Frank fucked him, the satisfying size of his cock, his
steady, rocking rhythm, the heft of his belly, made Ed squirt
without touching himself. Frank came out of the bathroom
with a warm washcloth and a towel. He tenderly wiped Ed
down, then dried him.

"What are you thinking about?" Frank asked.

"Nothing."

"What's wrong?"

Ed sat up. "Nothing. I just worry sometimes."

"You never have to worry about me!" Frank said.

"Maybe. But you've never been involved before. You don't
know how it can go wrong."

"I know enough."

"Frank, I'm afraid you're going to look at me one night and
say, 'I don't want this anymore,' and I will crumple up and die."

"I would never do that!" Frank said. "I love you."

Ed was quiet for a moment. "Then I had just better shut up."

Frank and Gene Crespo were in the locker room at the end of their shift. Crespo was pulling on his sweatpants. He jogged home every day. "Three miles!" he said too often. He was married and had two small kids. Short, wiry, with an antsy gleam in his eye, he figured if he played his cards right, he'd be the next Chief of Police. Somebody told him once that he looked like Al Pacino in *Serpico*, so he was always carefully bearded and tousled. Frank and Gene went through high school together but were never tight. He thought Frank was lazy.

"You were spotted going into a building in Newark. Do you live there now?"

"You with the FBI, too? I live with my mother."

Crespo frowned and started to walk away. He turned back and lowered his voice. "So, are you gay or what?"

"Why?" Frank said. No one had ever asked him that before, and he didn't like it.

"What do you mean why? Does that mean yes?"

Frank didn't answer.

"Frank, this is a small town. People talk."

"So what?"

"Look, it doesn't matter to me, but you just kissed any promotions goodbye."

Frank tied his sneakers. He didn't know what to say. He just looked up at Crespo and shrugged.

"Look, this ain't New York with all of them groups. You're all alone out here, man." He put on his knapsack. "Why, Frank? Can you tell me that?"

Frank met Crespo's therapeutic, condescending gaze. Even as a kid, Crespo was always pushing it, sticking his big nose where it didn't belong. He didn't really care about anybody else, he just had to separate himself from the herd. Frank stood up. He was a foot taller than Crespo.

"The way you worry about me gets me right here," Frank pounded his chest. "But I don't want you to worry about me, pal. I do my job and my private life is my business. I don't wear no buttons or make no speeches. I don't ask no questions and I don't want none. I'm happy with my life. Are you? Good!"

Crespo didn't answer. He started running in place. He turned and ran out of the locker room.

Frank was spooked. He never thought about being gay. He just liked having sex with men. Now, he was with a guy he could imagine settling down with. He heard about teachers being fired for being gay, could the same thing happen to a cop? He imagined grainy pictures of him and Ed fucking on the beach on the front page of the local paper or *The Enquirer*. Fuck it. He was happy.

They were at Trilogy on Christopher Street on a Tuesday night in May, and they were at a table, just finishing dinner. Frank was quiet.

Ed leaned forward. "Back home, when I used to fantasize about New York, this is the kind of place I used to imagine. You know, good-looking upscale guys, sophistication, ambiance…"

"Um." Frank cleared his throat.

"It means atmosphere."

"I know what the fuck ambiance means!"

"Sorry. Why are you so quiet?"

"Why are you so wired tonight?"

"It's a beautiful night. I'm out with you. All's right with the world." Ed leaned back in his chair and spread his arms.

"Uh huh." Frank's face was overcast and dark.

They were silent until their dinner plates were cleared.

"Are we gonna get a place together or what?" Frank blurted.

"Wait. Where did that come from?" Ed leaned forward.

"My ass is on the line here and you're dancing around…"

"Slow down, big boy. Did I miss something? Did we talk about this?"

"Where the hell is that kid?" Frank downed his gin and tonic and stood up. He waved at the young waiter.

"Calm down, baby. I like the idea of sharing a place, but I don't want to be rushed into anything. I'm just starting to get on my feet again after Nick."

"Nick. Again."

"Okay. Okay."

The waiter brought Frank another drink. They were silent while Frank thrummed his fingers on the table.

"Why don't you want to live with me?" Frank said.

"Look, if you do anything, do it because you're almost thirty-five-years-old, and it's time to get off your ass. Don't do anything because of me. I don't want that responsibility. You got out of your mother's house, and that was good, but you need to spend time on your own, then you think about settling down with somebody."

"Somebody? I want you. So, what does that mean? Yes, or no?"

"Oh, today's the deadline?" Ed said. "I'll never understand how you think. You let everything bubble up inside you, then you come out with three clear sentences: bim bam boom, and now it's the law. I've been through this before, officer, and I'm not rushing. Things are good right now. That's all I know."

That night in Ed's bed, their rhythm was off. Frank's heft felt oppressive and smothering. He was trying too hard.

Ed said, "Stop, get up for a minute. I can't breathe."

Frank jumped out of bed. "Can you breathe now?"

"Yes. You were just too heavy on me."

"Excuse me." Frank stood up. "I'll just take my fat self to the couch."

Ed heard the TV click on, and he imagined Frank's mug as he sat on the couch. He couldn't bring himself to go after him and fell asleep. He woke as, step by step, Frank made love to him. Two, three, four, Ed counted off in his head as Frank worked his way up to his neck. It was the familiar recipe, but tonight, it felt stale.

"Can we just go to sleep? I'm pretty tired," Ed said.

Frank plopped down with a big sigh and turned his back.

"Nothing's wrong, don't be upset," Ed said. "We'll talk in the morning. Come on. Where's my little trooper?"

"Here I is," Frank muttered into his pillow.

Frank was on his beat after a sleepless night. It was the early morning rush, and traffic sped down the hill to Newark. He didn't want to move, and it took an elderly woman with a walker waiting for him to escort her across the street to snap him out of his stupor when she yelled, "Hey!" He wanted to be home on the couch with a pillow over his head, hiding from the world. If a car swerved out of control and headed toward him, he might jump out of the way. Might.

Ed wanted to take a week off, a little breathing time was the way he put it. Oh, nothing was wrong. He just wanted to think about things.

What am I going to do tonight and the next night and the next? Don't call, he said. Be a little trooper. This terrible ache was all new to Frank, and he fucking hated it.

Ed ran around, straightening up the apartment; he changed clothes three times: sweatpants, jeans, shorts. He was listening to love songs on the radio, switched it off, and queued up Chuck Mangione and Esther Satterfield's "Feels So Good," one of Nick's favorite tunes. It was good sex music. Nick was on his way over. In the middle of balancing his checkbook, he impulsively called Nick and was surprised to find him low and mopey. Danny, little Babykins, was gone. It was quick. "I don't want this anymore," and he was off to Florida with kids his age. Ed tried to keep the delight out of his voice. He liked Nick best when he was mopey. He was much more malleable that way. There were some glib expressions of sympathy, then accusations, then reminiscences in their long conversation. There were also lengthy pauses that felt familiar and erotic. Finally, Nick asked, "Are you busy tonight?"

Ed took a beat and answered, "No," as casually as he could.

When the bell rang, he realized he was trembling. Nick walked past him and set a six-pack of Michelob in the refrigerator. He emptied his pockets, putting two fat joints on the kitchen table, a gold coke kit, and a bottle of poppers.

"Where is the KY?" Ed asked, putting his arms around him. Nick shuddered in his embrace. He looked terrible, his face gray, unshaven, his eyes bleary, his hair cut gruesomely short. He was dressed in black, which made him look both sinister and fragile.

"You didn't have to bring the goodies," Ed said. "I can stand you sober."

They got undressed. Nick was wearing his lucky gray jockstrap and a studded cock ring.

"You make me feel naked," Ed said.

"You are naked, stupid."

They started on the couch and wound up on the floor, each working off his grudges. The coke made them speedy, and they were at it a long time.

Nick straddled Ed's chest, mechanically pulling at his exhausted cock, his face dark and blank. Ed ran his hands over the sculpted stone of Nick's body and felt the birthmark on the base of his spine. He remembered how much he loved Nick's wiry, tense frame and its earthy smell. He liked him best unwashed and unshaven. His heart swelled with love for the man on top of him.

"I really hate your guts," Ed said.

Frank dreaded walking into his apartment. All day on the street, he tried but couldn't keep his mind off Ed. It was worse at home, where his imagination bounced off the shiny white walls. He had never felt the power of the phone before; it was always in the corner of his eye like some Twilight Zone terror with a life of its own. He thought if he primed it, it might ring. He called his mother. No answer. Bingo night.

Around eight, the phone rang, and his heart pounded. A woman's voice asked for Mr. Anto-line.

"Yes."

"Mr. Anto-line, I'm Sherry from Major Marketing. May I ask you some questions about soft drinks?"

He answered all her questions, each of which triggered a series of sub-questions about the sweetening and consumption of soft drinks. He imagined Sherry as a young, bleached blond, sitting alone in a dismal green office while her mother watched the baby. She had some trouble following her script, and he was patient with her.

Sherry was thanking him for his time and seemed reluctant to let him go. He wanted to ask her if she needed a ride. She sounded like someone who needed a ride. He wanted to say wait when she told him to expect some coupons in the mail.

He called Ed. Not home. He drove to his apartment and sat in the car, looking at the dark windows. He went to The Male Box. It was dollar night; the place was packed, and it was hard to get to the bar. A short, humpy dancer spread his pink cheeks to the crowd, pulling off his jockstrap in one motion. Frank wedged himself into a corner and stayed for an hour. He called Ed. No answer.

"Hi, stranger," John said, buzzing him into The Tubs. "There are only a few stragglers here. Are you sure you want to come in? Yes? Well, there's always me! I get off at two and every half hour after that."

Frank sat in his room with the door open and heard heavy footsteps upstairs. He took off his towel and lay back with his eyes closed. You made me do this, he thought. I don't care what happens. I don't care if I live or die. This thought frightened him. He never thought or felt this way before. He always just chugged along, getting by and mostly thinking about food and sex. Now, he wasn't sure about anything.

He started to fall asleep. Cold hands ran up his leg. He opened his eyes and saw a large, hairy shadow.

"Hi there, are you awake? What a surprise to find you here!" It was Al. He tried to snuggle in beside Frank.

"I don't wanna talk," Frank said, sitting up.

"What do you want, darling? What do you want?" Al said, sinking to his knees. For all his talk, he didn't know how to give a decent blow job. It was all teeth and noise. Frank tapped his head forcefully.

"Stop right now," he said in his cop voice. "You suck at... sucking."

Al stood up, adjusted his rug. "I've had better... and bigger."

"Beat it."

Frank called Ed Saturday morning. He answered and sounded surprised.

"Why are you surprised?" Frank asked.

"I'm not. I was thinking about you."

"And I was thinking about you. When am I going to see you?"

"Soon, Frank."

"What the fuck does that mean? What about tonight?"

"I think it's too soon. I haven't cleared all out all the cobwebs yet."

"You said a week. It's been a week."

Ed was silent.

"You better fucking talk to me, Ed. You better start talking."

There was a long silence.

"I need a little more time," Ed said.

"What happened? What did I do?" Frank choked up and could barely get the words out.

Ed got scared. "Nothing! It's nothing you did. It's just I need some time to myself."

"But…" Frank didn't know what else to say.

"Please let me go now. I will call you this week, and we can go out and talk. Let me get off now, please." Ed hung up.

Ed didn't call. Sherry from Major Marketing didn't call. The phone rang once. It was his mother.

"So, when are you coming down? I made some nice sausage and peppers."

"I don't know."

"When?'

"I don't fucking know, Ma!"

"Call me when you're normal." She hung up.

He lay on the couch and stared at the ceiling. There was a water stain that came to look like a Volkswagen Beetle. He had the phone on his chest and fingered the buttons of Ed's number. *How can he not care about me? Something must be very wrong. He would never do this.*

No answer. He tried every ten minutes, letting it ring ten, fifteen, twenty times. He drove to Ed's apartment. Lights out. He rang the bell. He sat in his car and waited until it was nearly three a.m. He woke up in his car at seven thirty and drove straight to work. After the morning rush, he drove the squad car to the middle school and went to the gym. A young black man led the boys in jumping jacks. Frank waited politely by the bleachers. There was a break while the boys pulled mats off the wall for wrestling.

"Hey, buddy," Frank said to the teacher. "I'm looking for Ed Webster."

"He's off this week. He'll be back on Monday."

Frank stumbled through the week, drinking himself to sleep, and felt the thump of every second. Saturday, he found himself at Trilogy, unwashed and unshaven, and he tried to drink away his nerves. Later, he stood swaying in the center of an adult bookstore backroom with his hand on his wallet. He plowed across Seventh Avenue, swept along on the piss tide foam of his own misery; the path was magically cleared for him by streetwise strollers.

An old woman wearing a blue winter coat and blue babushka stood by Cooper Union, pleading with passersby in a tiny pull-string voice, "Please help me. I'm hungry. Please help me." She kept her huge white hand extended. Frank got close enough to be spun around by the big hand and found himself looking into her pale, myopic eyes. She gave him a one-on-one version of her pitch, putting schmaltz into it.

"Lady, you got the wrong number." Frank tried to get past her.

"Give me some money, you fucking asshole. I know you got it!" She was clamped onto his left arm.

"I'm crazier than you are, lady," Frank said. "So you better let me go. I could kill you right now, and nobody would stop me."

"And you're a fucking asshole," she said, releasing him. She wandered up Third Avenue and resumed her litany with lunatic calm.

Frank kept walking east, not sure where he was headed.

He passed the Saint Marks Baths and doubled back. Inside, he stood before a black marble and gilt check-in counter. The snippy, bald concierge's brief glance made him feel as if he'd flunked the entrance physical. It seemed many dark flights up before he met his attendant, Angel, who let him past dim red rooms carrying two towels and a small cup of goop.

Frank's flat feet resounded in the hall as he bumped into walls and beautiful men. Every room he passed contained a living centerfold, perfectly lighted and poised. Beautiful men with blank faces and big cocks roamed the halls, sticking their noses and cocks into rooms and pulling out instantly. He gazed at cover boy faces that looked through him. A deeply tanned boy in a jockstrap lay on his stomach. Frank walked into his room.

"Just resting."

A mock construction worker, his face shadowed by a hardhat, stroked his big pink piece. Frank stopped, stepped in, and the hardhat shook vehemently.

In the ersatz moonlight of the orgy room, he saw muscular shadows that stared straight ahead as he walked through and back again slowly. No one stirred. Maybe he was dreaming. He might have passed out on the couch and burped up this morbid fantasy filled with desirable, untouchable men.

A tall shadow brushed past him, heading out of the dorm. This chance touch sent a shiver through him and stung him back into consciousness. He followed the shadow, a spectacularly built cowboy in a Stetson, downstairs to the showers and watched, dry-mouthed, as the cowboy lathered the length of his rosy, glistening skin.

He kept the Stetson on in the shower, which meant he must be bald or almost. The guy's face was pinched and mean, and his weak chin was covered with stubble. Frank stood alongside under cold drizzle, and the cowboy's eyes met his for a full second. Frank followed him up three flights of stairs, unable to catch his eye again.

He watched the cowboy offer his stiff, uncircumcised meat to open doors and pull back when a hand reached out. The cowboy turned a corner, and he lost him. Grunts and moans of pleasure drifted into the hall from unidentified rooms, and Frank imagined they might be piped in over the loudspeaker. He circled the third floor again and saw his dream man propped on a cot, stroking himself.

Frank stepped into the room, and the cowboy gave him the mean eye. His ears pounded as he reached for him with a cold hand.

"Just resting." He had a German accent.

Frank entered and closed the door behind him.

"Just let me touch you."

"No!" the cowboy shouted.

"Please!"

The cowboy jumped up.

"Get out!" He reached past Frank to open the door, keeping the towel modestly before him. Frank stumbled out and bumped into a thin, middle-aged black man who stepped into the room and slammed the door behind him. Frank heard the cowboy say, "Yes, give it to me, Daddy! Give it to me!"

Frank stared at the number on the door, 303. He fled to his room and threw himself on the cot, buried his face in the pillow, and fell asleep with his head under the pillow. A pounding on the wall woke him up. Someone was getting plowed in the next room. Frank sat up.

"Go home," he said to himself and immediately followed his own advice. He had a headache, but it was wonderful to be on the street. The Village was filled with lovers eating ice cream cones. It was wonderful to be in his car with the radio playing love songs.

At the end of the Holland Tunnel, what wafted through the windows felt like fresh country air. Safe, reliable Jersey air.

He scrambled four eggs, fried up a half pound of bacon, drank three glasses of apple juice, took a multi-vitamin, then stretched out on the couch. He fell asleep watching a rerun of *Laverne & Shirley*.

He got up early the next morning and ran in the park. He took all his clothes to the basement laundromat, vacuumed the whole apartment, and washed the floors with pine soap. He bought the *Star-Ledger* and read the sports section, the comics, and *Parade* magazine. His mother was surprised when he stopped by with a strawberry shortcake. He took his nephew to see *Star Wars* for the second time.

His momentum evaporated the moment he was inside the apartment again. He played hide and seek with the phone all evening, then stood by the window, hoping to see Ed's car. This helps me, he thought. "This is my life," he said to the window, "And I don't like it."

Ed jumped when the phone rang. He let it ring five times before he answered.

"Yes? Hello?" He knew who it was.

"Ed, how are you? It's Frank."

"Great. What's up?"

"Where you been. I haven't talked to you in a while."

"Been to Ohio, you know, to see my mom."

"Oh."

"And how are you?" Ed chirped.

There was a long silence. Ed listened to Frank breathe.

"I'm fucked in the head, man. I'm completely fucked in the head. When can I see you?"

"Give me a minute, okay? I just got back, and I've got to get my bearings."

"Can I come over now?"

"Um. No."

"I got to see you, Ed. It feels so bad. It feels like I'm going to die or something. Nothing makes sense, what did I do wrong? What did I do?"

"Take some deep breaths. You'll be okay, sweetie. I have to talk to you, too. Tuesday. I'll talk to you Tuesday."

"I won't make it. I know it. Tonight."

"I can't," Ed said. "Not tonight. My mom's here. She, um, came back with me."

Nick was sitting on the couch. When he heard this, he jumped off the couch and ran into the bathroom, shutting the door.

"Oh, that's nice." Frank didn't believe him.

"Keep taking deep breaths. You sound bad."

"Yes." Frank took deep breaths, then unrolled some paper towels, wiped his eyes, and blew his nose. "I really miss you."

"Will you be OK until Tuesday? We can clear the air then."

"What does that mean?"

"It means… Look, I'll talk to you Tuesday. I got to go. It's late and I'm beat."

"Ed?"

"Tuesday, okay sweetie? You go get some rest. Goodnight."

Ed put down the phone, walked into the kitchen, and made himself a drink.

"You can come out now."

"That really sucked," Nick said.

"What was I supposed to do?"

"Ask your 'mom,'" Nick said, making air quotes. "You should talk to him. Call him back. I'm going."

"No!"

"You should talk to him," Nick said.

"You and I are together again. That's all I care about. You are sticking around, right?" He kissed the top of Nick's head. He loved the new gray streaks in his hair.

"Yeah, yeah. But you should call the poor guy."

"I think it's too late."

The next morning at ten a.m. at Cedar Avenue Middle School, Ed grouped his eighth graders into two teams, Red and Blue, for volleyball. He put all his problem kids on the Blue Team, hoping the pressure of keeping the ball aloft would spark them into a little body English. The Blues were all precocious and chubby and probably stayed glued to their Ataris at night. And they were well-mannered. Not wishing to step on anyone's toes, they politely let the ball bounce past them. The Reds, tall, tough, and bony, were slaughtering them. Just then, the ball bounced off Shelly Feingold's curly blond head and back over the net into Red no-man's-land. This surprise point unified the Blues, and "Use your head, Shelly!" became their battle cry.

Ed laughed and ran his hands over his chest, folding his arms tight across it and flexing his pecs. Whenever Shelly and his friends imitated Mr. Webster, they puffed up like peacocks and hugged themselves. He was happy. Nick was back, and though they were still a little tentative, the old chemistry was still there. He felt bad about Frank, such a sweet man and a great fuck. Another time, they might have made a go of it—but Nick's hold on him obscured everything.

The Blue team scored four more points.

Frank drove to the Cedar Avenue Middle school and pulled into the parking lot. He just wanted to see Ed. He didn't know what he was going to do when he saw him.

He entered the school through a side door. A janitor swabbed the stairs with disinfectant. "Watch your step, buddy," he called. Frank fingered the gun in his holster. He hadn't used it in a year, and that was to fire a warning shot in the air at a fleeing purse snatcher. He entered the gym, saw the game in progress, and hesitated. Ed was on the sidelines, shouting, "Crank it up!" Frank's big footsteps went unheard in the din. He was a few feet away before Ed noticed him, and when he did, his eyes widened and darted left and right, looking for an exit.

No, let's get this over with now, Ed thought, much as he dreaded it. He had a free period at eleven, so they could talk for a bit then. *Sometimes things just don't work out,* he would say. *I loved the time I spent with you, but it's time for both of us to move on. Nick and I are back together.* Maybe it was best not to mention Nick.

Ed held up his hand, indicating, wait.

Frank could see in Ed's exasperated, frightened face that there was nothing there for him. The man he loved didn't want him anymore, the man he *thought* he loved. Something shifted inside of him as he looked at Ed's distraught face. He didn't recognize him. Where did he go?

He didn't know what to do. The gun was still in its holster; he rubbed the nub of its grip. From here, he could shoot Ed right between the eyes... but then what? He was supposed to preserve and protect, or something like that.

The ball bounced off Shelly's head again and landed at Frank's feet. All eyes were on the ball and him. He turned and walked out of the gym.

EGGHEAD PAYNE

My family came to Newark, New Jersey, on the Portuguese *Mayflower* in 1925. On paper, we were one of the first families of Newark's Little Portugal, the Ironbound section, but somehow, through a series of mishaps, scandals, tragedies, and just plain stupidity, we were always broke and just this side of the law. The Ironbound was Newark's other side of the tracks, its Lower East Side. Locals referred to it as Down Neck because of its location at the neck of the foaming Passaic River. It was where the character of Tony Soprano was born and raised, and if you saw *War of the Worlds* with Tom Cruise, the street where the church gets destroyed is Ferry Street, our main street, and that church was, and still is, St. Stephan's.

For a time, my best friend was Egghead Payne. We were in Mr. Blonsky's class in seventh and eighth grades at Lafayette Street School but didn't talk to each other until one day in the playground. I was throwing my Spaldeen high bouncer against the wall, and it got away from me. Egghead was walking by, handed it to me, and presto: best friends.

Egghead's hair was buzzed short, and his head was perfectly round like a melon, but Melon Head Payne was just too much trouble to think of and say, and Egghead just seemed to go with Eugene. His grandmother called him Egghead once, and it stuck. I never called him that since that would have been mean. He had brown skin, the color of an old football, sad brown eyes, and even features so symmetrical that he looked like a cartoon character: The Adventures of Egghead. My little sister said, "He looks like Charlie Brown!" His plummy lips were always slightly parted, somewhere between a sneer and a smile, so that you always saw his small, bright, even teeth. He never laughed out loud, but if he thought something was funny, he hissed through his pretty teeth and released a little puff of air. Our friendship ended in a big, ugly public way with a resounding slap across the face on the steps of the Church of Our Lady of Fatima in June 1961.

The Ironbound was ethnically and racially blended then in a way that didn't cause any disturbances—yet. Our block was all white, but there were black families on the next block. Being on the wrong side of the tracks was the grease that made it all seem to work on our narrow streets, but the tribes never occupied the same building. Though it was built on a grand scale, Newark was just a tired old city in its work clothes, trying to make it through the twentieth century in one piece. The trains screeched along the tracks, and the factories pounded out their essential widgets and flanges and belched their smoke. There was a layer of grime on everything, and on some humid summer days, an easterly breeze sent the fumes from the nearby slaughterhouse our way. To me and Egghead, it was all we knew, and it was paradise.

After school, we often went to a dusty pocket park near Penn Station to play stickball or read comic books. I read *Batman* and *The Green Lantern* out loud using different voices: Daffy Duck, Bullwinkle, and Walter Cronkite. Egghead liked Cronkite the best, it was my attempt at the voice of authority, and when I used it, I felt better. If I was Daffy too long, he nudged me.

"Cronkite. Do Cronkite." I basked in the steadfast trust of Egghead's big brown eyes. For a time, it was the safest place in my world, and, for a time, I was the safest place in his world.

Newark's Penn Station was an Art Deco limestone beauty with vestiges of its former glory. It was the gateway to the Ironbound, the dividing line between Uptown and Downtown, and once you crossed through it, you were in a different world. On weekends, we liked to play in Penn Station's echoing chambers. We pretended to be waiting for trains and looked impatiently at the imaginary watches on our bare, bony wrists. I tapped him on the shoulder as if he were a stranger.

"Excuse me, sir. When is the next train to Chattanooga?"

"Chattanooga Choo Choo! Chattanooga! Chattanooooga!" Egghead loved saying this.

I found a copy of Theodore Sturgeon's novel, *More Than Human*, on top of one of the garbage cans on the platform, and this magical find, with its lonely heroes and their superpowers, showed me there might be another dimension beyond the train tracks.

Sometimes, we walked uptown, where the big department stores and big movie theaters beckoned. We went to the movies every week. I had a paper route, so I always had a little money, and Egghead never had any, so I treated him. He was like my little brother, though he was a year older than me. I had three younger sisters I referred to as Nina, Pinta, and Santa Maria, and I was used to being a big brother.

When we saw *North by Northwest* at the Paramount, I was amazed that Cary Grant wore the same glorious blue-gray Saville Row suit for three days straight, something I would attempt with less success when I grew up. The Paramount was a couple of doors away from The Newark Evening News, New Jersey's biggest and best newspaper, and the bars around it were hangouts for its reporters in their rumpled suits and shiny ties. I dreamed I might be one of them someday.

Richard Beymer was the star of every movie at RKO Proctor's main theater: *West Side Story, Five Finger Exercise,* and *The Longest Day.* Did they just keep his name on the marquee and rearrange the words underneath it every week? He seemed sensitive and fragile, and when he sang "Something's Coming" in *West Side Story,* I had tears in my eyes. He was my first crush, though I didn't know then that I was gay.

My father went one flight up to the Proctor's Penthouse Cinema, where he could see racy foreign films with Brigitte Bardot and Marcello Mastroianni. He was the neighborhood Casanova and considered handsome, with big brown eyes and a rascally baby face. It was only when I saw *La Dolce Vita* as an adult that I understood my father's short, hectic life. He wanted to be Marcello Mastroianni splashing with Anita Ekberg in the Trevi Fountain, not work in a factory, and be saddled with four kids he barely knew.

My first memory was of him on top of me, pounding my head into the driveway of my grandmother's house. I was three years old, so I don't know what I could have done to cause his volcanic rage.

Our Lady of Fatima, our first Portuguese church, was completed in 1958. Despite my parents' objections and my scandalous father and divorced grandmother, I was one of its first altar boys, a job I took very seriously. The firstborn, I was a golden-haired baby, then a dirty blond boy, blue-eyed and tall. The church started a Boy Scout troop, and I had to lobby my parents to join that, too. I wanted to be brave, clean, and reverent. My sisters became Girl Scouts, and for us, being scouts with our handbooks, oaths, and rules was a respite from the tempestuous chaos that swirled around us. We developed our own underground railroad to subliminally transmit feelings, knowing there was no safe audience for them above ground.

I didn't look like the typical Portuguese boy or like anybody else in my family, a blue-eyed boy in a brown-eyed world. I had the long, sad face, moist eyes, and coloring of a bodega Jesus painting and was voted most pious-looking two years in a row. I was often pulled out of school to work funerals where my sad Jesus face got me good tips from grateful undertakers.

Lafayette Street School was two blocks from my grandmother's house, where we sometimes lived, depending on our finances. Whenever the *Newark Evening News* wanted to do a story about the city's cultural diversity, they would send a photographer to our school because we had an exotic mix that included Italians, Poles, Lithuanians, Irish, Puerto Ricans, Blacks, Galician Spaniards (Gallegos), and the last survivors of Newark's once lively Chinatown, the Eng cousins.

Immigration laws had just been eased, and more Portuguese poured into the neighborhood. We were called "Pork Chops" because it was the closest-sounding pejorative a moron could reach in a pinch. Those Irish, Polish, and Italian residents who resented the Portuguese invasion called us "Zekes." I'm not sure how they came up with it, probably in some midnight, white-hooded cabals, but when we overheard it murmured behind our backs, it stung. We could refer to ourselves as Pork Chops, but we never, ever used the Z word.

My tiny, iron-willed grandmother was forced into an arranged marriage as a teenager and had to flee Portugal with the husband she hated to escape his gambling debts. He looked like a monkey, beat her, and they had four daughters. She divorced his sorry ass when she was twenty-seven. This left her a dangerous, fallen woman, often whispered about by the genteel fishwives of the neighborhood. For her few visits to Our Lady of Fatima, she wore a wide-brim navy-blue hat and navy-blue suit. With her head held defiantly high, jaws clenched, and nostrils flaring, she sailed majestically down the aisle like the *Queen Mary of Fuck You*. When she was tired of a subject, she would imperiously snap, "Ponto. Final!" (Period. The End!) And that was that!

With her daughters to raise, she worked at a suitcase handle factory, did embroidery, watched neighborhood children, and took whatever piecework she could get. Like most immigrants, she was very thrifty, and through a combination of hard work, determination, and some mysterious lucky breaks, she eventually bought the biggest house on the block, formerly the mansion of a family known for their hot dogs. It was three stories tall and built on a grand scale with spacious rooms and high ceilings. The blooming garden was filled with roses of every color, all kinds of vegetables, fig trees, and a grape arbor. Ever enterprising, my grandmother turned the two upper floors into a rooming house for single immigrant men who filled the factories and ditches of the neighborhood. My father, fresh from Portugal and the Merchant Marine, was one of them, and that proximity resulted in my parents' turbulent marriage.

I was often my grandmother's sidekick as she cleaned the furnished rooms. It was a thrill to explore these secret sections of the big house. The men's rooms smelled tantalizingly of cigarettes, dirty socks, and whiskey. The men were at their construction jobs, but one day, I walked into a small corner room where a slender young man was in his bed, naked, with the bedsheet just about at his waist, his chest pale, and his arms brown, like most construction workers. He might have been drunk or hung over. He smiled and waved me in, and I could smell the funk and whiskey breath oozing from him. I froze, and my grandmother yanked me into the hallway and slammed the door shut. The image of him in the bed, his glittering eyes, his seductive wave, and his earthy aroma planted a flag in my consciousness.

At the end of the day, my grandmother liked to kick back with some strong, homemade red wine and was usually drunk and either woeful or nasty by seven p.m. That night she sneered at me, "Are you a sissy boy?"

My father sometimes didn't come home for a few days at a time. In the evening, he often went out in Italian suits from The Swank Shop on Ferry Street, and it was my job to polish his selection of size ten Florsheims. He was charming and popular out in the world, but at home, his unpredictable temper kept us on high alert. He once pounded the kitchen table so hard that a full soup tureen flew into the air and hit the ceiling. I tried to avoid him. When he wasn't around, I was the man of the house.

My mother was a compact, wiry bundle with sparkling, lively brown eyes and the long, expressive face of a great comedienne. She read classic novels and loved British films, anything with Alec Guinness and Trevor Howard. She had the willful temperament of a Bronte heroine, and my father was her Heathcliff, her reach for the stars of passion. She was hooked on his bad boy sizzle, and he on her unconditional love. Though she was often confined to shabby, small, second-floor apartments with four kids, her adventurous heart was running along the misty moors, chasing her Heathcliff with her wooly, wild hair cascading behind her. Her sharp tongue and love of language united one sweltering Fourth of July when non-stop firecrackers turned our beloved dog into a whimpering, quivering mess. My mother ran to the window and shouted to anyone within earshot: "Why don't you take those firecrackers and shove them up your mother's ass!"

Egghead envied me for having a father on hand, no matter how temperamental and inattentive. His father was in North Carolina with a whole new family. His mother lived uptown in the Stella Wright Homes, the projects. She had nothing to do with him. Egghead was sentenced to living with the smoldering, short-tempered Miss Irma, who was nicer to me than she was to him. And she wasn't very nice. Egghead called her Auntie.

After the second time I met her, he confessed that she was his grandmother, but she didn't want that known. She hoped to be able to snag gentleman callers, and being Grandma was not a selling point.

At home, she was a big, scowling woman in a grimy robe and a head rag, watching very loud television and eating Ritz Crackers with margarine and Nilla Wafers. She never cooked and sometimes shared a Swanson TV dinner with Egghead. No wonder he was always hungry. She noticed me looking at her and said, "What you lookin' at, Bright Eyes?" Like my grandmother, she liked to say disparaging things about his parents to anyone who would listen.

Sometimes in the early evening, I saw Miss Irma on Ferry Street, stuffed into a shiny dress with her ample cleavage overflowing, probably heading to a bar in her spiky heels. She topped off the whole ensemble with an elaborate copper-colored wig—Oh, Miss Irma! I wondered if, in their nighttime personae, Miss Irma and my father knew each other.

Egghead didn't like coming to Hayes Pool with me. But what else would he do? Hayes was a public pool at the far end of the Ironbound near the entrance to the Pulaski Skyway, a long walk from home. It was usually dirty and jammed with screaming kids, and you learned to negotiate the big, jagged cracks at its turquoise bottom. I never really learned to swim but loved being in the water and always jumped into the middle of the pool, where I spent a lot of time underwater, pretending I was a deep-sea diver. Egghead never wanted to get wet and sat on the side, staring into space. I noticed that his bathing suit said Fruit of the Loom on it and was just a pair of black boxer shorts.

One noisy afternoon, while I was resurfacing, I looked at him, sitting at the edge of the pool with his worried face. What the hell was he thinking about? He looked like a boy trapped in a well fifty feet deep, his soul struggling to reach the surface with nothing to hold on to. While I was looking at him, some roughhousing kids accidentally knocked him into the pool. He splashed frantically and blindly in every direction, eyes bulging with terror. His flailing arms pummeled me, fingers tore at me before I could walk him to the steps. Did I push him into the pool with my powerful mind like a character in a Theodore Sturgeon story just *because*... because he was sitting there moping in his sad underpants bathing suit? What was the word for that power? Right, telekinesis. It was the first time I saw real terror, and I'm reminded of it whenever I see a doomed wildebeest trapped in a crocodile's jaws on *Nat Geo Wild*.

Egghead looked like a doomed wildebeest in school, too, whenever Mr. Blonsky scanned the back of the classroom. I was one of Mr. Blonsky's favorite students, and Egghead was almost invisible to him. Blonsky looked like a soft-hearted Stalin with his short gray hair, crinkly eyes, and forest of nose hair. He was a dedicated teacher, and if you showed any promise whatsoever, he pushed you to do better. Otherwise, you collected dust in the back of the class, like Egghead did—and wondered what everybody was talking about.

IQ tests were all the rage. Three other kids and I, The Brains, had scored over 130. Three of us were Portuguese, I'm proud to say. The other Brain was the beautiful Paxton Phipps. His skin was the color of a sugar cookie, and his hair had a ginger blush. His eyes were brown and gold and sparkled when he flexed his enormous dimples. Paxton Phipps! Even his name was charismatic. He dressed better than the rest of us in crisp white shirts, pants with sharp creases, and shiny shoes. Everybody, white and black, boy and girl, had a crush on him, including me.

"Why are you wasting your time with Shithead?" Paxton asked in one of our many marathon evening phone calls. He had no use for Egghead and wouldn't listen to any defense of him. I winced, but I was so dazzled by Paxton that I kept my mouth shut.

"He's so ugly he hurts my feelings," Paxton said, quoting Moms Mabley. He played me her albums over the phone. They were filthy and hilarious, like a sneak peek into an even darker grown-up world.

"Ain't nothing an old man can do for me but bring me a message from a young one," Moms said. I repeated that line to my mother. She liked it when Paxton called.

"Is that Paxton? Tell him I said hello." She met him when Paxton and I starred in a class play, where I played a sap who got his hand stuck in a mailbox, and Paxton was a slick reporter covering the story. After the silly play, my mother gushed at Paxton like a star-struck fan but said my performance was "a little hammy." She usually referred to Egghead as "poor Egghead," or if she was feeling flinty, "Mortimer Snerd," after the goofy-looking ventriloquist puppet.

After school, Paxton waited at the corner until a gigantic Chrysler Imperial picked him up. I think he lived in a different neighborhood, but one of his parents worked nearby, so it was easier for them if he came to Lafayette. But then he just disappeared in the middle of eighth grade, and the phone chats stopped. Paxton! It is a mystery to me that such a remarkable boy with such a remarkable name—Paxton Phipps!—was never heard from again. Like Theodore Sturgeon, Paxton was a glimpse of another, more intricate and stylish world. I asked Mr. Blonsky what happened to Paxton, and he looked mystified, "I don't know. I really don't know. What a remarkable boy." Someone said his father was an FBI agent on special assignment.

One day, we had a substitute teacher, a round, thirtyish Black woman, Mrs. Bryant. She must have been a devout churchgoer who longed to take the pulpit because she preached fractured Bible stories to us all day long.

"Jonah was afraid to preach to the people of Nineveh, but I am not afraid to talk to you, predominantly." She liked the word predominantly. I wasn't exactly sure what it meant; I think she was using it incorrectly.

"When I look at your faces, I can tell that you are good children, predominantly."

"Wasn't that teacher stupid?" I said to Egghead as we walked to gym class. He said, "Yeah," which was his response to just about everything. When we got back to our classroom, Egghead, for the first time ever, raised his hand.

Mrs. Bryant looked at her seating chart and said, "Yes, Eugene?"

Egghead stood up and pointed at me. "Teacher, *that boy* said you was stupid." He smiled, hissed, and sat down.

"Thank you, Eugene," Mrs. Bryant said. "You see, children, it's just like I said. People are predominantly good, but you don't know how stupid somebody is until they open up their mouth and tell you, like *that boy* done." She pointed at me. The Revenge of Egghead.

After school, I walked away from Egghead in a huff. He caught up with me.

"Why did you do that?" I asked.

"Do what? I didn't do nothing."

"Just go away," I said. He didn't go away but got in step with me.

"Predominantly," he hissed. "I like that word. *Predominantly!"*

His big, bold betrayal shocked me. It made me look at Egghead in a new way. Mr. Blonsky made him feel stupid. I said Mrs. Bryant was stupid. Lines were being drawn, and like Hayes Pool, there was a big crack in our friendship.

Coming home from Hayes Pool with Egghead one summer afternoon, we came across my father's new Corvair parked on a busy street. He was passionately kissing a very pretty, young Latina. When he saw us, he ducked down and covered himself and his date with his Swank Shop trench coat. To me, that was more shameful than anything else.

"Hey, ain't that your father?" Egghead asked. I walked away quickly, looking at everything but the car. I was embarrassed that Egghead had witnessed the scene, and I didn't like his smug smile.

When my father came home later, he sought me out for a change and stared at me with his big brown eyes, silently pleading: *you won't say anything, right?* I saw the wheels turning behind the hot cocoa gaze; he was trying to melt me. Is that what all the ladies were so crazy about? I didn't get it and stopped looking at him. I was standing next to a window and didn't say anything, glad to be in control for once. I tapped on the window and looked at the blooming garden with its fat figs below. Finally, I nodded, just nodded—and a marriage was saved without a word being said. I was ten years old and realized that I was on my own; my parents had never raised me, were not going to raise me, nor be much help going forward.

A few weeks later, we were at Haven Beach in Point Pleasant. My mother and sisters were on the Boardwalk, and I was coming out of the rough surf. My father was on a blanket, tanning his beautiful machine, so he could share his bronze god-ness with his fan club when he got back to Newark. He looked at my long, scrawny frame.

"You have to *devil up* your body and *devil up* your muscles," he said. I just nodded and thought, *Devil up? It's DEVELOP! Speak English, you stupid spic.*

Mr. Blonsky loved *The New York Herald Tribune*. We read it every day and dissected its stories: Most of the stories were about Cuba. One day, a striking blond boy magically appeared in the class doorway, and everyone gasped, including Mr. Blonsky. This boy had green eyes, freckles, and wore a remarkable fringed buckskin jacket that a cowboy might wear at a rodeo. He was Carlos Castillo, our first Cuban refugee. The arrival of this exotic visitor began a Cuban invasion that rocked our neighborhood in every conceivable way.

Though they were refugees who left everything behind, the Cubans seemed smarter and better dressed than the rest of us, bringing a new sizzle and spicy music to Down Neck. They bristled with confidence and something else: sex. It had always simmered, undercover, all around us, but the Cubans owned it and were comfortable putting it on display.

Carlos had an older brother, Felix, who had the same green eyes and blond hair. He had been a bodybuilder in Cuba and liked to stretch out on the small patch of grass in their backyard in a Speedo. Neighbors found things to do in their backyards.

A few weeks later, it was two days after Memorial Day, and Egghead and I were walking down Lafayette Street on our way to the pool. Two blocks from my grandmother's house, we passed Carlos, the Cuban boy, sitting on the steps of his building, eating a sandwich of pale-yellow Cuban bread and thick, red guava jelly. He looked up.

"Where are you fellows going?" Carlos had only a slight accent.

"Hayes Pool," I said and held up my rolled-up towel.

"There's a pool. Oh boy! Can I come too?"

We waited for him to run upstairs and get his bathing suit, and he hopped with excitement as we walked.

"Hey, let me ask you fellows something. Did either one of you fellows ever try to suck your own dick?"

I wasn't even sure what that combination of words meant, but Egghead nodded. Carlos said he tried for a long time and finally got the hang of it. There was a cow on his family's farm in Cuba who did it like it was a lollipop, but the best thing was when a girl did it to you.

When we got to the pool, Carlos was horrified by the noise, grime, and cracked bottom, but that didn't stop him from cannonballing into the middle with a celebratory scream. He grew up in Manzanillo, with the Caribbean as his backyard, so water and air were of equal value to him. He left us behind in the kids' pool and went to the smaller, deeper *adult* pool, sixteen feet deep with a diving board. He spent the rest of the afternoon showing off, doing a combination of perfect and goofy dives accompanied by sound effects and faces. Half the pool just stopped and watched him, and if their attention flagged, he nudged it with: *Hey, look at this! Look at this!* Even Egghead looked up from time to time and seemed impressed.

Since Carlos lived a couple of blocks from me, he started to meet me on the way to school, and we walked home together, too. Carlos's father had been a dentist in Manzanillo and now worked as an assistant for a Cuban dentist in Union City. Carlos's mother, who had been a teacher, was the cleaning lady at that office. Carlos was a latchkey kid, and when we went to his apartment, we ate those guava sandwiches on Cuban bread. Felix was often in his tiny bedroom with a girl. When Carlos and I went to see *Psycho,* Felix tagged along. During the shower scene, Felix screamed and buried his face in my shoulder. I liked it.

I delivered the *Newark Star-Ledger* every morning and was done by seven thirty a.m. My route was Jefferson and Madison Streets, just below Ferry Street, where, just past the train tracks, they devolved into shabby or empty buildings and weedy lots filled with liquor bottles and syringes. Egghead and Miss Irma lived in one of those shabby buildings.

Below the Jersey Central tracks was an urban lover's lane, where early morning couples steamed up the windows of their cars, and shady characters lurked, smoking in the shadows day and night. I had to pass them to get to one of my customers, and one morning, a man whistled at me.

"Hey, little boy. I wanna pork you in the butt," he called and made a juicy kissing sound.

After that, to avoid the tracks, I walked around the whole block to wind up on the other side.

I collected from my customers in the afternoon and always tried to be done before dark. After I got home one night, a teenage boy delivering pizza was stabbed to death for fifty cents just a few blocks from my route. This senseless crime rattled the already shaky neighborhood.

"They'll take your money and kill you anyway!" my mother called out after that as I left to do my collections. I didn't blink. Danger was always part of the atmosphere, like carbon monoxide. Inhale, exhale, walk, run for your life.

"Bye, Mom!" I waved at her.

My paper route manager, Mr. Narkowitz, was an angry, ugly man. He looked like an angry Honey Badger with Coke bottle glasses, a gray crew cut like a spiky oven brush, his face sprayed with Perma-Scowl. Narkowitz! His name still feels like a curse. He followed me in his car most mornings as I made my deliveries. Why? Didn't he have grown stuff to do? Attendance was mandatory at his weekly meetings with all the carriers at his grimy, smoke-filled office. All he did was shout at us to get more subscribers. He often pulled me aside for special nagging with his harsh, gravelly voice because I smiled too much, according to him.

"Smiley, you think the world owes you a living!" he snarled.

My life was not a great adventure story, and my family had its problems, but I was just a boy, filled with goofy boy joy juice, and that was no crime. I thought about what he said. *Do* I think the world owes me a living? I wasn't sure what it meant, and I didn't think it was true.

"I don't think so," I said. He threw a lit cigarette at me and told me to get the fuck out of his office.

"Hey, Smiley, get your ass over here." Narkowitz honked his horn at me one morning as I delivered my papers. He got out of his putrid black Rambler and grabbed my elbow. He pointed down Jefferson Street. "There's at least a couple of hundred people living here. Why can't you squeeze some new subscribers out of all this?" He waved his arm as if it were a magic wand with a cigarette at the end of it. "The paper's having a promotion. Get twenty new customers, and you could win a Schwinn Bicycle, the Continental ten-speed."

That was exactly the bike I wanted! I saw it up at Bamberger's Department Store, and I was hoping to save enough to buy it someday. I had a clunky, rusted girl's bike that my father bought second-hand from a guy at the factory. I scraped off the rust, painted it silver, and called it Nellybelle, just like the jeep on *The Roy Rogers Show*. I rode Nellybelle all over town. I loved its homely, dependable charms, but I got teased about it. "Hey, Dale Evans, nice horse!"

I wanted that Continental ten-speed, so I hustled and got some new subscribers, but I was still five short. Time was running out. Egghead and Miss Irma's building was within the scope of Narkowitz's arm wave. I got a brilliant and terrible idea: what if I put Miss Irma down as a new subscriber but gave her the paper for free and paid for her myself?

I still hung out with Egghead sometimes, but he and Carlos didn't like each other, and, well, Carlos was more fun. I sometimes saw Egghead tagging along behind Tyrone Pendleberry, who was tall, lean, and tough. He smoked cigarettes and shoplifted from the Food Fair. He had a bouncing tough guy walk that Egghead tried to copy.

I took Egghead to see *The Absent-Minded Professor*. I bought him two hot dogs and a big bucket of popcorn. On the way home, I asked Egghead to talk to Miss Irma about the subscription while he practiced his new tough guy walk.

"No way. You do it," he hissed.

"I'm afraid of her."

"Me too," he said.

"Do it with me." I nudged him.

"No. Why should I?"

"When I get the new bike, I will give you my old one."

He disappeared before my eyes. His body was still there, but his eyes were blank. His soul went down to the well to check with the others trapped there. Then he popped back.

"Give me five dollars."

"Five?" I asked the new tough Egghead.

"Give me five dollars." I could tell he really liked saying that. "And the bike."

I had five dollars and I handed it to him. I liked doing that.

We almost marched into the apartment.

Miss Irma was watching *The Guiding Light* with the sound way up. She was eating a Ritz Cracker smothered in margarine. Egghead cleared his throat. She didn't hear him or look at us.

"Um… Auntie?

There was a commercial. She noticed us and glared.

"What?!" Her mouth was full.

I stepped forward.

"Ma'am, would you like to get the *Star-Ledger* for free?"

"Ain't nothing for free. What do I have to do for it?" she asked.

"Nothing. Absolutely nothing." I gave her my most pious altar-boy look and squeezed out a shy smile. Is this how my father started?

"You best not be shitting me, Bright Eyes." She pointed a manicured finger at me.

Egghead walked down the stairs with me.

♥

"When do I get that bike?"

"When I get mine," I said.

We weren't friends anymore, just two shady little con artists pulling a scam.

I signed Miss Irma up for the phantom subscription.

The whole idea was wrong. I was an altar boy and a Boy Scout. The Scout Oath was my compass in the Ironbound's rusty jungle, the slippery olive-oiled morality of my world. I tried to be trustworthy, loyal, helpful, friendly, courteous, kind, obedient, cheerful, thrifty, brave, clean, and reverent every day for my own sake.

I didn't lie. To survive, I learned not to share everything I knew, but I never told an outright lie—and this was one. I thought about my lie every day. I felt a stain spread across me, something that anyone could see. I wanted Narkowitz off my back and I wanted that bike. Is this the way adults felt most of the time? I had no respect for them and now I was just like them.

I spent most of my time with Carlos now. He was an explorer discovering Newark's exotic brick jungle, and I was his native guide. His enthusiasm added a shine to the old, grimy buildings and narrow streets—and beyond. Carlos got a used bike, and I still had Nellybelle (until that new Schwinn!), and we rode out to the ghost city of Port Newark with its wide empty streets and bulging container ships. Then we would ride to Newark Airport, which included a dangerous stretch of highway, but being so close to the planes and the important-looking travelers made it worthwhile. It was exciting seeing my familiar world through Carlos' green eyes.

On the way home from the airport, a car on the highway almost clipped me. The angry driver pulled over and yelled at me.

"You fucking moron! You almost got killed. I wish I could drag you home to your parents and tell them what you did!" I wished he could, too.

Carlos wanted to see a dirty movie at The Little Theater uptown. He told the burly woman in the box office window that we had to get in there and look for our father because our mother was having a baby. He was so persuasive and insistent that I almost believed him. So that's what good lying looks like!

I imagined my father inside, all dressed up in a Swank suit. The burly woman didn't buy it and I was relieved. I was eleven and Carlos was twelve years old.

One Saturday morning, we got on a train at Penn Station and went to Monmouth Racetrack. Carlos said he had horses in Cuba, followed racing in the paper, had some hunches, and wanted to place bets. I learned the drill in a couple of minutes before we went up to the window and placed money bets. I expected someone to stop us, but nobody blinked. I bet on Brief Encounter in the second race because my mother loved that movie. She came in second. Carlos won with Stylish Abby in the third. We stuck around for the fourth and left with close to fifty dollars in our pockets. We got back to Newark by five.

One morning, I delivered my papers, including my complementary one for Miss Irma, and Narkowitz didn't trail me as usual. I went home, changed for school, and walked to Carlos's building where he waited in front for me. When I got there, I heard a car horn honk. There was the dusty black Rambler and the glint of Coke bottle glasses.

"Hey, Smiley, get in the car," Narkowitz said.

"I can't. I'm with my friend and we're going to school now."

"Get in. I'll give yous both a ride."

"It's two blocks."

"Get the fuck in the car. NOW!"

Carlos and I got in the back seat of the smelly car, loaded with newspapers, cigarette butts, Slim Jim wrappers, torn potato chip bags, and empty bottles of Ballantine Beer. Narkowitz drove two blocks and parked across the street from the school. He sat facing straight ahead, both hands gripping the steering wheel.

"Tell me about Mrs. Irma Payne."

"What?" My body went cold.

"Irma Payne, goddammit!"

"She's at 155 Jefferson Street. Third floor."

"I know. I paid her a visit."

"Oh." I felt a bead of cold sweat form between my shoulder blades.

"She don't want the paper. She never did. You put her down just so you could get that bike!" He turned to face us, his ugly mug pulsing with rage. I was scared to death.

"I... I..." The big fat bead of sweat wandered down my spine.

"Shut the fuck up, you little piece of shit! You lied to me. *You lied to me!*"

I watched him raise his flabby arm, watched his dirty hand with its chewed fingernails come swinging toward me. It landed, hard, on my cheek.

Carlos screamed and jumped out of the car. I sat there for a moment, the sound still ringing in my ears, the sting burning my face. Narkowitz's purple face was contorted in a mixture of horror, glee, and something else that I just did not want to know about. I stumbled out of the car and stumbled through the rest of the day in shock.

The next morning, I didn't want to deliver papers anymore. Narkowitz was waiting for me in the black Rambler.

"You'd better get moving," my mother said.

"I can't. I don't want to."

I was an A student, a Boy Scout, and an Altar Boy who always did the right thing. This was not like me.

"Why?" Her eyes were wide.

"He makes me nervous."

My mother picked up all the nuances in a heartbeat.

"Stay here." She ran to the kitchen, grabbed a broom, and ran out onto the street.

"Get the hell out of here, you creep, or I'll beat your ugly face in!" she shouted, wielding the broom as if it were a sledgehammer.

I heard Narkowitz peel away and could almost smell the rubber. She decided not to tell my father because he would kill Narkowitz, and we had enough trouble as it was. The end of Narkowitz. Ponto. Final!

As more Cubans came to the neighborhood, so did more Portuguese, some of them refugees from the colonial wars in Mozambique and Angola. One of them was my shiftless Uncle Tito.

"Great. Just what we need," old Mr. Firpo, the barber, said as I sat in his chair. "More spics and Zekes." He pointed toward the street with his scissors as a blond man wearing a beret walked by. It was Uncle Tito.

He was my father's older brother, and with his blond hair and watery blue eyes, he looked like a cad from a screwball comedy. The brothers never got along. After a few drinks, there were shouting matches and punches got thrown. They would patch it up for a bit, but it didn't last long. Tito chain-smoked Du Mauriers and liked good brandy and flashy clothes. He'd been a desk clerk in Luanda in his Portuguese Army service but made it sound like he engaged in hand-to-hand combat with restless natives. My father got Tito jobs that never worked out—until he became a security guard. That's how he found his career track: the security guard/unemployment Ferris wheel that goes round and round but never up. Now I understood what Narkowitz meant: *he thinks the world owes him a living!*

Our Lady of Fatima held its first Feast of Saint Anthony in 1959. By 1961, it was a huge event that reverberated through the Ironbound. The church's parking lot was set up with picnic tables, and stands were selling all the Portuguese favorites, their enticing fragrances filling the whole neighborhood. Even the Zeke Haters showed up because the food was so good.

My whole family went to the Feast of Saint Anthony. On the way to the parking lot, I thought I saw Egghead, but I lost him in the crowd. My parents, sisters, grandmother, and Tito shared a long picnic table, and we took turns going up to the food stands. There were open grills where sardines and chouriço sausages sizzled. There was a spit filled with carne de espeto, tender barbequed cubes of beef that melted in your mouth, and delicious pork cubes marinated in Madeira wine. There were of tremocos, small yellow Portuguese beans served cold. Everything was accompanied by Portuguese rolls with a gentle crust and soft interior. People drank strong red wine from white porcelain bowls, and everybody's chins were covered in crumbs of bread, sardines, and chouriço.

My father and Tito drank a lot of wine and were kicking back shots of cachaça, sweet Portuguese firewater. Their voices were loud but still brotherly and friendly so far, but my poor mother's wide eyes indicated she heard the ticking of a time bomb.

I went to the front of the church on Jefferson Street, where there were more traditional carnival stands: pizza, sausage, zeppoles, pretzels, and the low-rent rides like The Whip, and a twelve-foot Ferris wheel with six tiny baskets, which I was too tall to fit into. Some kids were throwing firecrackers into the middle of the crowd.

I saw Egghead standing next to the pizza stand, looking at it wistfully and hungrily as if the guy behind the counter might read his mind, like I always did, and give him a free slice.

I went up to him. "Hey."

He looked sad for a moment, but then he smiled, the pretty teeth, the little puff of breath.

I figured he was hungry, and we started walking to the parking lot where all the stands were. I knew my parents would spot us for some grub. As we got closer to the fragrant, sizzling stands, Egghead stopped. He saw that wall of white people, heard the loud foreign voices, and would not go further, no matter how hungry he was.

We turned back and sat on the church steps. We didn't say anything, just sat side by side, looking at the crowd. It felt good to be next to Egghead again. From the back, I could hear a woman yodeling a mournful Fado; in front of us, the crowd lined up for the rides, and everything was punctuated by the pop of firecrackers.

Egghead was staring at the pizza stand. Oh right. That was my cue to march up there and buy two slices. I didn't have a paper route anymore and I didn't have any money. I had saved up $200, but my parents borrowed it for some emergency.

I felt Egghead getting restless. He spit a big, high gob into the crowd and jumped up.

"Where's my bike?"

"I didn't get the new one, so…"

"So what? You owe me. You owe me!"

"*If* I get a new one, you can have Nellybelle."

"When?"

"I don't know," I said.

"Give me some money."

"I don't have any."

"You lie. You always got money." His voice had steel in it. I was afraid of him, and I didn't like it.

"No, really."

"How come?" He was right in my face.

"I don't deliver papers anymore." (Thanks to your stupid grandmother.)

"You lie."

"No. It's true."

"Come on." He pushed me a little too hard.

"No." I pushed him back.

"All I find I keep." He started frisking me. His hands dug into my pockets.

A firecracker or M80 blew up at our feet. We jumped and I couldn't hear anything. The force of it seemed to pull Egghead high into the air, and his shirt was over his head. Then, behind him, I saw my uncle Tito, his red face twisted with rage. He'd grabbed Egghead by his shirt and yanked him away from me. He turned Egghead around, slapped him across the face, and threw him to the ground, shouting at him in Portuguese.

"Stop! Stop! He's my friend." I got between them and got what may or may not have been an intentional whack from Tito.

Tito grabbed me by the shoulders. His red face was in mine and ripe with cachaça.

"You are OK? You are OK?"

"Yes. Yes."

Tito pushed me aside and stumbled down the steps, down Jefferson Street toward Ferry Street, where the bars were. I imagined in his drunken mind that this hero of the Portuguese Army had spotted an incipient native uprising and strategically, bravely squashed it. Or so the story would go.

I helped Egghead get up. His shirt was torn. He was rubbing his face, and I knew what that sting felt like. His face was terrible to see, the same horror from when he fell in the pool, but there was a new dark shadow behind it. Resentment. Hate. Rage. All sorting themselves out in front of me, trying to take over his worried little face.

"Let's go," I said and took his arm. Where, I didn't know yet.

He shook free and shook his head.

"Come on. Please." I was going to ask my mother for money to buy him a slice of pizza.

He shook his head and walked down the steps and down Jefferson Street, back home to Miss Irma, where he was now safer than being with me. I told a stupid lie for the sake of a bike that I didn't get. I got slapped for it and then Egghead got slapped for it. I was going on to East Side High School. Egghead got left back. I never saw him again.

INSIDE THE
SHOW BUSINESS

oses and Diandra Treadwell were the charismatic
ministers at the Second Baptist Church in Oxford,
Mississippi. Moses was short, robust, and indigo
with a booming voice; Diandra, tall, slender, and cream-colored
with long, straight hair. They adored each other, and though
they once made noises about having a child, someday, Elijah
was a surprise late in their marriage. On the day he was born,
October 13th, 1970, he seemed fully aware, fully assembled, and
on a path of his own. His skin was the color of caramel, and his
large, almond-shaped eyes seemed to look right into Moses's
and Diandra's souls and challenge them. Spooked, they kept
busy with their church duties and assigned most of his day-to-
day care to their devoted housekeeper, Miss Quality, a sweet,
diminutive older woman who was as interested in her "stories"
on TV as she was in Elijah.

When Elijah was five, he sat himself at the old church organ, which hadn't been touched in over a year, and spontaneously began to play and then sing. He became the precious delight of the entire congregation. A retired music professor, Dr. Eugene Poole, confirmed that Elijah was not only a prodigy on the organ but that he had perfect vocal pitch as well. Moses and Diandra realized that their son was a draw and leaned on his talents to raise funds. They wanted new bibles, new choir robes, and a new organ. Whenever he saw himself in the mirror in his Sunday best, a white suit with a white bow tie and white shoes, Elijah understood why the congregation loved him, though he didn't think his parents did.

On his first day at school, accompanied by Miss Quality, he fell on the steps and sprained his wrist. Because he was too valuable to be sidelined, Moses took him out of school and hired the music professor, Dr. Poole, as his private tutor.

Dr. Poole had Elijah listen to and learn the music of black composers like Florence Price, Samuel Coleridge Taylor, and William Grant Still. "I was in the orchestra when Doctor Still conducted the New Orleans Symphony. You look a bit like him."

One sparkling Sunday morning when he was eleven years old, Elijah played and sang one of his favorite hymns, the stirring, straightforward "To Worship, Work, and Witness" for the adoring congregation. Nothing his parents said or did made him feel any closer to God; he just sat at the organ and waited for his next song cue. But when he looked out into the pews where the devout women rhythmically fanned themselves and the devout men wiped their faces with crisp white handkerchiefs, he understood the Almighty. He thought of the word *exaltation*, but he wasn't sure what it meant.

Suddenly, he felt something wet and warm slither up his right leg. It rested around his genitals and gently massaged them before it squeezed around into his backside and entered him. It felt like a mud puppy, the giant, four-legged salamander he found once in the Tallahatchie River, but deep down, he knew that it was really Satan, that he was being tested, and he was failing. The persistent ripple beneath his skin and the satisfying occupation of his lower body stimulated all his senses. Satan liked to visit him while he played before the congregation at first but then slipped into his bed most nights.

Moses thundered every Sunday about sin and sinners. He never mentioned saints because he, like most Baptists, had a direct line to Jesus and didn't need some saint tampering with the message. Elijah didn't know who to talk to about his brushes with Satan. He couldn't talk to Moses about this or anything else.

This is where a saint would come in handy. Wasn't there one that killed a dragon?

Elijah went to Square Books, a fairly new bookstore in the heart of Oxford. He asked the white woman at the desk for books about saints. She smiled and led him to the Comparative Religion shelf. He found something called *The History of Saints* with lots of pictures and found a picture of a handsome young saint, Saint George, killing a dragon. Saint George was hounded by the Roman emperor Diocletian around 304 AD. Besides killing the dragon, he survived many trials before he was beheaded. He decided George would be his patron saint and help him kill the little dragon that possessed him.

When he turned the page, he was struck by the picture of the bust of a beautiful, pale young man with long hair, a sliver of mustache, a goatee, and the saddest eyes Elijah had ever seen in a person or a picture. The young man had a red slit on his neck. He was Saint Acisclus, and he had been beheaded along with his sister, Victoria, for being Christian in Cordoba, Spain, during Diocletian's reign. Diocletian again! He wished he could have known this lovely young saint, but he knew this delicate martyr couldn't be his protector. So, he would think about Saint George and keep Acisclus as a backup, even though they were both white.

Elijah didn't know any white people, and whenever he was around them, he held his breath. There was safety in the tight-knit Second Baptist congregation, as well as protection against the picture-postcard white community that surrounded them. Its polite condescension shrouded a simmering resentment that made him feel that something was lying in wait for him.

When he was thirteen, he half-listened to Moses thunder from the pulpit one summer Sunday morning while he gazed through the window and watched a cardinal hop from branch to branch on the big old magnolia overlooking the parking lot.

"My friends," the Reverend bellowed, "I want to read you this from Romans 1:27."

Then, in his deeper "scriptures" voice, he read, "In the same way, the men also abandoned natural relations with women and were inflamed with lust for one another. Men committed shameful acts with other men and received in themselves the due penalty for their error."

Moses looked over the heads of the congregation, as always, to the Scenes from the Bible crochet mural on the church's back wall. Then he continued, "My friends, there is also this from Leviticus: 'Do not have sexual relations with a man as one does with a woman. That is detestable.'" Then he turned and looked to the magnolia out the window and hissed, "Detestable!"

"Detestable!" Diandra hissed as well.

The congregation nodded its collective head and shouted, "Amen!"

Outside, the cardinal emitted several metallic squeaks, flew up against the window, and then away.

Elijah's ears burned. Could his father and the rest of the congregation see the mark of Satan on him? Just for fun, Satan, that rascal, squeezed his genitals. The next day, his voice cracked, dropped an octave, and lost its sweetness. He stopped singing and knew he had to get as far away from Oxford as possible. New York City popped into his head, though he knew little about it.

Dr. Poole tutored him until he was sixteen, but despite his promising start, Elijah had no gift for composition, and Dr. Poole gave up scolding him for his clumsy fingering and lack of focus. He helped Elijah get a music scholarship to his alma mater, historically black Lincoln University in Pennsylvania, which put him within bus or train distance of New York City. His parents looked relieved as he boarded the Greyhound bus in Oxford, and Elijah didn't exhale until the bus reached Memphis.

Life at Lincoln was an adjustment, but it was refreshing to be around people his own age who didn't think he was a precious angel. He kept to himself at first, and Satan still occasionally crept into his cot at night.

Students from Lincoln's music and theater departments took a trip to New York City to see the musical "Dreamgirls." On the trip, Elijah shared his Milford Plaza Hotel room with Darnay Womble, the willowy star of Lincoln's theater department. Darnay sang well enough, moved gracefully, and got all the male leads. Once the "Dreamgirls" overture started, Elijah's body seemed to float from his plush seat in the Imperial Theater and hover over the stage as if he were a character in the show. When Curtis sang "When I First Saw You" to Deena, Darnay grasped his hand and held on to it. Elijah, caught up in the moment, let him.

The drama teacher had arranged for an onstage chat with one of the show's stars, Ben Harney, who spoke to the students as he stood next to the ghost light. Darnay asked a few too many silly questions, so Elijah tuned him out and took in the velvety splendor of the orchestra; then he gazed into the wings, which were bathed in a misty lavender light that beckoned him. He wandered off on his own through the drafty, narrow corridors backstage, peeking into the empty dressing rooms, and passed a room with racks and racks of costumes and shelves full of props. Another room was filled with hundreds of wigs on mannequin heads, their purpose written on the front: *Loretta: One Night Only.*

He inhaled the theater's earthy, exotic perfume: sweat, dust, the bubble gum scent that he recognized as greasepaint and had a vision of himself working behind the scenes on a magnificent show like this. Midtown Manhattan's grimy, congested streets, the stench from the garbage cans and the unwashed street crazies who picked through them, the oozing discarded McDonald's milkshakes, the rancid cigarette smoke, the unrelenting cornet blasts of taxis, the blinking lights of the adult emporiums—the thoughtless, heedless chaos of it all, thrilled him. He remembered Leviticus, "And these are unclean to you, among the swarming things." He liked being among the swarming things, these urban mud puppies, in Satan's hometown. He passed a newsstand and saw the cover of a Mandate magazine with a shirtless, muscled young Latino pulling at his waistband. It sent shockwaves through him, and on cue, Satan squeezed him.

When they got back to their hotel room, he and Darnay sat on their respective beds and chattered excitedly about the show, the dirty streets, the peep shows. Darnay suddenly leaned forward, kissed Elijah on the lips, and they tumbled into his bed. One movement flowed into another, and soon, Darnay occupied Elijah's lower regions the way Satan once had. Oh, he realized, he wasn't possessed after all; he was just gay.

Back at school, he switched his major to mass communications. Senior year brought him an internship in New York City where he lived in student housing at Fordham, within sight of Lincoln Center. He made a point of walking through its magnificent plaza every day. He was placed in the office of Adele Fiterstein, a music publicist who had once repped Carnegie Hall and some classical music legends but now worked with individual artists who weren't marquee names.

A gaunt, glamorous woman in her seventies, Adele's champagne blond French twist, mink coat, and extra-long Nat Sherman cigarettes were her trademarks. When a reviewer asked how he would recognize her in the lobby, she said, "I'll be the haggard blond in the mink coat, smoking a foot-long Nat Sherman." When someone referred to her as the Queen of PR, she responded, "Nah, I'm just the Dowager Duchess."

Another trademark was her luxurious false eyelashes. "I never go anywhere without my batwings," she said when she noticed Elijah staring at them.

She worked from her small, musty apartment above Carnegie Hall. When she was on duty, between ten a.m. and six p.m., Adele kept her door open.

"Darling, I have nothing to hide," she said. "Who knows? Murray Perahia or Manny Ax might need a publicist and come looking for me. You know, Marlon Brando lived down the hall, but nothing ever happened between us."

Behind her desk, an airbrushed, Scavullo-like portrait of her filled one wall, while another wall held smaller photos of Adele with some of the biggest names in music: Heifetz, Horovitz, Bernstein, Menuhin, and Tiny Tim. A small pantry off the living/dining room was big enough to hold a desk. That was Elijah's station.

The office smelled like an ashtray, and everything was nicotine-stained: her pink silk drapes, her pink couch, her pink divan, and the pink satin bedspread in her bedroom. Adele had four pastel Chanel suits she wore for events, and at home, she liked caftans in various shades of pink.

"I was the toast of Altoona, PA," she told him on his first day. "The little blonde girl at the big black piano. My mother booked me into every temple and Masonic Hall in western Pennsylvania. I got a scholarship to the Curtis Institute, and from there, I came to New York. It's all in my book, of course," she said.

"Your book?" Elijah asked.

"Yes. *Little Adele and Her Magic Fingers*. The manuscript is here somewhere. My dream was to play Carnegie Hall, of course, but I never thought I would be living here. After a few years, I gave up the piano when I realized I didn't have IT!" Adele snapped her fingers for emphasis.

Elijah enjoyed her monologue but had to ask. "Do you have any questions for me?"

"Can you work the infernal word processing and fax machines that your predecessor talked me into?"

"Yes."

"Can you make coffee?"

"Yes."

"Darling, you're hired."

Before Elijah, Adele stabbed out her correspondence on an old Olivetti Underwood typewriter, her magic fingers not so nimble anymore. An Adele Fiterstein Public Relations press release was always riddled with typos, and most of its recipients were charmed by the handwritten squiggle at the bottom: "Darling, please forgive the false notes!"

When she was busy, she paid people to do her typing, and that was Elijah's job in his first summer with her. He proofread, retyped, and eventually rewrote her press releases and got them to the printer. When they returned, he stuffed them into envelopes he had labeled and took them to the nearest post office.

"Darling, you're a godsend!" Adele exclaimed. She called everyone darling, even messengers and delivery boys. "Saves time," she said.

Her specialty was to work the phones, pitching one idea after another to whoever would take her calls.

"Darling, he plays the cello with his feet!" Elijah heard her say to a music writer for *The New York Times*. One morning, in her phone call frenzy, she called out, "Darling, you're black. What's the area code for Detroit?"

Elijah gasped, then burst out laughing.

He kept his hair short and sported a pencil mustache to look more sophisticated. "Darling, you look like a baby William Grant Still."

"I've heard that before. You know him?"

"Oh yes. My mother made me trot out the usual Chopin and Mozart for the concerts, but I met Dr. Still when I was at Curtis, and I liked to play his *Summerland*. It spoke to me."

Elijah became familiar with the music press, and his musical background helped him sound knowledgeable. When he graduated, Adele asked him to work with her full-time. She changed her letterhead to Adele Fiterstein Associates.

"I adore you, darling!"

He found an apartment he could barely afford on the fifth floor of a rundown six-story walk-up on East Ninety-Third Street near First Avenue. Elijah liked the neighborhood; it had its own personality and was just far away enough from the midtown frenzy to give him some breathing room. He bought a small television with a built-in VCR. There was a good video store on First Avenue, and one of the clerks, a grizzled older man with long gray hair, recommended his favorite films: *Casablanca, The Third Man, Out of the Past, Scarlet Street,* and *Lolita.* Elijah liked his picks. He never watched movies in Oxford.

The video store had a gay porn section, and with AIDS surging through the city, watching porn was the extent of his romantic life; he stored away the moves he saw on film in case he ever got his hands on another man again.

On weekends, he walked for miles exploring the city. One Sunday, he found himself at the Hispanic Museum and Library on upper Broadway at 155th Street. As he strolled past the vivid portraits and statues, one stopped him in his tracks. There was the bust of Saint Acisclus that he had seen in the saints book in Oxford. His haunted eyes were filled with an exquisite pain that reached out to Elijah as if he were asking for his help. Disoriented, he sat on the nearest bench to recover. Saint Acisclus instantly slipped into his soul to keep him soothing company, the way Satan's mud puppy had once invaded his body.

Adele's good-natured befuddlement and helplessness softened Elijah's negative feelings about white people. He didn't hold his breath around her. Here, he found white people tolerable and even sometimes entertaining. As he got used to New York and the entertainment business, he realized it was nothing like most people imagined. Midtown Manhattan was like a stifling greenhouse filled with exotic human orchids that couldn't survive anywhere else, and its streets were littered with their broken blossoms. Adele, bless her heart, was one of them.

The office had a new client, a young tenor named Anthony Scagliotti, who was making his debut at Town Hall. Elijah overheard one of Adele's frenzied phone pitches: "And he drives a garbage truck on Staten Island during the day!"

The Scagliottis owned Dependable Dump and were funding their beloved son's debut.

Elijah wrote something up about Anthony and pitched it to the *New York Post*. They ran the story with a whole set of photos of beefy young Anthony in his green Dependable Dump jumpsuit, sitting in his truck, hoisting a garbage can, and in a tux onstage.

The morning TV show *Good Day New York* saw the *New York Post* story and did an interview with Anthony while he drove his truck, then filmed him onstage.

Elijah supervised both those shoots and was dismayed when sweet Anthony, with his full baby face and whisper of stubble, opened his mouth to sing an off-key "Largo al factotum" from *The Barber of Seville*. The producer looked to Elijah, who shrugged to cover his embarrassment.

"He's not very good," Elijah told Adele the next day.

"That's okay, darling," Adele said, taking a life-giving pull on her Nat Sherman. "They can't all be Placido Domingo. We just spray a little Chanel No. 5 on them and get them out there."

Between the good press and all the relatives, Anthony's concert sold out. The grateful Scagliottis paid Adele in cash and gave her a little something extra. She gave Elijah a five-hundred-dollar bonus.

"Well done!" she said. "You're a real publicist now, darling."

Even when you get the story, Elijah realized, the artist can stink, and your work can be better than theirs. But he liked all of it, the pitching, talking to editors, working with TV crews. He even liked the words *public relations*. They made him feel legitimate. PR was all castles in the air, and every once in a while, you got hold of a castle, yanked it to earth, and got it into the *New York Post* and on television, which proved that you really existed, you were heard. Placement equaled personhood. Elijah thought he had cracked the code and climbed out of the great swamp of the unseen in show business. That feeling was another castle in the air, and he knew it could evaporate at any moment.

One afternoon, Adele called out to him, "Darling, I have two tickets to Andre Watts downstairs tonight. You want them?"

"Yes!" he said, "But don't you want to go?"

"Nah. Unless they're paying me, I'm not interested. I'd rather rinse out my tights." She blew out a balloon of smoke to make her point.

For his twenty-fifth birthday, Adele took him to dinner at The Russian Tea Room.

"Thank you for coming into my life, my beautiful sunbeam," Adele said, and they toasted with Veuve Clicquot. "Darling, we're happy, aren't we? This is still working, isn't it?"

"Yes, Darling!" he answered.

Ten days later, when he reported for duty, Adele's door was locked. He buzzed and knocked, but there was no answer. He found the super and got him to open the door. They found Adele in her bed, wearing her pink Schiaparelli peignoir, a full ashtray, and a hard-cover copy of Barbara Cartland's *A Hazard of Hearts* on her nightstand. With her hair in a pink snood and no bat wings, she looked like Little Adele from Altoona.

"Good night, my duchess," he whispered as he walked away.

What now?

His resume wasn't dynamic enough yet to get him hired by one of the bigger offices, and because Adele's bookkeeping was erratic, he was denied unemployment benefits while they investigated his case. He started falling behind in the rent.

He had a job interview in the West Village with a one-woman theatrical publicity firm; the woman weighed almost three hundred pounds and could not leave her apartment. She needed someone to be her legs. When she opened the door, she seemed unpleasantly surprised that he was black and blurted, "Oh!" There was nowhere to go from there. Elijah walked aimlessly around the West Village, hoping for inspiration. He saw a help-wanted sign in the window of the Duane Reade on Sixth Avenue and walked in, past the scrawny man who shook an angry paper cup at anyone who entered. The entrance smelled like piss.

This Duane Reade grew like a split-level tumor out of the West Fourth Street subway station. Inside, the store looked like it may have been dropped there from a great height and never settled itself. A layer of dust and grime covered the narrow aisles and sparsely stocked shelves, and dust balls roamed the floors.

He spoke to the cashier, Prudence Pinderloo, her name tag said, who glared at him and summoned the manager, Nigel Pinderloo, *his* name tag read, a short, stout brown man who glared at him as well and asked him a few terse questions.

"What did you do before?" Nigel's voice was high and clipped.

"Public relations."

"What is that?"

"Um… typing." He was hired.

When he reported for duty the next morning, Elijah was planted at the high impact, temperamental register after a brief, brusque lesson from Prudence. He struggled to master its complicated keyboard and wondered if the thorny Pinderloos had designed it themselves. The staff, mostly Pinderloos, oozed hostility and ignored customers while they stocked, or pretended to stock, the shelves. The Pinderloos were from Guyana, and Elijah suspected it was French Guyana, where they had managed the Duane Reade on Devil's Island.

Nigel's mother, Priti Pinderloo, worked at the store part time. She was a tiny woman with a cherubic face and wore her gray hair in a ponytail over a foot long. Priti spent her time humming while she dreamily tickled the barren shelves with a feather duster.

After he punched in, Elijah went directly to the register, where he remained until one of his two fifteen-minute breaks or his half-hour lunch. The Pinderloos had found a way to bark at him without looking at him, and every day he asked himself, *Am I here?*

Despite the nonstop volume, Elijah liked dealing with the customers. They were mostly Greenwich Village regulars. Dazed painters and sculptors in splattered sweatshirts on breaks from their masterpieces bought cigarettes, Slim Jims, and paper towels. Interwoven among them were actors, dancers, writers, and the neighborhood psychos who were just trying to get warm or cool while they shoplifted. One regular customer looked like Peter Lorre at the end of his career. He always scanned Elijah with his enormous headlights.

"Elijah. What a beautiful name," he said one day and winked.

He liked it best when the kids got out of school at three p.m. and poured into the store to buy candy, soda, and chips. They were loud and out of control, but Elijah enjoyed their energy as the well-behaved ones tried to get the most for their money, and the shady ones, with wily, innocent faces, bought the cheapest thing and stuffed their pockets with as much swag as they could fit. In Oxford, trapped at the organ, he had never been a boy, a carefree, goofy boy who might be tempted to steal Kit Kat bars.

Though he wasn't the most efficient cashier and could never figure out coupons and returns, the customers preferred him to Pinderloos. One regular asked, "How can you stand them?"

He didn't know, either, but he was able to make the rent that month.

On Valentine's Day, he was on duty for eight hours when every last-minute shopper below Fourteenth Street jammed the store to buy last-minute, heart-shaped boxes of Russell Stover's discounted, thoughtless candy, thoughtless cards, and faded red roses for their beloveds. If he loved someone, he would be embarrassed to hand them these shoddy love tokens on this manufactured Hallmark holiday. Looking at the tense, unhappy faces at his register, he imagined the disappointed ones who would be presented with these cheap, inconsiderate trinkets.

His register jammed several times, and Nigel angrily fixed it without looking at him. The lines of last-minute lovers snaked through the tight aisles and thrummed with anger and frustration as time stood still in the pitiless fluorescent light. The thrumming was punctuated by peppy computerized voices promoting Valentine's specials and flu shots.

The smell of the cheap chocolate seeped from the bright red, heart-shaped boxes and gave him a headache. When he got a short bathroom break, he went to the pain reliever aisle, but the shelves were empty. Mother Pinderloo was dreamily massaging them with her feather duster.

After five hours of his eight-hour shift, red hearts swam before his eyes, and he began to hallucinate. How did he wind up here? A line popped into his head, "Constantly risking absurdity and death when he performs above the heads of his audience." Where was that from? Right, from a poem in Lawrence Ferlinghetti's book, *A Coney Island of the Mind.*

He realized he had fallen into a Duane Reade of the Soul, an existential sinkhole where everything is advertised, but nothing is available on the dusty, puke-green shelves. A place where kindness shriveled like ancient roses and dignity was impossible without a fight. He was ashamed of himself for having this miserable, minimum wage job, being bad at it, and for having no Valentine on this idiotic holiday.

Drenched in flop sweat, he was afraid that either he or the store would implode, collapsing onto the subway tracks below. He punched out after ten p.m. and crawled into bed, where he hid the whole next day. When Nigel called to find out where he was, he quit.

"I knew you were a pussy," Nigel said.

What now? He was twenty-six years old, and the Duane Reade fiasco shook his confidence. Two nights later, he went to the bar, Julius, in the West Village, where the drinks were cheap and the burgers delicious. As he bit into his cheeseburger, someone tapped his arm.

"You look down in the dumps, kiddo." It was the Peter Lorre guy from the store.

Elijah shrugged. He didn't want to engage with this funny-looking, middle-aged man with the tired pick-up line.

"So, the joke is as follows," the man, unencouraged, said. "A queen goes to his proctologist. The doctor reaches into his ass and pulls out a dozen roses. 'Where did these roses come from?' he asks. 'Read the card,' the queen says."

Elijah laughed and they shook hands.

"I remember your name tag. Elijah, right? I'm Martin Krantz."

Elijah nodded in his direction.

So... what's the trouble—in ten words or less?" he asked.

Elijah told him about Duane Reade firing him and that he didn't know what to do.

"That was fifteen words. BUT! I am a publicist, and I could use some help. Do you like theater?"

"Yes!"

"Great. You're hired," Martin said.

1501 Broadway, in the heart of Times Square, was the majestic Paramount Building, with its sandy, Egyptian-themed façade. Built by the movie studio in 1927, the building's thirty-three floors hosted a hodgepodge of businesses mostly related to entertainment: producers, agents, managers, casting directors, and publicists and the lawyers, accountants, ophthalmologists, and dentists who serviced them. Two noble institutions, The Dramatists Guild and Theatre Development Fund, twenty floors apart, gracefully anchored her majesty, and her stately rear end abutted the New York Times castle on Forty-Third Street.

Elijah entered through the ornate golden doors and waited for an elevator in the Art Deco splendor of the black marble lobby. When one descended, he entered and pressed the button for the fifteenth floor. Before the doors closed, there was a commotion, and two slender young men kept the door open for another passenger. Her shrill, breathless monologue preceded her and filled the lobby, then her voluminous body filled the elevator. It was Shelley Winters in a black tracksuit under a purple duster, a black beret on her head.

She prattled, breathlessly merry, as if she had just been released from solitary. Her babbling gave Elijah no room to interrupt and tell her how much he loved her in *Lolita*, his favorite film. She did not look anything like the love-starved, voluptuous Charlotte Haze, though she sounded like her on steroids. Shelley and her devoted attendants glanced at Elijah and then looked away, relieved that he was a nobody and that they were alone in the elevator and could speak freely. He stood there, invisible, until he got off on the fifteenth floor.

As he walked down the hall, he took a deep breath and hoped he would rematerialize before he reached the Krantz office, Suite 1508.

"What do you want me to do?" Elijah asked Martin that morning.

"Make yourself indispensable!" Martin snapped. "This is not a teaching hospital!" Then he smiled. Martin had the bigger office in the back. Like Adele, his wall was adorned with photos of him with celebrities: Geraldine Page, Annie Ross, Elizabeth Ashley, and the ubiquitous Tiny Tim. Elijah had the smaller cubicle alongside it. From their large, smudged windows, you could see the rear end of the New York Times building, a sliver of Forty-Second Street and its peep shows, and the rooftop water towers of Midtown. Martin usually wore a white shirt and a clip-on bowtie. He arranged the dark, restless tendrils of his thinning hair into new exotic patterns daily.

He had been a boy soprano in Detroit and came to New York to be in musicals. After a few chorus jobs and a lot of unemployment, he started answering phones in a publicist's office and eventually opened one of his own. Martin worked on some acclaimed Broadway, off-Broadway shows, and stellar cabaret acts and had a good reputation. Thirty years later, he still loved the business but knew its dark side.

"A dozen press agents working overtime can do terrible things to the human spirit," Martin said one day.

"You really think so? I thought we helped people."

"That's from *Sunset Boulevard*, kiddo. Since there's only two of us, we must work that much harder to destroy those spirits."

Martin spat out snappy lines all the time. Eventually, Elijah realized he was quoting his favorite films, like *All About Eve*, *The Boys in the Band*, and *A Letter to Three Wives*.

Elijah discovered that his dark, internal Allegheny River flowed easily into Martin's caustic Monongahela, which made the office the Ohio River of PR. Though they had occasional squabbles, they made a formidable team, and they made each other laugh.

Martin Krantz Associates currently had three clients: a production of Dostoevsky's *The Idiot*, staged by an avant-garde Hungarian theater company; a dingy nightclub, The Hideaway, just south of restaurant row on Forty-Sixth Street; and a stage version of the old television series *Gilligan's Island*.

Elijah took over writing the press releases after an angry call from the listings editor of *New York Magazine*.

"I have no idea what this show is about! What am I supposed to do with this?"

Like Adele, Martin wrote vague, flowery prose borrowed from the producer's notes. Elijah studied the theater listings and realized that he had a maximum of two punchy paragraphs to convince a listings editor to list the show, a critic to review it, and a reader to buy a ticket. Thinking of the angry listings editor, he rewrote *The Idiot* press release, trimmed the descriptions down to the essentials with all the important information and a snappy headline into one, at-a-glance page.

When *The Village Voice* reviewed the show, they dismissed it as misguided and said that the press release was better than the show. Again, for the moment, Elijah felt like a real publicist. *The Idiot* closed a few days later, which left the office with two clients: The Hideaway, with its third-rate cabaret performers, and *Gilligan's Island: President Gilligan*, the office's main source of income. Elijah had never seen the television show.

Now in its sixth month, it was a loose, interactive stage version of the popular TV show, staged cabaret style in a church basement in Midtown. It was based on the episode "President Gilligan," where the four male characters compete to run the island. The audience voted for the winner, which was usually Gilligan. Put together as a goof by a bunch of midwestern college roommates, it was popular with suburban theater parties and attracted the attention of television crews from around the world, especially Japan. This meant that Elijah had to be at the show a couple of nights a week to monitor the rambunctious TV crews to make sure they followed Actors Equity guidelines. The cast was comprised mostly of non-equity beginners of varying skill. Elijah referred to them as Frosted Mini-Talents.

Despite his annoyance, working on a hit show like this one was making his reputation; it was his first experience working on a show that people actually wanted to see.

To keep the buzz going, the producers would cast a minor celebrity. A television traffic reporter had just ended her run as the character Mary Ann, and now, a former pitcher for the Mets was playing Gilligan or at least wearing the costume and reciting the lines. The only consolation for Elijah was that the pitcher was a modest, good-looking Dominican, Fernando Luna, who said, "I always feel better when you are here. When you watch television, you never know what it is really like to be inside the show business."

Elijah pitched him to the *Daily News*, which did a photo spread on him that included him at his restaurant in Washington Heights, La Luna. Then *Good Day New York* filmed him at the show and at the restaurant, making his specialty, chivo guiado picante, a spicy goat stew. None of the cast would speak to him after that.

At The Hideaway, Daria Sobel, a singer and comedienne, rehearsed her new show, *Jazz Baby*. With her mop of frizzy black hair and slash of red lipstick, Daria played the heroine's dumpy, wisecracking sidekick in a couple of movies and a short-lived sitcom. Her performance ten years ago as Miss Marmelstein, the put-upon secretary in a revival of *I Can Get It for You Wholesale*, reignited her stalled career. The role that launched Streisand turned out to be a lucky one for Daria; she stole the show. *The New York Times* considered giving her a coveted Hirschfeld drawing, but Daria got bumped by Kaye Ballard, who was in *The Pirates of Penzance*. There was talk of a Broadway revival of *Funny Girl*, but it never happened. There were featured roles in a succession of Broadway and off-Broadway flops, then cabaret rooms—starting at the top with The Carlyle and steadily sinking to The Hideaway.

Her impressive resume cloaked the fact that nobody wanted to work with her. She started off every job as a charming ray of sunlight, bringing Entenmann's cookies and bags of black jellybeans to rehearsals. After about three weeks, exit Miss Marmelstein, enter Madame Defarge. She realizes that she's not getting enough attention, so she adopts a wide, joyless smile and simpering voice that masks her rage. In her fifties, Daria lived off the rent from an apartment building in Rochester that her parents had left her.

Her tearful overnight voice message insisted that an exclamation point be added to the show's title: *Jazz Baby!* Though it was a time-consuming pain in the ass, Elijah decided to add the exclamation point by hand on all the three hundred copies of the release. He had heard that they did the same thing with "Oklahoma!"

Martin didn't take her calls anymore, so Elijah half-listened to her endless complaints. His background in music seeped into their conversations, so Daria used him as a sounding board for songs she might use in the act.

She asked Elijah to come to a rehearsal. "I could use your ear, and I am dying to meet you. You know I adore you, right?"

"Oh, I don't know…"

"Please!" Daria's voice choked.

He asked Martin for his opinion.

"Just do it. It may shut her up." Martin sighed.

"She said she adores me." Elijah shuddered.

"Listen, kiddo," Martin's voice dropped an octave. "There is no greater love than showbiz love—which is like no love at all. When they say they love you, head for the hills."

Elijah went to The Hideaway the next afternoon; the small dingy room was empty and smelled of mold and stale beer. He heard a vacuum cleaner whining somewhere nearby and muffled voices from what he guessed was backstage. There were about twenty rickety wooden tables ringed by equally rickety wooden chairs surrounding a tiny stage with an upright black Yamaha piano on it.

"Hello?" he called out.

"Be right there!" Daria said and emerged in a bright red sweat suit that matched her bright red lips.

"Elijah!" she squealed and ran to him. She planted a big, too-wet kiss on his lips, held his face, and said, "You're even more gorgeous than I imagined!"

"What's all the uproar, darlings?" a male voice asked.

A slight, attractive man stood in shadow at the edge of the stage. He wore a black suit with no tie.

"Elijah, this is Etienne Pichegru, my pianist."

When he stepped onto the stage, Elijah gasped. With his soulful brown eyes, delicate features, facial scruff, and halo of curly dark hair, he looked just like his beloved Saint Acisclus, except that he was smiling. Was he Spanish, too?

"Brilliant," Etienne said. "Daria raves, so I been buzzin' to meet you." His sprightly, cultured voice had a slight Cockney trace that sounded a bit like Cary Grant. He sat at the piano.

"I'm introducing a new song into the show," Daria said. "Do you know Michel Legrand's 'Watch What Happens'?"

"I do. It's challenging. Good for you," Elijah said, keeping his eyes on Etienne.

Daria couldn't hit the C-sharp at the top of the tune: "Cold, I can't believe your heart is cold." Her attempts to reach the note sounded like yodeling, while Etienne dutifully hit C-sharp. To keep from giggling, Elijah kept his focus on Etienne, who beamed cheekily. With such an exotic name, Etienne Pichegru! Elijah imagined he might be Spanish or French, which only added to his allure.

Daria staggered to the end of the song and said, "I need a break," and walked off. Etienne remained onstage.

"I will now sing 'Nessum Dorma,'" he announced, then struck a dramatic chord on the piano.

Elijah cackled. "Is that in the act?" he asked.

"You like it?"

Elijah nodded.

"Then it's in. I'll do it during her ladyship's break." Etienne smiled, took a breath, and then launched into a touching rendition of "A Nightingale Sang in Berkeley Square."

As Elijah watched Etienne onstage, something fundamental moved in his chest, the same kind of thump he felt at the Imperial Theatre; this was something he wanted. It blended with the ache he felt when he saw Saint Acisclus. This exotic French refugee from a Goya painting was throwing him off his non-existent romantic trajectory. He wanted to rush the stage and kiss him. He'd never felt this way before.

"I hope I'm not interrupting." Daria had returned, and the sour milk tone in her voice sent a shiver through Elijah, as it was supposed to. "You will be happy to know that I've decided NOT to sing 'Watch What Happens.' Instead, I will sing Leonard Cohen's 'Dress Rehearsal Rag.'"

"Why?" Elijah blurted.

Etienne's eyes widened, and he covered his mouth.

Elijah continued; he couldn't stop himself. "You call the show Jazz Baby, but you have no jazz in it. How about something like 'Black Coffee' or 'Take the A Train'?"

Daria gasped, then burst into tears, covering her face with her hands.

"Get out! Get out! Get out!" she sobbed and pointed to the door.

"How was rehearsal?" Martin asked the next morning.

"Grueling. People put up with Stritch because she delivers. Sobel ain't no Stritch!"

"I know, kiddo, but these little shit shows pay the rent," Martin sighed. The phone rang, and Martin picked up.

"No! That is not acceptable! If you continue this way, I will quit you and your show!" Martin's voice was unusually loud. He hung up. "That was Daria. She wants me to fire you. Fuck her."

"Thank you."

"Listen, kiddo. It's not personal with people like her." Martin sighed a deep theatrical sigh and continued. "We're just props to them, same as a microphone, a wig or a… folding chair. Do you remember the last folding chair you sat on? We serve the cause, and if we don't, we don't exist to them."

Daria kept her trap shut. Martin and Elijah dutifully sent out the releases, made the phone calls. The third string critic from *The New York Times* came to the second preview. The audience was sparse that night, supplemented by a comped contingent from the Stein Senior Center, dependable but noisy seat fillers. *The New York Times* review headline read: "Jazz Baby? Where's the jazz?" The review went on to call the show "earnest but undernourished" and singled out Etienne's charm and his "Nessun Dorma" moment. *Jazz Baby!* lasted a week. Elijah was glad to be rid of Daria but heartbroken that he would never see his beloved Etienne Pichegru again.

Martin and Elijah hoped for a Broadway or off-Broadway show on a lucrative union contract but would take just about any show, even trained seals. They were hired by an experimental Polish theatre troupe, which was doing *The Cherry Orchard* in modern dress and in Polish. Audience members wore headsets, which piped in the English translation. Elijah went to a rehearsal and loved what he saw. He pitched it to *The New York Times*, which did a preview, then gave the show a rave review. Its four-week run was sold out, so the show extended. He had broken the code: a smart press release, a thoughtful pitch letter, and a follow-up call usually got a response.

The success of *Gilligan's Island* attracted a team of young African American producers who were bringing in a stage version of the old sitcom *Good Times*. They wanted a black publicist, and, at that moment, Elijah was the only black game in town.

Elijah found himself thinking about Etienne Pichegru. Etienne Pichegru! He loved saying the name to himself, even just thinking it. He wanted to sit across the table from Etienne in a cozy French or Spanish restaurant and listen to him tell his story in that bewitching Cary Grant accent. But there was nothing to be done about it.

Until... four months later, he went to The New Yorker office on Forty-Third Street to drop off *Gilligan's Island* photos. Coming out of the building, he came face to face with Etienne.

"You!" he exclaimed.

"You!" Etienne responded. They kissed.

Etienne was performing in a new restaurant a few doors down.

"Are you hungry?" Etienne asked. "They comp my meals, and I can get you comped too. They like to make the room look busy." They held hands walking to the restaurant. Etienne's was small and furry with calloused fingers.

The restaurant, which didn't have a name yet, looked like a cafeteria inside with orange Formica tables and blue Formica chairs.

They held hands across the distractingly shiny table and ordered the special, the Branzino.

"Looks and tastes like the lining of an Albanian drag queen's espadrille," Etienne said. He sent it back and ordered them salmon. "It's harder to fuck up salmon."

"Are you French?" Elijah asked.

Etienne shrugged. "I belong to the world."

"How is Daria?"

"Dunno. She took off for Rochester to nurse her wounds."

The sparkle and wattage coming from this animated Saint Acisclus made him lightheaded. He impulsively touched Etienne's face and stroked his cheek to make sure he was real.

"I… like you," Elijah stammered.

"I like everything about you," Etienne said. He leaned forward and whispered, "I would like to lie down with you."

It was time for Etienne's set, and he took the small stage and sat behind a small white piano. Etienne sang "And a Nightingale Sang in Berkely Square" and did the "Nessum Dorma" bit, then sang a song in Spanish and one in French, gazing at Elijah the whole time. He loved seeing his beloved work so passionately before a handful of distracted diners in this sterile, soon-to-be-extinct restaurant on a drizzly Tuesday night. That was the special paradox of show business. Sometimes you sucked and got away with it, and sometimes you were brilliant, as Etienne was tonight, and no one noticed. He felt deeply connected to this other, still unknown soldier, busting his butt to be "inside the show business."

They took the six train uptown and stood face to face, holding onto a pole. As soon as they were inside the apartment, they started kissing. Etienne's kisses were soft and tremulous; his darting tongue felt like a frantic little bird. Elijah devoured him, pulling Etienne so close that he gasped for breath. They stumbled a few feet to the futon and fell onto it, their clothes in a tangle on the floor, and fucked. Etienne had a dancer's lean body and a lovely plump ass. He squeaked in the heat of passion. Elijah liked it.

"I'm knackered," Etienne sighed as he nestled in the crook of Elijah's arm. "But this is nice, ain't it?"

"Yes, it is," Elijah sighed. For the first time ever, he was very happy.

"It's all a matter of kinetics. I'm chuffed that we finally… connected," Etienne sighed.

Elijah detected a slight, contradictory ripple in Etienne's accent. Was he French Canadian?

He held Etienne's face in his hands. "Seriously, where were you born?"

"Rochester," Etienne replied.

"Is that northern England? I mean, the UK?"

"No. Rochester in upstate New York."

"What? You're kidding, right?"

"No. I was born there and studied at Eastman. To make money, I worked at a Renaissance Faire in Trumansburg for five seasons. Juggled, sang, danced, and played the fool. I liked the accent, so I held on to it."

Elijah was silent as he absorbed this new information.

Etienne nudged him, "And what about you?"

"Just a little Black boy from Mississippi. So, is your name really Etienne Pichegru? Is it on your birth certificate?"

"When I was in Paris, I saw the name Charles Pichegru inscribed on the Arc de Triomphe. He was a general who led a conspiracy to overthrow Napoleon. Like with the accent, I liked the name, so I borrowed it, then added Etienne to spice it up. It beats David."

"Your real name is David?"

"Yes, David Sobel. I'm just a nice Jewish boy from Rochester."

"Sobel?"

"Yeah. Daria is my sister," he said with no accent whatsoever. "Because of her reputation, I thought it best not to advertise it."

Elijah felt a shiver, withdrew his arm, and sat up in the suddenly cramped futon. If it weren't his own apartment, he would have made an excuse and left. Etienne/David yawned and stretched.

"I am so bloody knackered," he said, a Brit again, and snuggled against Elijah, clearly intending to spend the night. Elijah stood up.

"Are you okay?" David Sobel asked.

Elijah looked at Etienne/David/Acisclus's angelic face, then straddled him and stuffed his cock into his lying mouth. Afterward, whoever this stranger was burrowed up against him again and fell asleep. Elijah listened to him breathe. His warm, furry body felt just right, and he looked like a little boy, a happy little Saint Acisclus. Did he lie? Well, not really. He just made up an exotic character he could play, and he played him well. Exhausted, Elijah decided to see how he felt in the morning.

MADAM CLUZET

"Pi is the ratio of the circumference of a circle to its diameter. Pi is the ratio of the circumference of a circle to its diameter," I whisper this to myself and into the headset before I attempt my first call.

Okay. Go!

"Hello. This is Brett Helvig from *Pension Plus Monthly*. May I speak to Erik Kever Ryle?"

"Yeah. What?" the deep, unenthusiastic voice on the other end of the line responds.

"Oh, hi, Mr. Kever Ryle. Our February issue is running a feature on indexing, and I want to ask you a few questions for our survey... Hello?" I lost him somewhere after indexing. What the hell is indexing anyway?

A voice behind me barks, "No. No. No. No. No!" It's the boss, Charlotte, who was pointed out to me when I interviewed. I turn and see she is holding her cell phone. She blows kisses into it. Are all those nos for me or her phone friend?

"Adieu, mon amour!" She blows a big kiss into the phone. That's not for me.

I turn my swivel chair around and give her big, blue actor eyes.

"Hello." I drop my voice an octave.

"Mon mari—sorry, my husband. He's French." Charlotte puts her phone away. "Hello, I'm Charlotte Hopper. And you must be Bruce from the Actors Fund. Hiring you people is my way of contributing, I suppose."

"I'm Brett," I say. "Brett Helvig. Good to meet you."

Charlotte is about fifty, I think, wearing a smart gray pantsuit that looks like Chanel, as do the shoes. The perfume is definitely Chanel No. 5. Her dark hair is cropped in a stylish pixie. Her gray eyes match her suit. They look like they might sparkle if she wanted them to. Just not now. She's a handsome woman who looks to be about ten feet tall as she towers over me. I'm a classic movie buff, and she reminds me a little of my beloved Joan Bennett, the dark hair, the light eyes.

"OK. I *just* got in from Paris, so I wasn't here to set you up properly," Charlotte takes a breath. "BUT you must never, never, NEVER use the word survey. No surveys. That's a dirty word around here." Charlotte's voice is cultured and melodious with a fetching little croak in it. Her eyes go steely as she continues. "Please write this down in stone. We get phone ballots. We call them BALLOTS. We call pension fund managers and ask them questions about specific investment topics. It's a quarterly feature in the magazine. You are collecting ballots."

I give her my big, *genuine* smile to go with the big eyes. "Ballots. Got it."

"You were recommended by the Actors Fund. Are you an actor?"

No, I want to say. But I am an actor, just not a working one. I clear my throat. "Yes. I—"

"Someday, I will want to hear all about your brilliant career, but today, I need you to hit the ground running. For this issue, we are asking pension fund managers about indexing. Do you know what indexing is?

"I do not."

"Dammit," Charlotte spits. "Indexing is... It's managing assets to match the performance of an index."

"An index," I repeat. I have no idea what an index is.

"Have you heard of Dow Jones? The S&P 500?"

"Yes." The fog is lifting.

"Well, those are indexes," she says and looks around the office to check on the rest of the troops. "I really need you to get started on this, so I can't go into the whole history of indexing right now. You started off on the wrong foot, but I'm sure you'll get it right. Are *you* sure?"

"Yes, I am," I say. I give her the deep voice, the eyes, the smile. But I'm not sure at all.

"Brilliant," Charlotte says. "First, let me give you the rules and regulations of my department. You are expected to make at least fifty calls a day. That's the bare minimum. You are not allowed to make or receive personal calls on the company phone. You are not allowed to make or answer cell phone calls at your desk. The computer is strictly for company use only. It's not your gateway to the outside world. You were not hired to post Facebook updates, shop at Amazon, or watch kittens on YouTube."

She's given this speech a thousand times, and like the star of a long-running Broadway show, say *Sunset Boulevard*, she's figured out its beats and breaths. She's found its resting spots and where to pick up the pace. It's a Sunday matinee performance, but I don't feel cheated.

She pushes through. It feels like she's coming to her big aria.

"The computers and phones are monitored. We know what you do and who you're talking to. You are NOT here to make new friends, meet your soul mate, or write your novel. As far as I'm concerned, there is no you. You are not here. What is here is a voice attached to a headset and fingers that enter data. This is not a reality show; this is reality, and there's no pot of gold at the end of the rainbow. There is no rainbow. Repeat. There is no rainbow. If there was a rainbow, you wouldn't know anyway. There are no windows in your area. Do you understand?"

"Yes. I understand," I say, "but you can put down the sledgehammer. I've had many jobs, and I know the drill."

There is a beat that could bounce in any direction. I'm proud of myself, but I'll probably be unemployed in a second. Her gray eyes look off into the middle distance, the way the great actor Herbert Marshall did in every movie. Then she looks right at me.

"Hmmm… Do you now?" Charlotte lets it and me hang there. Suddenly, her face brightens. "Look. I don't mean to sound harsh, but every week, I have to make the same speech. The last few years, I'm getting the same kind of person. They resent that they have to take a job like this. They don't want to hear suggestions about improving their performance. We have 'check-ins' to work things out, and I dread them. More often than not, the check-ins don't end with a resolution to do better; they end in tears. And, oops, someone just doesn't show up the next day. Some people start out capably enough and then realize that, oh, this *is* the job. This thing they're doing IS the job—and they don't like it. Too bad. You can either do it or you cannot. Hence, the 'sledgehammer.' I need it for my protection."

"Understood," I say. "Hence, I like that… *hence.* You don't hear it much anymore."

I'm out on a limb.

"What? Oh. Okay." She shakes her head. "I have three mainstays in my department: Ken, Mark, and Maddie, who came through the Actors Fund. They come in every day, assume the position, and start making calls. They take their half-hour lunches, and they sign out at the end of the day. The calls get made. The ballots are produced. If they have lives outside of the office, I don't know about them. Right now, there is no cubicle free near the other three, so we had to put you here in Siberia. If you have any questions, come to me, and don't ask Ken, Mark, or Maddie. I don't want them slowed down. Okay? But don't worry. I will check on you regularly to keep you company. Got it?"

"Yes." I need this job.

"Now, I want to hear you make another call."

I look at the next name on the screen and press the phone icon, and the dialing begins. I take a breath.

"Hello. This is Brett from *Pension Plus Monthly*. May I speak to Craig Fox? Oh, hi, Mr. Fox. Our February issue is running a feature on indexing, and I want to ask you a few questions about indexing for our sur… upcoming issue… Hello?" I look at Charlotte and shrug. "He hung up."

"Okay. That is more like it. Stay with that. I'll leave you to it. One thing to remember is that a good ranking from us helps these pension fund managers. They're sitting on trillions of dollars, and a good ranking from us means more people jump when they say jump."

"Ah, subtext. I understand. Thank you!"

Charlotte shakes her head again. "Now, get on that phone, and I will check back with you."

She spins around and marches through the maze of cubicles filled with unfortunate souls like me. I hear her crisp voice soar above the partitions. For her, this IS rocket science and open-heart surgery and atom splitting and all those endeavors that prohibit you from asking yourself why. For her, ballots are the core of life itself. Good for her. She has a mission.

Time for another call and another approach.

"John Martello? This is Brett Helvig from *Pension Plus Monthly*. How are you today? I'm glad to hear it. I'm just fine, too, thank you. We talked to you in October for our Investor Relations issue." He's still there.

"Okay. Shoot," Martello says.

"Thank you! This time around, I'd like to ask you about indexing. We could really use your input. It will take ten minutes, tops, and I will zip right along. These are multiple-choice questions, as you may remember."

I read him the questions and try to make it sound like I'm thinking them up on the spot.

He plays along pleasantly, and I sound like I know what I'm doing. Phew!

For the rest of the day, I just put my head down and push through, one call after another, no chatting because there's nobody to chat with in Siberia. Passing heads check me out, and I'm not sure if it's because I'm good, bad, or just new. The only breaks are a half-hour lunch and bathroom time, and I begin to look forward to my bathroom time. How long can you spend washing your hands?

I try not to look at my trapped, unhappy face in this cruel and unusual lighting. A designer would call this light plot Prison Break.

Pi is the ratio of the circumference of a circle to its diameter.

Pi is the ratio of the circumference of a circle to its diameter.

That's my mantra. I read it in a textbook when I was ten, and it made me happy. It was like a bowl of good, hearty alphabet soup filled with big, crunchy vegetables. I use it to settle me down, to fix me in time and space. I am here, and this is this, and all is well. I run number sequences in my head. I sit and watch the numbers change on a computer screen. I can calculate percentages and equations in my head, and I love to write the sigma notation; it's like a flag to me. I play Zombie Math on my iPad. It soothes me. It's like the visual equivalent of a babbling brook. Or, like Bette Davis and her lacework in *The Letter*, it soothes the troubled soul.

I only pass Ken, Mark, and Maddie on my way to the bathroom, and they are always hunched over their computers and don't even look up when I walk by.

I did not come to New York from Fergus Falls, Minnesota, fifty-five miles from Fargo, North Dakota, to bob for ballots. All those classes, workshops, and showcases landed me here? Fergus Falls is a picture-perfect small town with about 13,000 residents. The Otter Tail River runs through Fergus Falls, and there is a waterfall in the heart of town.

I was an only child. My parents were older, distant, secret drinkers in our spotless, tense ranch house. If I'd stayed, I'd be the overweight drama teacher at the high school and be in and out of AA. Every year, there are at least fifty days when the temperature is below zero. So, you skate and ice fish and drink and seethe.

I've had this job before, just with better lighting and nicer people. I sit in a cubicle all by myself, surrounded by the white noise of high finance. Seven more hours. Seven more days. Seven more years. No rainbows. No windows. I need this job. *We* need this job. Otherwise, we move in with his unhappy family in Union City. My partner, Al, wants to keep his days free for auditions. Pi is the ratio of the circumference of a circle to its diameter. Somehow, dragging its broken leg and my broken spirit behind it, this ugly baboon butt of a day comes to an end, and I have collected ten ballots. Ballots!

The next day, I notice people hovering around my cubicle, listening to my ballot pitch.

They don't talk to me, so I have no idea what they think. Somewhere in the middle of the day, I figure out who I'm playing in this scene: I'm Brett Helvig, investigative reporter on the financial beat, and I want to get to the bottom of this indexing thing. I even drop my voice half a register.

It makes me feel less detached from the mothership of sanity and—it gets results. I get eighteen ballots.

When I go to the men's room, I pass a burly woman with donut crumbs on her sweater. She was one of the hoverers, and she gives me a thumbs up.

The next morning, I turn on my computer, and I get a whiff of Chanel. Charlotte is standing behind me.

"Good work," she says. "You really got the hang of it."

"Thank you." I turn my chair around to face her. She's wearing a charcoal-gray suit today.

"This project ends the week after next, but I should have another one coming up shortly. Are you going to be available?"

"Yes." Dammit.

"What about the acting? Anything on the horizon?"

"That's on hold for the time being," I say, and I hate saying it. "I have a project, but…"

Charlotte looks startled, her gray eyes lasers. "But? I need to know if I can count on you."

"I am completely free." Dammit.

"Good. Well then, I should be able to keep you busy for a while."

"Great!" That's acting!

Charlotte's eyes de-laser. "Are you... connected to someone?"

"Yes."

"What does he do?" Presumptuous but on the money.

"He's an actor too. But he does IT between gigs." I look at my list and hit the phone icon.

She's right behind me, so I have to show her how dedicated I am. And I'd rather not talk about my personal life.

"Hello, is this John Wernke? Hi, John, this is Brett Helvig from *Pension Plus Monthly*..."

"My husband is...." Charlotte says.

I tap my headset and try to look interested, but I have to get back to Mr. Wernke.

"...an actor, too," she says as she steps away. Wernke puts me on hold, and I hear Charlotte softly but clearly murmur to herself, "Mon existence est une campagne triste ou il pleut toujours."

I write it down in the margins of the masthead page of the magazine. Did I hear it right?

Wernke comes back, and I score my first ballot of the day.

I look at what I scribbled. I think it means: *My life is a sad country where it rains all the time.*

When I go to the bathroom, I Google it. "My life is a sad *campaign* where it rains all the time."

It's attributed to Leon Bloy, a French writer I never heard of. Does Charlotte, the all-powerful, really feel that way about her life, or is she—gasp—an intellectual?

I'm plugging along the next day. The ballots are coming in. My style is getting looser. I'm talking to someone from the pension department of a well-known fried chicken conglomerate. My antennae are honed now, and I can tell in a few breaths if someone will answer my ballot questions. This guy is challenging and cheeky, ready to dust the lowly phone solicitor. I go for broke.

"I buy your extra crispy fried chicken. Why not take my extra crispy ballot?"

He inhales. "Shoot."

I hear some gasps outside the cubicle. Word of my fried chicken gambit spreads across the floor, maybe through the building. I get significant looks when I walk to the men's room but no thumbs up. I'm braced for a scolding from Charlotte. At eleven thirty, I get a whiff of Chanel, and she is behind me again.

"How many ballots?" she asks.

"Ten so far," I say.

"Good! You know we have something in common," she says with a smile. She's not looking at me, though, but at the dusty beige wall behind Maddie's head. Does she try to limit eye contact with the staff, or is she reading from an imaginary teleprompter? I want to ask if she likes fried chicken too, but instead, I say, "Oh?"

"Yes. My husband is an actor, too," she says proudly, her eyes on the wall.

"Is he? Nice."

"He's French."

"Great." I don't know what else to say.

"You may have heard of him."

"Oh?"

"My husband is Francois Cluzet." It's like an announcement. "Do you know him?"

I do, I think. "Francois Cluzet, Francois Cluzet. I know that name."

"He's quite famous."

"Yes. Yes. Francois Cluzet. Yes."

"He's a movie star. My husband, the movie star." Charlotte is beaming, and she's giving me her laser-gray eyes. "You may know him from *Round Midnight, Chocolat, Tell No One...*"

"*Tell No One... Tell No One.*" I'm getting an image. I loved that film. "Yes! He was the lead, the... the doctor, right?"

"Yes, that's my husband. He won the César Best Actor Award for that. His name was Alex in the film. Dr. Alex Beck." She's giving me her full attention.

"Oh, he's wonderful! Such a good actor. Very French. That's your husband?"

"Oh yes. He's VERY French. Mon mari, le movie star." She is triumphant.

"How wonderful."

"Oh yes. Wonderful."

Now I'm beaming, too, just being next to the glamorous wife of a famous French actor—and a good one. But wait. Then what is she doing here? I'd be in Paris or Cannes if I were her.

"But what are you doing *here*?" I blurt and regret.

Charlotte is unfazed. She's explained this countless times before.

"Ah, well. It's a long story. I've been at the magazine for almost twenty years. I like my job. What I do is important. I'm good at it, and, unfortunately, I'm indispensable." Then, she repeats it in French. "*Indispensable!* One more year and I can retire on a full pension with lots of perks... so..."

"I understand," I say, but I'm not sure I do.

"I knew you would. Anyway, one can't just be the movie star's wife. Still, it's a struggle. He's there. I'm here. I live for the weekend."

"What happens on the weekend?"

"More often than not, I fly to Paris."

"Yikes! Just for a weekend?"

"Oh yes. I used to take the Concorde. Now, I pretty much live on Air France. Fly out Friday night, fly in Monday morning. So, if I'm a little late and look a little the worse for wear on a Monday, that's the reason."

"Wow. I... I don't know what to say. It must be wonderful to be married to him—and terrible, I guess, to be apart."

"Yes. Wonderful and terrible," Charlotte says with a sigh. "I don't really like to talk about it, but, well, the cat's out of the bag. And I thought you might understand. You're an actor, involved with an actor."

"Yes. I guess." But Al and I aren't on the celestial plane. "Francois... I mean, your husband, is so good. What's he like? Oh, stupid question, but... what's he like?"

Charlotte beams. She looks like a new woman, a pearly light shining from her gray eyes, like the pearly skies of Paris. "Well, he's very French, with all that that implies. Vain, earthy, opinionated... and, well..."

"Well?" Wait. She's my boss so she shouldn't tell me *everything*.

"Well, very sexy. He's very driven and works all the time. He's the French Everyman. His face, his body... it's like a map of France. Taut, seasoned, saucy, with a deep earthy smell of French soil, the lush foliage of the countryside, a burnished gold in the center of his dark chocolate eyes. Thick, mossy hair. A beautiful, big French honker. And oh, his Pyrenees. I love his Pyrenees."

Yikes! She's going in. I have nothing to say. Wait. Yes, I do.

"And he lives in, you live in Paris?"

"Yes. We have an apartment in Paris. And a place in the country. Do you know Paris?"

"I've been there several times for... Yes. It is beautiful."

"Our place is in the fifteenth arrondissement, slightly off the beaten path. The neighborhood is called Commerce. Do you know it?"

"No," I say.

"Most Americans don't. It's not jammed with tourists and riffraff. We have a lovely little flat on Rue Du Commerce, a few steps from the Metro. The entrance is wedged between a boulangerie and a pecherie, I mean, a bakery and a fish market. Heavenly."

"How wonderful. And where is your place in the country?"

Charlotte looks startled. "Oh. Do you know France?"

"Yes. I traveled around it a bit for... Yes. Where is your country place?"

"It's... well, I really can't say. You know, for security reasons."

Give me a break. Security reasons?

"Oh. Yes. I understand." I don't. "Well, I would love to meet Francois."

"Yes. I'm sure you would. Well, maybe someday you can. I don't like to talk about my husband here."

"I understand... Well... I should really get back to work."

She puts her hand on my shoulder and squeezes. "Oh yes. Work, work, work!"

I turn and give her a wan smile, the "I don't see you" one that is the specialty of Midwestern white women of a certain age and the gay men who aspire to be like them.

After I've been there a week, I have a nodding acquaintance with Ken, Mark, and Maddie. I bump into Ken in the men's room while I'm at the urinal.

"I like your style," he says. I suspect he's not talking about the way I pee. "Overheard you a couple of times. Smooth, man, smooth." He's a handsome black man in his fifties with a deep, melodious voice—the Voice of God or James Earl Jones.

I've overheard his pitch. It's like a friendly God who puts his arm around your shoulder to give you the inside scoop: it's all bullshit, brother. I'd take his ballot and ask for seconds.

While he's shaking off, he says, "Don't let the Dragon Lady get to you."

Dragon Lady. Of course!

I bump into him again a few days later as we head to the elevator.

"How you doing with the Dragon Lady?" he asks.

"Getting by," I say. "That's something about her husband, huh?"

He looks surprised. "She has a husband? I thought she was married to the job."

I guess that means I'm special. The chosen one.

When Mark looks up as I pass, he gives me a wan, crooked smile, and his brown hair flops into his face. He looks to be a boyish forty-something and like a man recovering from something.

His pitch is whispery and urgent with a hint of a lateral lisp. He sucks you into his intense, top-secret ballot; it's just between the two of you.

Maddie is small and pretty with a halo of curly blonde hair and big blue eyes. When she looks up, all I read is, "Help!" Her small voice is inaudible in the white noise of finance, so I don't know her pitch. She always snags the most ballots, and it looks like doing so takes everything out of her. I haven't seen either of them away from their desks, so I don't know if they can walk.

The office is on lower Park Avenue, a few blocks from Union Square. When it's nice out, I buy half a sandwich at Pret a Manger and sit in the park. I always have a *New Yorker* with me, trying to read through my ten-year backlog. I've been at *Pension Plus Monthly* (we call it PPM) for almost two weeks and am starting to get used to feeling my soul drain out of my body. On this particular day, I see Susan Sarandon get out of a cab near Sixteenth Street. She's petite, and I imagined her being seven feet tall. There's nobody to tell this to, and when I get back to my desk, Charlotte is standing there in a nimbus of Chanel No. 5.

"Ah, there you are." She's smiling.

"I was at lunch," I say. "I just saw—"

"Oh, I know. Your desk phone was ringing, and I picked it up."

"Oh." I mean—uh oh.

"Yes. It was your husband," she says. We're not married. Don't ask. I think "no personal calls" was one of her ten or twenty commandments, so I guess I'm in trouble.

"Sorry about that," I say, "I left my phone at home in the charger."

Charlotte beams, "No worries. We had a nice chat. He's quite charming, and he has a lovely, deep voice." She growls a little.

"Yes. He does"

"What's his name?"

"Al, Alex, Alejandro"

"How's that?"

"He was born Alejandro Castillo; his stage name is Alex Castillo; everybody calls him Al."

I'd rather be making calls than having this conversation with her.

Charlotte's eyes light up. "Oh, he's Latin. Very nice."

"Cuban. Cuban American. He was born here. His family came over on the Cuban *Mayflower* in 1960." Al said that to me on our first real date.

"He has a lovely, deep voice."

"Yes. You said that."

"He called once before, looking for you, and got transferred to my line by mistake. We talked for quite a long time."

"Oh. You never told me," I say. And Al never told me. Something I can add to the list of things he doesn't tell me as we slip into a tenth-anniversary slump.

"I am NOT your answering service!" she snaps. Then she takes a breath and smiles. "Do you have a picture of him?"

"You mean in my wallet? Um. No. Does anyone do that anymore?"

"How about on your phone? I'm just curious. He *sounds* handsome. Is he?"

Wait a minute. Is no-nonsense Charlotte… boy crazy?

"Yes," I say. "Well, I think so. Most people do. Anyway, I left my phone at home, remember?"

"Oh, right. Oh well. I would just love to match that voice with a face. Too bad. Too bad."

Instead of keeping my trap shut and going back to work, I give her this tasty tidbit. "There's his website. He has pictures on that. Headshots, scenes from plays, and a video reel."

I see the words waft out of my mouth like smoke rings, and there's no way to lasso them back home.

Charlotte claps her hands together. "Oh great. Pull it up."

Is this a test? Will I set off alarms or get tasered if I visit his site while I'm on duty?

I say, "Right now? I, um, should be making calls."

"I'm giving you permission. Just this once."

She leans in as I type in the site address and puts a hand on my right shoulder.

Al's striking, smiling face fills the screen. It's weird to have his face on this screen with her hand on my shoulder.

"Yummy!" Charlotte says. "You are a lucky boy."

I usually think so. The first three years were wonderful, magical, but every second after that has been renegotiated. I love him. I want to get married. He doesn't, doesn't believe in that for gay men. "We're outcasts, rebels, and should stay that way!" is how the speech goes. I've managed to be faithful, pretty much, but it's hard for Alejandro to keep it in his pants. He suffers from RDS, Restless Dick Syndrome, so we don't ask and don't tell. Still pound for pound, minute by minute, it's not bad. I like being around him; there's a sizzle in the air that keeps me alert. And I love that face. It is home to me.

"There he is. There's my platano," I say, but that feels way too intimate. But if she can talk about her husband's Pyrenees, I guess the lid is off.

"Platano?"

"Oh, that's my nickname for him. It means plantain, you know, the fruit, like a starchy banana?"

"Oh," she says, but she doesn't know.

"Because he's Cuban and he likes plantains."

"I see. My, my. He looks a lot like Antonio Banderas." Her voice is oddly girlish and gooey.

"We all look alike to you gringos," Al likes to say.

"You think so? I don't."

This is getting weird. I exit the website. "Well, I'd better start making some calls."

"Does he speak Spanish?"

I put on my headset, hoping to end this scene. "Yes."

"You are very lucky."

"I guess. So are you, Madam Cluzet."

Charlotte removes her hand from my shoulder and lifts her chin. "Yes, I am. I really am. But, for the record, it's *Madame* Cluzet." Charlotte has her boss voice back. "Maybe all four of us can get together the next time Francois is in town."

"Sure," I say, knowing it will never happen, and that's just on my end.

"How many ballots do you have so far today?"

"Eleven."

"Back to work," Charlotte says, as if we just hadn't shared those handsome husband moments.

Before I slip on my headset, I hear her say something to herself, "Faites-vous des amis prompts à vous censurer."

I write it down on my scratch pad and think about it while I make my next few calls.

An hour later, it comes to me, "Make friends with those who would be quick to criticize you."

Was that stage whisper meant for me? Am I being played? Who is she quoting?

The next day is a warm and sunny one, and I take my little half chicken salad Pret sandwich and a bottle of beet juice and sit in Union Square with my trusty *New Yorker*. I haven't seen Charlotte yet today. Has she been in meetings all morning, or is she in Paris climbing Cluzet's Pyrenees?

As I think this, I see a determined figure stride across the square heading toward Park Avenue. As it gets closer, it looks like a shapely eggplant. It is Charlotte. She cuts north of me and my sad little sandwich and doesn't notice me, nor, I imagine, anything else that isn't *PPM*-related. She has a great walk and a very nice ass in her eggplant pantsuit, and her determined stride reminds me of Teresa Wright marching to the library in *Shadow of a Doubt*. I don't see her again for the rest of the day.

I google Francois Cluzet and see his extensive film credits, but Wikipedia doesn't have much on his personal life. He has one son with Marie Trintignant and three other children, but the entry doesn't mention their mother. Charlotte didn't mention children. There is nothing motherly about her. Is she wife number two, three, or four?

As a ballot collector, I have good days and bad days. My early triumphs have faded, and my pitch doesn't generate any interest from eavesdroppers, or from me for that matter. This role wasn't very interesting to begin with, and it's turned from a three-week showcase into a long, dull run. Charlotte hasn't checked on me much. She is away or locked up in meetings or something. Then, one rainy day, I dig into my HB Studio training, refine my performance, and get into a groove. I turn in twenty-three ballots. The next morning, Charlotte is at my desk.

"Twenty-three completed ballots. Twenty-three in one day! I think that's a record."

I don't know what to say. This is not a talent I care about, but I did see one of Cluzet's films.

"Great!" I chirp. "You know, I saw *Untouchable* last night."

"*Untouchable?*" It's a sneer.

"Yes, your husband's film. It was on Netflix the other night. It's wonderful. He's wonderful."

She brightens and forgives my French.

"Oh. *Intouchable.* Oh yes." *Ontooshable.*

"*Intouchable.* Right. I loved it."

"That's nice," she says without enthusiasm. She's thinking of something else, and her eyes are fixed on that dreary wall again. "I think next week I'm going to call a meeting. I want you to tell the others about your technique. They're slacking off a bit. Maybe you can tell them your secret."

"Oh, there's no secret. I just put my head down and charge ahead."

I stare at the wall with her and imagine what she sees: a PowerPoint presentation of my technique. Something she can record and present to new hires instead of making her introductory speech. *I don't have time to explain it all to you. Just click on this link.*

Ken stands in his cubicle, stretches, and walks through our shared middle-distance projection, disrupting it.

"I just do the best I can."

"Well, whatever you do, next week, I want you to share that with the others," she commands. "I won't be in tomorrow, and I won't be back in the office until Wednesday. I'll call in from time to time. Frank has a few days off, and I will be spending time with him in Paris."

"Frank?" Who's Frank?

"Oh, my husband, Francois. It's a little joke between us. He loves all things American, so I call him Frank. I love France, so his pet name for me is Chantal. At home, we're Frank and Chantal."

"Sweet." I imagine them in sweats in front of a widescreen TV. He's eating Taco Bell, and she's tucking into foie gras.

"You think so? Do you and Alejandro have pet names? Oh, right. You call him Platano?"

"How did you meet Francois?" I ask. "I think it must be a great story." I want to see where she goes with this. I want her to make me believe. Maybe her story is true, but I have a pesky feeling that something is wrong with it. Is it just me, or, in the current climate, does the debunking start before the myth is even created? Like the story of Jesus, I want to believe in Francois and Charlotte, or Frank and Chantal. Sing it, sister.

"How did we meet? How did we meet? Yes, it is a great story." She's taxiing the runway.

"I'm sure... But you don't have to tell me."

"Oh, I'd be glad to. How *did* we meet? Well... in 1994, I was working in the London office, and I had a fortnight's holiday, so I went to Paris."

"Ah, of course." Fortnight? She has a Mid-Atlantic accent, like Constance Bennet in *Topper*.

"I thought, well, let me do the grand thing, really do it up, you know? So I stayed at the George V, probably the grandest hotel in Paris."

"Oh yes. I've walked by it."

"The hotel was to be my vacation. The rooms are beautiful, there's a magnificent pool, and it's near everything. My plan was to be an invisible tourist with a lovely room, just re-charging my batteries and drinking in the sights."

"How wonderful."

"Yes. But there was a lot of fuss in the lobby and in front of the building," she continues. "A film crew was there, and they made getting to and fro very tiresome. They were filming *French Kiss* with Meg Ryan and Kevin Kline. Frank had a nice little part in it. Have you seen it?"

"Yes. Who was Francois in it? Wait. Was he the guy who steals Meg Ryan's bag?" It's coming back to me. "And then Jean Reno arrests him and says, 'OK, Bob, tu connais le musique.'"

Charlotte frowns. I'm interrupting her aria.

"I think it's a dreadful film, BUT I will always love it—for special reasons. There I was in Paris, in April. April in Paris, and I was out all the glorious day. I came back to the hotel exhausted. I just wanted to have a bath, a lie down before going out to dinner with some friends. When I got to the hotel, the front door was blocked by those awful production people on headsets. I started to make a fuss: I'm a guest, this is an outrage. I have to get in there. I said it in English, I said it in French, and I was getting nowhere." She's deep into reliving the scene, and she's pointing at the awful film crew, then she stops. A glow infuses her face and spreads to the air around her as she recalls the scene.

I realize I'm smiling, too, absorbed by the glow.

"A very handsome man was standing in front of the hotel, smoking a cigarette. He was watching the scene with a twinkle in his eye. Then the handsome man came up to the production people and said, 'This is my wife. She is my guest. Kasdan has given permission for her to visit me.' I was going to protest... but thought better of it. Then I felt his rugged hand on the small of my back as he guided me past the riffraff and into the elevator."

"Wow!" I can't help it. This is good stuff.

She holds up her hand, wait. "'Thank you so much,' I said to him. 'I can take it from here.' Then, he winked at me. One little wink and I was completely undone. One little wink from this gorgeous man and my heart stood still. I forgot what I was saying and just stood there, sputtering. His hand felt so right on my back, so natural and strong that I let him escort me to my room."

"Incredible. That scene is better than the stupid film."

"Yes. Well, we were inseparable from then on. I saw him every day I was in Paris, and when I went back to London, I visited him every weekend. If he wasn't working, he came to London. We were married in Paris six months later."

"That is a great story. So romantic." She sold me.

"Oh yes. But in 1996, I got a big promotion and was assigned to head the New York division. It was bittersweet. I really missed New York. I grew up in Connecticut and came to NYU for a Masters in French Comparative Literature. I started here part-time because they needed French speakers in the international division, and well, I just kept moving up and was sent to London. I still have the same apartment on West Fifty-First Street that I got when I moved here. But the downside is I have to spend time away from my husband. He's always working, going from one film to another. I had hoped that with *Tell No One* he would get some American films, but that hasn't happened."

Now that I think of it, I don't understand it either. Cluzet has a Bogie quality, and he's like a cooler Dustin Hoffman. "I don't know how you do it," I wind up saying.

"Neither do I," she says. "Anyway, one more year, and then I go to Paris and live with Frank full time."

"Sounds good to me. What would you do?"

"Nothing. Everything. Live! I will just be Madame Cluzet. I'll cook wonderful meals in our little flat. We'll have dinner parties, and Deneuve will sit next to me and smoke up the joint and give me all the dirt. We'll wander around Paris like teenagers, holding hands, and we'll give each other foot rubs at night. I'll visit his sets and play bit parts in his films. And... we'll spend time at our rundown little country place. Yes! I'll... I'll milk the goats and make cheese. I'll romp around with our dogs, two big golden labs, Chanel and Dior. I'll learn how to do embroidery, and I'll catch up on all this *Fifty Shades* and *Harry Potter* crap and read all of Jackie Collins. That's ten years right there."

"Nice!" I say. It sounds good to me.

"When Frank comes to New York, we must go out, the four of us. I would love to meet Alejandro. We've become quite chummy on the phone." There's a purr in her smile. "Until Frank comes, maybe the three of us can meet."

I shudder involuntarily. I don't like this one bit.

"Why?" I say, and she looks shocked.

"Why?" she echoes. "Why not?"

I don't want her anywhere near Al. I just want to meet the movie star. Al is taller, better looking, more talented, and more charming than I am. Whenever I see him onstage, I get lost in his stardust. I can imagine her latching onto him and turning him into her boyfriend, real or imaginary.

"Al's schedule is very erratic. It's hard to make plans with him. He's always on call, so…"

"Just a thought. Or. We could have lunch."

I want to change the subject.

"Does Frank ever call you here?"

"We talk every day on our mobiles." Suddenly, her face gets grim, and she changes her tone. "Next week, when I'm not here, I want you to unofficially be my eyes and ears. I've requested that they bump up your hourly rate, and if you're interested, I can fast-track you for a permanent position. Would you be interested?"

"Yes! Thank you." I say, too brightly. She's asking me to nark for a few more coins, and I'm willing. Who the fuck am I now?

That night, Al and I have comps to *Phantom of the Opera*. A friend is in the chorus. It's fun to be sophisticated New York actors in an audience of talky, tickled tourists. Al gets a few double-takes because he looks like he could be famous. We plan to go to Joe Allen for a bite afterward. Al used to work there, and we always bump into people we know. The grub is good, and the place makes you happy to be in showbiz. When we get out of *Phantom*, we head the two blocks up Eighth Avenue to Forty-Sixth Street. I see someone who looks just like Charlotte coming out of Shake Shack, carrying a very big take-out bag. Is Frank in town, and they're having an All-American touristy take-out binge with Netflix? Or is she all alone? It's Friday night—shouldn't she be on her way to Paris by now? I nudge Al and see his eyes have been following the bouncing buttocks of a young blond boy, fresh from dance class, wearing electric blue tights.

"Hey, that's Charlotte," I say.

We follow her for a few blocks.

"That's the Dragon Lady? She looks a little basic and a bit fragile," he says.

Yes, it is Charlotte, the same determined Teresa Wright walk. She's wearing a gray sweat suit, and her body jiggles inside all the cotton, no need for shapewear when she's off duty. In the bright light of garish store windows hawking I LOVE NY memorabilia, her hair looks flat and dirty, and she's wearing glasses and a pair of tan Uggs.

"Aren't you going to say hello?" Al asks, but I can't do it. "Or I will. It's always nice to meet a fan." I grab his arm to stop him.

On Monday morning, I'm back at my desk when the phone rings. It's Charlotte on a crackling line.

"Hi. Where are you?" I ask.

"Paris. We didn't go to the country. There was so much to do here."

"Right. I can't believe you're calling me from Paris." Then I add, "When did you leave?"

"Friday night, the last flight. So how is it going? What was the ballot count for Friday?"

"Forty-four altogether between the four of us," I say.

"Oh dear, that's not very impressive. Who had the most ballots?"

"Maddie, of course. Everything is just the same. What's the weather like in Paris? Can you see those pearly skies from your window?"

"Yes, I am, and there's a hint of a rainbow. The weather has been glorious. Just glorious. Has the new program for the European ballots been installed yet?"

"No. They are doing that tomorrow."

"Next week, we start the All-Europe ballots, and I need you to come in at six a.m."

"Six?" is all I can say.

"Yes. I want you to start, and then I'll bring the rest of the team in that early. You're my lead pony."

"Great!" I say, glad that she can't see my face. "How is your husband?"

"Oh, he's yummy, as usual." She releases a long sigh. "He's in the shower, so I thought I would check in with you. He's off for a few weeks, and he's grown this hideous beard. He always does that whenever he has any time off between projects. I hate it, but it makes him happy."

"I rented one of his films, *The Story of Women,* with Isabelle Huppert," I say proudly. "It's very, um, rigorous, but he's wonderful in it, and of course, so is she. Do you know her?"

"Huppert? We've met. How many ballots did Ken turn in?"

"Um, ten. I think. What's Francois's—your husband's next project?" I'm imagining Francois in the shower.

"How many ballots did Mark and Maddie turn in?"

"Mark had twelve and Maddie had fifteen." Why is she asking me about ballots when her movie star husband is soaping his taut, sinewy body?

"Okay. That's tolerable."

"Will Francois be in New York for the French film festival at Lincoln Center?" I ask though I know she will change the subject.

"I have to sign off. We're going to the opera tonight."

"How wonderful! I went on a tour of it, and I thought it was gorgeous. What are you seeing?" I hear sirens on her end of the phone, those distinctive French low *high*, low *high* wails.

"Well, it's always a mob scene when we go. But he's an opera buff, so…" she says as the sirens get louder. "Damn those sirens! Well, I must dash."

"See you next week," I say, but she's gone.

I imagine her standing in her charming flat on the Rue du Commerce, wearing a fluffy white robe while Francois sings in the shower, something smart like an art song by Reynaldo Hahn. The water stops, the singing stops, and he enters the living room in his fluffy white robe and scoots behind her. His strong, wiry arms pull her close to him while his sexy Gallic mug nuzzles her white neck. Together, they gaze out the window at the Parisian rainbow and think about what they will wear to the opera tonight. I hope they're seeing something French, like *The Pearl Fishers*.

And then... and then... I get this other image. Charlotte in those gray sweats, standing in the middle of a non-descript living room in a dingy apartment on West Fifty-First Street. She's holding the phone in one hand and a remote in the other. She has a French crime drama on TV, maybe *Tell No One*, and she's cued up the siren sound to usher her out of our conversation. Once I'm gone, she drops the remote and digs into another giant bag of Shake Shack goodies like the Shake Stack and a peanut butter shake. That's what I would get.

I do some more googling on Francois Cluzet—it takes a while to sort through his tangled love life. It's not like here, where TMZ tells you too much about everybody. But from what I can see, monsieur is currently married to a woman named Narjiss, who looks nothing like Charlotte. They are arm in arm at an opening in Paris. Maybe that's over. Maybe Charlotte *was* married to him.

Maybe she and Francois are like Tracy and Hepburn; they are each other's great loves, but it's not... official, you know?

How can I judge her?

I have my handsome boyfriend, and I feel like I'm struggling to keep him. Al is a much better actor than I am. When I see him onstage, I still think, wow, this is my boyfriend? He gives himself over to his performances and lets them inhabit him. I just can't do that. I don't have his toolbox. That's why he needs to keep his options open, and I need this job.

I start bright and early at six a.m. on Monday, the only one in the big, lonely office. I am a little groggy, and I don't get many ballots. On the plus side, I get out at two, but I am lost about what to do the rest of the day. Charlotte is due back from Paris or West Fifty-First on Wednesday.

I'm at my desk on Wednesday when she breezes in around seven.

"Oh. I didn't think you'd be in this early," I say.

"Well, my flight was delayed, and we landed just a few hours ago. I couldn't get to sleep. I was still so wired from the weekend. Going from one premiere and party to another, tottering around Paris in heels, giggling like teenagers. Sometimes, Frank just has to play the movie star because they love him so. I hate to talk about it. Anyway, what's been going on around here?"

"Everything is pretty much the same. You should go back home and try to get some sleep."

I can say that kind of thing because I'm her lead pony. Yes, I am.

"I might, later. There's a department head meeting at ten. And besides, since I asked you to come in at six, I didn't want you to be here all alone. When the rest switch to this schedule next week, we'll have a few ballots under our belts. And it takes a while to adjust to calling Europe, so I want you to get a feel for it. When you're calling Europe, because of the time difference, it's best to start as far east as you can—Russia, Poland, Scandinavia—and start working your way west. I hope this new schedule doesn't bother Alejandro."

"Nope. We're struggling—so we go where the work is. Anyway, he was still asleep when I left this morning."

"Yummy!" Then she growls and rubs her hands together.

"Hmmm?"

"Do you speak any other languages?"

"Not really. Some bad French maybe."

"That's not a problem. Most of the admins speak English, as do the Fund Managers."

Charlotte looks a little rumpled today. Her hair is flattish, and her makeup is off. Her suit is wrinkled, and there's something on her left shoulder. So I say, "You have something on your shoulder."

"I do? Where?"

"Yes. Left side, looks like hair."

She swipes at it and misses. It's on her arm, too.

"Let me... May I?"

I run my hand down her shoulder and left arm and scoop it off. It's hair. Red hair. It looks like cat hair. I show it to her, and she is flustered.

"Oh dear. Damn. Thanks."

"I think I got everything." I deposit the fur ball in the nearest waste basket.

"Thank you. Frank jumped all over me as I was leaving this morning," she says.

"Your husband is in New York?"

"No. Frank, the cat."

"Your cat is named Frank too?" I knew there was a cat. "Oh. Do you have any children?" I blurt. Well, the sick old cat is out of the bag, so why not? "Sorry. I guess that's none of my business."

She looks over my shoulder, like a long-suffering Ann Harding, takes a beat, and says, "Frank has children... from previous... entanglements." She lasers in on me again and snaps. "I think it's time we started making some calls, don't you?"

I stumble through the rest of the week, punchy from the new schedule. I start the morning by calling Russia and working my way west. It's true that the admins speak English, but I can't seem to crack the code until a sweet guy in Copenhagen takes my ballot. I go to the staged reading of a friend's new play and fall asleep. It will be a while before she talks to me again. I learn that I have to go to sleep by ten p.m. to wake up by four a.m. Somehow, my life has slipped away from me, and I've become a thing that goes to a place and does a thing. Is this what most working Americans feel like every day?

Ken, Mark, and Maddie all switch to the new dawn schedule, but only Maddie and I make it every day on time. In the relative quiet, I can hear her pitch now. It's delicate and whispery, and she often says, "It would mean the world to me if you would take my ballot." Brilliant!

Charlotte lets me know that she's going to Paris again that weekend, and I'm to be her eyes and ears. She talked about more money, but I haven't seen it yet. She doesn't come in on Friday, so I imagine she's on her way to Paris... or to Shake Shack.

When I get up Saturday morning, Al is gone. He slipped out before dawn to catch a bus to Atlantic City for a Comic-Con convention. He's a cosplay nerd and wants to play the first Hispanic superhero. A friend made him a snug, flattering body suit in the colors of the Cuban flag. It showcases his arrogant, bulbous cock and bubble butt, so I'm sure, like a good action hero, he'll see a lot of action this weekend. I was hoping for a note with "Love you!" on it, but all I got was a text, "Be back Monday xo."

So, I'm alone all weekend: me, TCM, and junk food. I should be working on my show. What show? Let me tell you about my show, *Emilie!* Emilie du Chatelet was a scientist and mathematician, and Voltaire was her lover. I want to develop it into a piece about their love affair. It was pi that led me to Newton and from Newton I stumbled onto Emilie du Chatelet who wrote about him.

She was born in 1704 and was married to the Marquis du Chatelet when she met Voltaire and fell in love with him. Their affair was an open secret, and they had their own Chateau. Maybe, if I'm generous, that's the kind of arrangement Charlotte has with Francois.

Al and I visited their home, Chateau de Cirey, when we were in France. Voltaire's real name was Francois, just like Charlotte's man. Francois Marie Arouet. Once I finish the first draft, I have to figure out if I can find an actress to play Emilie or whether I do it in drag, ala Charles Busch, if I have the nerve. The idea is that Al would be Voltaire. He may not have the wit, but he does have the temperament. Like Lucy and Desi, it might be a way to keep our marriage together—if we ever get married.

"Judge me for my own merits, or lack of them, but do not look upon me as a mere appendage to this great general or that great scholar, this star that shines at the court of France or that famed author. When I add the sum total of my graces, I confess I am inferior to no one."

That's Madame du Chatelet, my Emilie, writing to Frederick the Great of Prussia in 1725. It's the cornerstone of the piece I'm making about her. What courage she had! I would love to stand on a stage and proudly say those words. I'm a privileged white male in the twenty-first century, and I don't have the balls to make that kind of declaration. I have a crappy temp job where my possibly insane boss claims I'm her lead pony and leads me around on a pony ride. I haven't seen any of that extra money yet. Since Charlotte has her masters in French Comparative Lit, in another world, I would have liked to talk to her about Voltaire and Emilie, but I don't want her anywhere near my baby.

Charlotte is in Paris with her movie star husband, Al is in Atlantic City doing a threesome with a wannabe Batman and a fake Green Lantern, their costumes in a pile on the floor, and I'm all alone in my small apartment in my noisy neighborhood, and even my trusty TCM has let me down. They've programmed a twenty-four-hour tribute to John Wayne. I've been working on *Emilie!* for three hours, and I have two new sentences and no new thoughts.

I want a drink. I have a bottle of gin but no tonic or limes or cucumbers. I might be able to get them at the rundown bodega down the street where the dairy products have exceeded their expiration dates, and the fruit looks bruised and unhappy. I could go to Joe Allen, but that's a lot of money and trouble for one drink. Mickeys on Ninth Avenue is a possibility; they have drink specials, and the grub is decent. Yeah, why not?

I get off the train at Fiftieth Street, and instead of going to Forty-Ninth, I decide to walk up to Fifty-First.

Charlotte has a place somewhere on this street, and I want to get an idea of the Dragon Lady's lair, though I don't know the address. I want to stumble upon her sitting on her front stoop with a fifteen-year-old orange cat on her lap and a giant Shake Shack bag beside her. There are some classic brick five-story walk-ups on the south side of the street where I imagine she might live. If I see her, we can finally put an end to this movie star husband fantasia. While we're at it, why not put an end to all our fantasias? Charlotte's movie star husband dream and Al's superhero reveries and our stalled partnership and my idea that my sad little show about a female mathematician who lived in the eighteenth century will be something that someone would want to see—*if* I ever write it.

What makes me, Charlotte, and Al think we can get away with these fantasies? Because... *Because* we came from our respective hamlets to live in Manhattan, to live inside the genie's smudged lamp. It's crowded and dirty in here, but we think we are that much closer to our dreams, and like compulsive gamblers, we hope the right combination of rubs and our own hubris will free us into a wider, sunlit world and give us the things we really want. To be seen and to be loved. We know the genie is capricious, and we are at his mercy, trapped inside the lamp by the promise of wishes fulfilled and the lure of glamorous scraps that sometimes land at our feet. This Manhattan Lamp Life is the opposite of my placid, passive Minnesotan upbringing with its frozen winters, secret drinking, and simmering resentments. I'm happier inside the tarnished lamp. At least it's warm, and I'm not alone.

I sip my gin. Time and I dissolve at the same stately pace, and now we're all in its big pot of goo on a jumpy Saturday night on Ninth Avenue.

I realize that I'm drunk and lost. Where am I? What am I doing here? I'm not horny; I'm lonely and soggy. I need to get my ass home. Maybe just hop in a cab, but that would be a long, jumpy, and expensive ride. Back to the C train.

I walk up to Fiftieth and turn right, and, boom, in the middle of the block, there's Charlotte ahead of me. She's got a big plastic bag from Duane Reade and a big paper bag from McDonald's.

She's wearing rumpled black sweats dusted with red fur and flip-flops. There is no Teresa Wright purpose in her walk, and her ass jiggles. I'm drunk, with nothing to lose, so I come up alongside her.

She is wearing glasses, her hair is flat, and she has no makeup on. Without the skillful war paint, she looks to be in her mid-sixties.

"Can I give you a hand?" I ask.

She jumps. "Oh!" Her eyes are wide and horrified, recalculating everything about her life, her real life. I can see that she's trying to remember what she's told me.

"No. I'm fine," she says. "What are you doing here? I mean, in this neighborhood." It sounds like an accusation.

"Having a drink at a pub." I try not to sound buzzed. "I'm surprised to see you. I thought you were going to Paris this weekend. Did you change your plans?"

Charlotte looks flustered. "Yes. My plans were changed... I changed them."

"Oh. Is your husband here? I would love to meet him."

"No."

"That's too bad. Is everything OK?"

"Oh yes. I really must dash." She takes a step.

"Right. Are you still going to Paris?"

"No. No. Something came up." She can't wait to get away from me.

"Nothing bad, I hope."

"No. Well, yes. Frank is sick."

"I'm sorry to hear that. Are you going to be with him?"

"Be with him? No. Frank, the cat, is sick. Since he is so... precarious... I couldn't leave him alone. And the woman who watches him is away this weekend."

"I understand."

"And of course, Frank, my husband, is heartbroken."

"Of course."

"Yes. He's just hanging around the Paris apartment, a lost puppy. He calls me every ten minutes, poor baby." She smiles at the thought of her handsome imaginary husband as a puppy.

I do, too.

"Of course."

"Well, I had better get home." Charlotte straightens her shoulders and becomes the Dragon Lady again. "I really must dash. Good to see you," she declares and marches off like Teresa Wright in flip-flops.

I get home without remembering how, and the next day, chastened, I clean the apartment, do the laundry, and cook a few meals that I freeze for during the week. What a good partner I am!

I even make a banana cream pie, his favorite. Today, I try on my benevolent Herbert Marshall face, serenely gazing out over the tangled webs of those less self-possessed than me. I have a clean apartment, clean laundry, a full refrigerator, and a pie waiting for my man. He's supposed to come home tomorrow, and we haven't talked all weekend.

I'm surprised by a text from him around eight p.m. "On my way home. Bus stuck in traffic on turnpike. Love you."

I respond with a heart emoji and "There's plenty of food."

I'm asleep when he gets in after midnight. He snuggles up against me. Whatever happened this weekend doesn't matter. He's back where he belongs. Don't ask, don't tell.

Al is still asleep when I leave at five the next morning. Will Charlotte be in today, or is she in Paris? Let's call it Paris.

I see Charlotte come in at ten. She glances at me and, I assume, the others while she marches toward the conference room at the end of the hall.

I score my first German ballot from a perky guy in Bonn, and I'm proud of myself.

At eleven thirty, the whiff of Chanel returns, and Charlotte is behind me. She looks like her pulled-together daytime self, including shapewear. She looks grim and gives me the bad news: the budget has been cut, and there's not enough money to keep me, the extra person, on. Ken, Maddie, and Mark will finish up the balloting.

"Perhaps if you had worked harder, I could have kept you," she snaps.

If I had a scimitar, I would decapitate her on the spot and walk out of this hellhole. Though she's playing Madame Cluzet again, all I can see is the frazzled, frumpy woman I bumped into on Fiftieth Street. I am not going to let this pass.

"Well, my work never changed. Remember me, twenty-three ballots in one day? A record?"

"And then, and then NOT twenty-three…"

"I see," I say, but I don't see what she wants me to see. I do see that my number was up when I bumped into her last night. I see that she isn't married to a movie star and that she's probably bipolar or schizophrenic or both.

"If you had kept up that pace, if you had been more focused, I could have fought harder to keep you. Here we are all about the numbers and… well, your numbers didn't add up."

"*Your* numbers don't add up," I blurt.

"What?"

"Nothing."

"Start making some calls."

I turn and look at her, really look at her. I channel Brett Helvig, investigative reporter, and I want to get to the bottom of this story. Her gray eyes meet mine and don't flinch. A showdown with the Dragon Lady. She would spit fireballs at me if she could. I keep my eyes clamped on hers.

When I look deep into Charlotte's eyes, I'm blocked but not by fire; there is a wall of ice. She's not a Dragon Lady; she's an iceberg, and there is a broken little woman trapped inside. I'm not afraid of the ice. I'm from Minnesota, and I know a cold, frightened heart when I see one. If I must, I can do this for an hour, maybe more. *Pi is the ratio of the circumference of a circle to its diameter. Pi is the ratio of the circumference of a circle to its diameter.*

Charlotte blinks.

About RIZE Press

RIZE publishes great stories and great writing across genres written by People of Color and other underrepresented groups. Our team consists of:

Lisa Diane Kastner, Founder and Executive Editor
Joelle Mitchell, Licensing and Strategy Lead
Cody Sisco, Acquisition Editor, RIZE
Benjamin White, Acquisition Editor, Running Wild
Peter A. Wright, Acquisition Editor, Running Wild
Resa Alboher, Editor
Angela Andrews, Editor
Sandra Bush, Editor

Ashley Crantas, Editor
Rebecca Dimyan, Editor
Abigail Efird, Editor
Aimee Hardy, Editor
Henry L. Herz, Editor
Cecilia Kennedy, Editor
Barbara Lockwood, Editor
AE Williams, Editor
Scott Schultz, Editor
Rod Gilley, Editor
Kelly Ottiano, Editor
Carolyn Banks, Editor

Evangeline Estropia, Product Manager
Pulp Art Studios, Cover Design
Standout Books, Interior Design
Polgarus Studios, Interior Design

Learn more about us and our stories at
www.runningwildpublishing.com

Loved these stories and want more?
Follow us at
www.runningwildpublishing.com,
www.facebook.com/runningwildpress,
on Twitter @lisadkastner @RunWildBooks @RwpRIZE

RUNNING WILD

RIZE